Three Days of Snow
and other stories

by Ward M. Clark

Cover Design by Hanna Al-Shaer

Contents

*Dedicated to the Glibertarians,
the most interesting, inspiring, and sometimes
baffling group of people that have ever existed.*

Preface

Some years back, my wife and I were driving cross country, and as we usually do while in the truck, we had some music playing. Both of us favor classic rock, and on that day, I had a long playlist up on the stereo, all songs by one of my favorite artists, America's Songwriter, Bob Dylan.

I've long thought that Dylan's best bodies of work may be found on his 1976 album Desire, and of those songs, perhaps the best is the ballad, Isis. As the song concluded on that day, I remember telling my wife, "You know, I could write a novel based that song." Well, it didn't end up being a novel but instead ended up a rather long short story. That story, Mystical Child, recounting the 1886 saga of a man named "Cairo Bob" Allen, was the first of several short stories I wrote based on Bob Dylan's work. You will find several of those stories in this collection.

Not long after that, I took my first shot at writing a fantasy story; that two-part work developed a life of its own, as fiction sometimes does, and ended up going in a completely different direction than I had initially intended. Also in this collection, you will find Season of Ice and Fire and Ice. I don't think that story is done yet. But then, I'm not done yet either.

Writing is a species of madness, I think. When you have the bug, you can't not do it. What you have before you now are some of the results of that madness. I sincerely hope you enjoy it. There will be more in time.

Mystical Child
Inspired by Bob Dylan's "Isis"

May 5, 1886 – Carson City, Nevada

She kicked me out this morning, a year to the day since we wed. Reckon it's been too long since I was in civilized country to hold on to a wife for long. Egypt ain't the place to learn fine manners. So, I may as well find some sort of work. I'm back in Carson City for now, if there's any sort of paying work to be had, it is likely to be here. Droving, I reckon, or maybe I'll take up prospecting. Maybe something else. Fellow who's good with a gun can always find a way. With a bit of luck, something here might set me on the right track. Might even get enough gold ahead to entice my wife to let me come back home.

— From the diary of Robert "Cairo Bob" Allen, 1841-1928

November 6, 1886:

Bob walked into the Dollar, his favorite Carson City saloon, and slapped the dust off his threadbare gray trousers. He was a tall, lean, hard-faced man in his middle forties, with icy blue eyes, bushy side whiskers, and thick brown hair that he had worn long since the War of the Northern Aggression, over twenty years since. Four years as a cavalry scout under General Wade Hampton, and ten years in the Egyptian Khedive's army had left him embittered and broke; Ismail the Magnificent's generosity did not live up to his name, not even with the former Confederate soldiers he retained to train his army. The only thing Bob had managed to retain from his years of service was his old Colt's Navy revolver, which hung now in a battered old Texas loop holster on his worn leather belt, and the nickname some of the other former Rebels serving the Khedive had hung on him: Cairo Bob.

Now, in early November, Carson City was enjoying a stretch of unusually fine fall weather, but that didn't help Bob's mood any. The sight of the Dollar didn't help; it was a long, narrow, dusty room, with a few tables along the wall opposite the narrow, grimy bar. Hal Ketch, the bartender, stood behind the bar, slowly polishing a glass with a dirty towel, his usual expression of eternal boredom etched on his square face. At one of the tables, two old men sat, playing a card game, tiredly. Bob didn't know their names.

"Morning, Bob," the bartender greeted him. It was a few minutes shy of noon, railroad time.

"Morning, Hal," Bob groused.

"Any word from the Missus?"

"Not since she kicked me out," Bob drawled. "Six goddamn months ago now. Gimme a whiskey. Need something to open m'eyes." He still missed Isis terribly; when he closed his eyes, he could still feel her lean, long body, could still smell her long, black hair, sage overlain with something musky. She was still there, as far as he knew, in the cabin up Clear Creek canyon. He hadn't been back since that last day.

The bartender placed a glass and a bottle of cheap rotgut in front of Bob. "What will you do?" he asked.

Bob poured out some whiskey and swallowed it at a gulp; it burned going down, as though he had swallowed a strand of barbed wire. "Dunno. Thought about goin' home to South

Carolina. Don't know as I want to do that. Bad memories." Like many former Confederates, he had a hard time accepting the loss, even now, over twenty years later.

"Long time ago," Hal observed.

"Don't make it no easier," Bob snapped. As Hal turned away, Bob thought he heard him mutter, "Damn stubborn Reb," but not so loud as to allow Bob to take offense and start up a scrap—besides which, if he did that, he wouldn't be able to come in and drink again.

Not that his dwindling supply of cash would allow that much longer in any case.

"Hey, Reb," one of the old men playing cards called. Bob bristled a little, but the old fellow hadn't meant anything by it; it was just a label, and Bob realized that, with his Low Country accent and the old gray Confederate trousers he still wore, he could hardly deny it.

"What do you want?"

"You still lookin' for payin' work?"

"Hell, yeah," Bob replied. "Got myself kicked off my own damn place. Man has to eat somehow."

"Fella was through here yesterday," the old man went on, "looking for someone to help him with some kind of big job. Said he was headed north, up towards Nez Perce country. If'n you was to get on the road right sharp, you might catch up with him."

"What's he look like?" Bob wanted to know.

"Short, kind of a gut on 'im, no hair. Kind of funny-looking, you ask me."

"Said he was headed north?"

"He did."

Bob poured himself another whiskey and stared at it moodily. *Almost out of money*, he reminded himself. *Long ride up to Nez Perce country. Five days, maybe six.*

His horse was across town at a stable, as was the rest of his traps; nothing more than a few clean shirts, a bedroll, his saddle, and a battered old Spencer rifle that dated back to the war. Bob had in fact been sleeping in the stable himself these last months, ever since his wife had kicked him out.

Well, hell, he thought, *it's not like I got anything to lose.*

He downed the whiskey, dropped some coins on the bar and headed out into the street.

On an impulse, perhaps driven by the prospect of a fresh start, he went into the town's only barber shop and laid down a precious ten cents for a haircut and shave. Bob emerged onto the street with a close-cropped head and a clean-shaven face for the first time since the end of the war. Feeling somehow renewed, he went to the stable, settled with the stable keeper for board of his horse, saddled the animal and rode off north.

Long stretch of wild country ahead of me, he thought, as he reached the edge of town and spurred his horse to a canter. He sat in the saddle with the ease of a veteran cavalryman, and his horse moved effortlessly; in spite of his poverty Bob had made sure to keep the animal in fine fettle, and his horse furniture was in good condition. The horse soldier's creed of *the horse, the saddle, the man* was still deeply ingrained in his soul.

He reached forward and tapped the stock of the Spencer. He had only one seven-shot magazine full of rounds for the rifle but figured he could find some more if he needed to. *Don't know why,* he told himself, *but feels like things might finally be turning my way. Things can't go too far wrong–either way, I'm better off than sitting around Carson City feeling sorry for myself.*

Get to see some new country, anyway. Never been that far north before.

The weather was turning. A light snow started to fall as he took the road north towards Boise and the Nez Perce nation.

November 10, 1886 – Boise, Idaho Territory

Four days hard riding has brought me to Boise in Idaho Territory. There's some fuss going on in town just now, people all upset about Chinese living in the town. Not sure why everyone is so riled up, it ain't like they were freedmen–I can see how some folks would be unhappy about that, although I ain't never had a problem with colored folks myself. But in Reno, I had run into a man who saw the same fellow I'm looking for, and said he was headed for some place northwards of Boise. I picked up on his trail again when I heard tell of his passage from an Indian in some little place called Jordan Valley in Oregon, so figure I'm on the right track. Man sure isn't taking any pains to keep his movements a secret or anything.

— From the diary of Robert "Cairo Bob" Allen, 1841-1928

November 10, 1886

Bob rode into Boise on a cloudy, cold day, with a chill wind blowing pellets of wet snow in his face. His old gray coat was wet through. He was wearing an old pair of corduroy trousers he had happened to acquire along the way, and two hickory shirts, along with his mule-ear trooper boots and ancient slouch hat; all were dirty, all were soaked.

"I'd kill for clean, dry duds and a warm bed," he muttered to himself as he walked his horse down what appeared to be the main drag. He knew the warm bed was unlikely, given his current state of poverty, but he had enough money left for a stable stall and a laundry, if such a thing were to be had; Boise looked to be a good-sized town, so the odds of getting his clothes cleaned up was reasonable, and he could always sleep in a stall with his horse.

He pulled out his wallet and went through the few remaining

banknotes—no, bills, he reminded himself—green Yankee bills, he noted with a slight frown, still not happy about how the whole thing had turned out. *Something better break loose pretty soon*, he reminded himself, *or I'm going to be broke myself.*

Bob rode down the street. As he turned onto an east-west street lined with businesses, the clouds broke open, allowing a weak, watery sunshine to peek through.

The sun was low in the sky, and after four days in the wilds, it was odd to ride from sun to shadow as he went in and out of the shade cast by the buildings along the south side of the street. Bob spotted a man standing on a corner, and angled his horse over towards the local.

"Hey, friend," Bob called. "Can you point me towards a place where a fella can get cleaned up?"

"Been on the trail a while?" the local asked.

"You might say that."

The Boisean's gaze narrowed on hearing Bob's accent. "Reb, are you?"

"*Was*," Bob agreed, trying a soft answer to turn away any possible wrath. "Wade Hampton's cavalry. Long time ago now."

"Yeah," the man agreed, relaxing some. "Served in a Wisconsin volunteer infantry regiment myself. Took a bullet in the arm at Second Wilderness... Well, anyway, as you say, friend, all a long time ago now. What did you say you were looking for?"

Bob slapped the leg of his muddy trousers. "Place to get cleaned up. Bath, laundry if there is such a thing."

The local pointed up the street. "There's a boarding house up two blocks, in what used to be Chinatown. Figure you can get a bath there, and Mrs. Olson across the street from there took over Chang's laundry, she can clean up your clothes right quick. That's where I get my stuff cleaned up."

"Took over?"

"Yeah," the Boisean said. "Big fuss around here lately about the Chinese. Territorial legislature passed a tax on 'em, and the folks around here made things pretty hot for anyone and anything Chinese. Most of the Chinese have left the territory now. Lots of them just up and abandoned houses and businesses, so the local folks took over. Big fuss earlier in the year, but it's mostly blown over now. I'm here to tell you, though, the line was drawn awfully strong between old Chinatown and the rest of the city for a while there, and that's for sure and for certain."

Uncertain as to how to react to that, Bob simply thanked the man and rode on.

"Sure as shooting" he said to himself a few minutes later: There, on the right-hand side of the street, was a big rambling wooden house with a sign:

MONARCH BOARDING HOUSE.

There was a hitching rail at the front of the house. Bob rode over, dismounted, tied his horse off, and went inside. A bell jingled as he closed the big oak door behind him and stepped into a warm entry room lit by a gas mantle. *Right civilized place*, this is, he told himself. Inside, he could see a large dining table. A lean man with the look of a drummer sat there, reading a newspaper. Somewhere a clock ticked loudly. The house smelled of fresh bread.

A large, gray-haired woman met him in the entry. "I'm Mrs. Dalby," she said. "I run the house here."

Bob nodded, removed his old slouch hat, and gave his name. "Looking for a place to spend a night or two," he told her. "Get cleaned up, get some hot food, if I can, ma'am."

"You're welcome, of course," the old woman said with a sniff. "Fifty cents a night. Another quarter for the hot supper. If it's a bath you want, go across the street to Broadman's Laundry, they can clean your clothes up and provide a hot shower-bath; it's the latest thing. Ten cents for shirts, fifteen for trousers, nickel for each item of small clothes. Quarter for the shower bath."

"That sounds right fine, ma'am. Is there a place I can put up my horse?"

"Stable is in back. Use of the stable is part of the rent, but I'll need a quarter for hay and oats for your animal if you want to feed it."

"I will, ma'am, thank you." Bob reached into his wallet and pulled out two one-dollar Yankee greenbacks. "Let's call it two nights for now," he said, handing her the bills. "Much obliged."

"I thank you," Mrs. Dalby said. "Supper is in at six o'clock sharp, so you have a couple of hours."

"Thank you, ma'am," Bob said. "Reckon I'll put up my horse, then see about that laundry."

"I'll send my boy Andy out to get you some feed," Mrs. Dalby said, and walked off.

Bob took his gelding to the stable, unsaddled him, put up the horse tack, and brushed the animal down. A boy of about ten or so came in as Bob was checking the horse's feet and filled the trough in the stall Bob was using with a mix of chopped hay and oats. The horse set to with a will.

With that done, Bob walked across the street to the building marked LAUNDRY AND HOT BATH

He didn't notice the short, portly fellow watching him from a rocking chair on the boarding house's porch. The round man watched Bob go into the laundry, then got up and went into the boarding house.

November 11, 1886 – Boise, Idaho Territory

> *I'd figured on having to ride up into the Nez Perce*
> *nation to find the man I was following, but sure enough,*
> *he found me, and on my second day in Boise, too. He was*
> *an odd fellow, too, just like the old man back in Carson*

City described him. Don't think he had any worries about being scalped, that's for sure, not with that pate of his. He had a hell of a proposition, too, and his timing was great, as I was pretty near out of money. I couldn't have stayed in the Monarch Boarding House more than a couple more days, my wallet was getting as thin as a March wind in the mountains.

— From the diary of Robert "Cairo Bob" Allen, 1841-1928

November 11, 1886

"Good God in the foothills, man, how long can this idiot Cleveland stay in office?" the drummer at the other side of the table was expounding—again. This time, at Bob's second supper at the Monarch Boarding House, he was going on about silver-backed currency.

The only thing Bob knew about silver was that he'd never had much of it in his hands, and rarely less so than now.

"I tell you, he ought to be run out of Washington City," the drummer went on. He slammed a fist down on the table, making the china jump. "Him and his bastard child."

"Ma, Ma, where's my Pa?" laughed another boarder. "Gone to the White House, haw, haw, haw!"

"Gentlemen!" Mrs. Dalby was just entering the room, bearing a large cauldron of chicken and dumplings. "I remind you, no talk of religion or politics at the table. If you wish to argue politics, kindly do so outside on the porch."

Bob had learned quickly that Mrs. Dalby, although a widow lady well past middle age, was in fact a formidable woman with a will of iron and the voice of a top sergeant when events called for it. The drummer grinned sheepishly as Mrs. Dalby handed him a huge bowl full of steaming chicken and dumplings. "Sorry, ma'am," he grinned. "Got a bit carried away, I did."

"Kindly see that you do not do so again," the Monarch Boarding House's proprietor replied.

Bob ate up quickly—the supper was long on dumplings and somewhat short on chicken—and went outside to the porch to smoke a cigar he had won earlier in the day playing cards with the drummer. He had little interest in what he still thought of as Yankee politics, although the fact that Cleveland was apparently a Democrat appealed somewhat to the former Confederate that still lived within him.

Almost out of money, he reminded himself as he struck a match on the sole of his trooper's boot and lit the cigar. He drew on the stogie; it was dry and acid-tasting, but he hadn't had a smoke in weeks. *Tomorrow, I either find some sort of work here in Boise or light out again.*

A figure materialized on the corner of the porch and drifted towards Bob. Seeing the movement out of the dark in the corner of his eye, Bob instinctively grabbed at his holster, but his revolver was up in his room. At Mrs. Dalby's command, no sidearms were to be worn in the house.

"Relax, friend, just wanted to speak with you," a high-pitched, scratchy voice said. The man stepped into the light from the window; a short, rotund man, his bald pate shining in the dim light.

That's him, Bob realized. *That's the man I'm looking for.*

"Got another match?"

"Sure thing, friend," Bob said. He took the matchbook from his jacket pocket and handed it to the man.

"Samuel P.C.E. Evans," the short man said by way of introduction. He extracted a tobacco pouch and papers from his jacket pocket and quickly, expertly rolled a cigarette. Striking a match on the porch rail, he took a long drag and exhaled contentedly. He didn't explain why he carried around the flock of initials.

"Bob Allen," Bob said. The two shook hands formally. "They call me Cairo Bob." He wasn't sure why he had added that last. There was something odd about the round man, something that reminded Bob of someone.

"Cairo Bob?" Evans asked.

"Spent ten years in Egypt," Bob explained. "After the war. The Khedive was building an Army, wanted help training his troops, and I had nothin' else to do, so…"

"Ah," Evans said. "Southron, then, are you?"

"That's right. South Carolina."

"From Virginia myself," Evans nodded. "Well, the part they call West Virginia now. Spent three years in Lee's Army of Northern Virginia. You?"

"Wade Hampton's cavalry, purt near the whole war."

"You and I, we may have been on the same field a time or two, then."

"Reckon we were."

Evans took another drag and looked at Bob sidelong. "Heard one of the boarders say you was looking for some work."

"That I am," Bob agreed. "Damn near down to my last dollar."

"Would you be interested in heading up north into Canada for a while? Got a lead on something up north of the border; might be something pretty big. Need someone to ride up there with me, find a place called Pyramid Peak. We'd be looking for the grave of a fella buried up there somewhere."

"What terms did you have in mind?" Bob asked.

"Fifty-fifty split of whatever we find," Evans said.

"Well, fine. What are you expecting to find?"

"Ever hear tell of a Spanish explorer name of de Vaca?" Bob shook his head. "Story goes that he criss-crossed the country, looking for seven lost cities of gold. Now, history says he failed, but according to the Nez Perce, one of his soldiers, man name of Ruiz, found one of the cities. Streets not paved with gold, but plenty of bar and sculpted gold to be had. He recovered as much as he could carry but died up there in the mountains, up in Canada. He had a partner, who buried him up there and brought word back to the Nez Perce of the place called Pyramid Peak, where Ruiz's grave is and where the gold is stashed, but the partner died before he could get back to civilization."

"Why didn't the Nez Perce chase this thing down, if they know all about it?"

Evans shrugged. "Who knows? Maybe they think the old boy was lying. Maybe they just don't care. Anyway, I've been through that country up in Canada, and I think I may know the peak they're talking about. I need a partner to help me get up there, find this place, dig up the gold, and bring it back. What do you say?"

"Long ways up there," Bob said reflectively. "We'd need a grubstake, maybe a pack horse each. All I got is my saddle horse and damn near no money."

"Don't worry none about that," Evans shook his head. "I'll arrange for grub and pack horses. If we find anything, I'll take that stake back out of the gold before we divide it up."

"That's fair," Bob agreed. "Nothing but. When you want to leave?"

"Best we do not draw too much attention," Evans said. "Tomorrow, you go to see Colonel Appleton on the west edge of town. He sells horses. Find a couple of good strong pack animals. I'll stake you, oh, ten dollars per horse; that should get a couple of decent ones. While you're doing that, I'll arrange for a month's worth of flour, bacon, and beans. How you fixed for guns and ammo?"

Bob frowned. "Give me a moment to weigh that." He thought hard on the contents of his saddlebags. "Reckon I got enough powder and ball for my revolver. Got a Spencer rifle, almost out of rounds for it; got one full magazine and three empty ones. If anyone in town has any .56 Spencer, I could sure use some."

"I'll see what I can do. Do we have a deal, then, sir?"

"We do," Bob said. They shook hands again, and Evans faded away into the dark, disappearing just as he had appeared.

November 17, 1886 – Somewhere in the Canadian Rockies

Cold up here, in Canada. Never been up in these parts before, and I see now why. In November back in South Carolina when I was a boy, can't hardly remember even wearing a jacket in November, but up here, even in the saddle and moving, I'm bundled up in damn near every piece of clothing I own, and wrapped up in a blanket to boot. Sleeping isn't easy, either. Especially since we aren't up here legal and don't want to draw attention to ourselves, so we're only making small fires to cook at night. Reminds me of back during the War of the Northern Aggression, when we were raiding up into Yankee territory. Not rightly sure how folk can live in a climate like this.

— From the diary of Robert "Cairo Bob" Allen, 1841-1928

November 17, 1886

It was nearing sundown on the fifth day.

The two men had snuck across the border into Canada two days before. Bob's skills as a cavalry scout stood them in good stead; they had once spent a half-hour hiding in a small copse of trees as a patrol of Mounties went past, but they had neatly evaded the Canucks. "J.E.B. Stuart couldn't have done her any better," Sam Evans observed, which made Bob grin.

But that had been some time since, and the weather was turning worse.

"Five days," Bob groused from the saddle. "Five days since we left Boise. Just keeps getting colder every damn day."

"This here sure as hell ain't Dixie," Evans agreed easily. He let out an audible gasp as a gust of wind drove snow into his thin coat. A coughing fit seized him. "Wish I'd thought to have bought a better coat. I been through these parts once before, but that was in summer."

"Here." Bob untied a spare blanket from his saddle and reached across to hand it to Evans. "Can't have you catching the grippe or something and dyin' before we find this here dead Spaniard."

"I sure do thank you," Evans said, wrapping the old wool blanket around his shoulders. "Damned if it ain't as cold as a Yankee banker's heart up here. But I'll get you to where we're going, don't you worry none—you got my word on that."

"Dark soon," Bob pointed out. "See that line of trees ahead? Must be a creek. Good place to shelter for the night."

"Looks like," Evans said.

An hour later, the horses were tended, and Bob was stirring a small pot of beans over a cavalryman's fire. He was mulling over the comment he had made to Evans earlier in the day, about Evans dying of the grippe. On the other side of the fire Evans was squatting, cutting up chunks of bacon to go into the beans. Another coughing fit seized him as Bob watched.

At least the snow's stopped, Bob thought. The sun was gone; Bob looked up at the glimmering, ice-chip stars shining through gaps in the clouds.

"Say," Bob said at last, "you do know where we're headed, right?"

"Think so," Evans said. He took out a dirty handkerchief and wiped his mouth with it. "About another forty miles or so—call it two day's ride. The Nez Perce I talked to called it what amounts to "straight-sided mountain" or "cone mountain." The one I talked to didn't know exactly how to savvy it in English. But when I had passed through these parts the summer before, I do remember seeing a mountain, straight sided, looked just like one of them ancient pyramids over Egypt way. Say, you were there; ever see them things for-real?"

"Couple times," Bob replied. "Some big ones not far from Cairo. I was there a few times. That's where I picked up the 'Cairo Bob' handle."

"Well, this here mountain, she looked just like the pyramids I saw once in a picture book. We've got some nasty badlands to ride through, but as long as the weather doesn't get worse, I reckon we'll be all right."

"So how are we supposed to find this Spaniard's grave, anyway?"

"Now that's the interesting part," Evans said. "The Indian said he didn't rightly see the man himself, you understand. But on the east side of the mountain, there's a big stone mostly blocking a cave entrance, and there's a Spanish cross carved into the stone. That's how we'll know where it is."

"So, all we have to do Is move that stone, and the grave's inside?"

"That's how I see it," Evans agreed. "Grave, tomb, whatever."

"I sure do hope you're right about all this."

Bob stirred the bacon Evans had cut up into the beans. After a little while, they were ready to eat. Each man had a tin plate and a spoon. They divvied up the beans and bacon and ate in contemplative silence.

When they were done, Evans offered to wash up the dishes in the creek. He gathered everything up and walked the few paces to the little stream. Bob could hear the pot and plates clattering as Evans dunked them in the cold water. Bob could also hear Evans coughing again.

Wonder if he's consumptive? Bob shook his head. *Reckon not.*

Everyone I ever heard of with the consumption couldn't hardly eat. Say the flesh just melts right off them. This Evans, whatever ails him, it ain't that.

Presently Evans came back. He handed Bob his plate and spoon. With an old field soldier's care, Bob tilted them towards the fire so he could look them over. They looked clean enough, so he stowed them in his saddlebag while Evans stowed the pot and his own eating gear. He knew all too well how dirty eating gear could make a man sick, and he had no desire to pick up a case of the quickstep in this weather.

"Two more days ride, you say," Bob asked.

Evans nodded. He rolled another cigarette, lit it with a brand from the fire, and took a long, contented drag. "Two more, maybe a day finding the grave."

"And then, what, a week getting back? Figure on going back to Boise?"

"Sure," Evans said. "There's enough mining in the area, I figure we should be able to cash in the gold. We can always melt it down into chunks, so they don't suspect we stole it. Ought to be able to make it look like credible nuggets."

"Won't folks wonder when we don't file any claims?"

"I doubt it," Evans assured Bob. "Claims office isn't even in the same building as the assay office. Even if someone did wonder, we'll be long gone by the time they put it all together."

"You say so."

Evans took another drag on the cigarette. "I reckon we'll be back to civilization by, oh, third or fourth of December. Not that long."

"Well," Bob said, "that ain't the worst news I ever heard."

They rolled up in bedrolls to sleep close beside the fire. As he was drifting off, Bob heard Evans coughing again.

November 18, 1886 – Somewhere in the Canadian Rockies

Evening at last. Fire isn't helping us get warm, not much. Evans keeps coughing. Afraid he's going to keel over. We rode through some bad country today. I'm thinking this trip is going to take longer than this man Evans thinks. We went up this steep-sided canyon, following a creek that's froze hard as rock, and made camp up near where it starts, on the edge of a little pond, also froze hard as rock. We'll have to hammer out some ice to melt for drinking, cooking, and necessary. Just keeps getting colder, and colder. Sure do hope it ends up being worth all this hardship. But, if I can just come out of this set up well enough to maybe win Isis back, it will have all been worth it.

— *From the diary of Robert "Cairo Bob" Allen, 1841-1928*

November 19, 1886

The two men had passed an uncomfortable night. Figuring they were far enough from the border, Bob had insisted on building the fire up enough to keep them from freezing solid, but he still slept poorly. Several times in the night he roused to throw more wood on the fire, but the supply ran out a couple of hours before dawn and, by the time the sun came up the South Carolinian was truly miserable. Evans coughed sporadically all through the night but other than that, hardly moved; Bob kept up the fire by himself, and when morning finally dawned pale and watery, he was more than a little resentful.

Think of what's ahead, he reminded himself, *and keep your damn mouth shut.*

The horses seemed to be faring well, at least. Bob had insisted on bringing along a sack of corn and another of oats. With that and the abundant dry grass, the horses were probably feeding better than the men.

Bob saddled the riding horses while Evans loaded the pack animals. Bob went over this saddle horse with a cavalryman's care, checking teeth, hooves, and eyes; the animal seemed fine. The pack horses were holding up. Evans climbed on his saddle horse without apparently giving a thought to the beast's state.

"Ready?" he asked Bob.

"I reckon." Bob said, as he climbed into his well-worn saddle.

"All right then," Evans said, and spurred his horse to a walk.

As they started out, Evans was rolling another cigarette and coughing. He seemed to have an inexhaustible supply of makings. He rode along, silent for once, leading one of the pack horses. Bob rode along behind, leading the other, in a contemplative silence.

Gold, he told himself. *Amazing how everything seems to turn on that. With gold, a man can have damn near anything. Without it, he doesn't have much.*

I don't want a palace in Egypt, or even a mansion in San Francisco. All I want is my cabin on Clear Creek and my wife back. I guess when she hooked up with me, she didn't have it clear what life was like on a little farm out in the boonies like that, but she sure didn't give it much of a chance. Barely that year.

But with gold, he thought, *I can do a lot more for her.*

This pans out, I'll bring her back a big old diamond necklace, maybe some other jewelry, so she'll know right off I've hit it big. I'll get some men out to add onto the cabin, bring in a real iron stove so she doesn't have to cook over the fire, maybe even get a well drilled. Hauling water from the creek sure ain't no fun.

I suppose if she wants, we could move into Carson City. Damn lot of Yankees there, but if it means keeping Isis or losing her again...

The thought trailed off.

Dammit, he thought, *war's over, and long since. I got to stop thinking that way. Hell, Isis herself said she's from Kansas—Bloody*

Kansas, John Brown's Kansas, and I never thought I'd be so besotted with a woman as I am with her.

He remembered during that good year, when he had brought Isis into Carson City to do some trading. A shop there sold women's pretties, and Isis's eye had fallen on an Indian necklace of silver and turquoise, but Bob hadn't the money to buy it. *That's the thing*, he thought, remembering that bright summer's day with Isis on his arm. *If that's still there in that store, I'll buy that right off, or something like it at least.*

The two riders had just crested a small ridge when Evans spoke up. "Look there," he called. Bob rode up alongside, looked to where Evans was pointing.

And there it was, in the weak morning light—a mountain, with an almost perfect pyramid shape. To the east there was another, smaller peak of similar construction.

"So," Bob asked, "which one is it?"

"Well," Evans said, "The Indian said he heard tell it was on the eastern slope. Figure we may as well check that eastern peak first. See how the two sort of run together and form a saddle? Doesn't look like there'd be any cave or any such in there."

"Makes sense." Bob stood in his saddle and examined what he could see of the ground ahead. "Looks like another waterway yonder, that might could lead us off to the east of that little mountain. Worth a try, anyway."

"You're the cavalry scout," Evans agreed. He was rolling another cigarette. A sharp, barking cough escaped him. He hawked and spat, and Bob thought he saw blood in the spittle before it landed in the tall, dry grass.

"I suppose," Bob said. "I'll lead, then. Another damn canyon, likely, but at least this time we're headed down, not up."

Bob rode ahead, glancing once over his shoulder to make sure Evans was following. The man was just lighting up his smoke. He dropped the match into a patch of snow and booted his horse.

Imagine what Isis would have thought of this little adventure, Bob reflected. *She would have thought it reckless as hell, that's what she would have thought.*

She won't think so if I come back with a fat wallet, he thought. He could hear Evan's horse's hooves on the ground behind him, so he didn't look back again. He went back to thinking of his wife, back there in the cabin on Clear Creek. Her long, black hair, her skin like new ivory, her full lips; the swell of her bosom, the curve of her hip, her biting, scratching passion in the bed when the light was out...

Don't know how the hell we never had a kid, Bob thought bitterly. *We may have had our problems, but good God that woman loves to fuck.* He felt himself growing hard in his faded gray trousers and cursed silently.

This man Evans, he mused, *damn well better know what he's up to. Half a mind to shoot him and leave him here otherwise.*

November 21, 1886 –Pyramid Peak

We arrived at the base of the smaller mountain at mid-morning, stopped in a patch of low brush near a small creek, built a fire, cooked up some bacon and biscuits, and planned our next move. Evans was of a mind that we should split up, one of us move off north, the other south, and check out any likely spots. I didn't cotton to that and told him so. We don't either of us know the other all that well, I said to him, and trust runs mightily lean in these sorts of doings. But he was pretty insistent, and to prove it he proposed to leave the pack horses and most of the gear where we'd stopped as a base camp, and both of us return every evening. This seemed to make a certain amount of sense, as I had to admit. So, we determined that we'd take the rest of the day to build some sort of shelter, let the horses rest and graze, and try to get the chill out of our bones before commencing to look for the Spaniard's tomb in the morning. We built a lean-to of brush and built a big fire in front of it, and I think that was the warmest I'd been since the Monarch Boarding House in Boise. Oh, and towards evening I took my Spencer, went out into a patch of woods, and shot a big doe. Fresh meat!

— *From the diary of Robert "Cairo Bob" Allen, 1841-1928*

November 22, 1886

Breakfast was venison tenderloin fried in bacon grease served up with leftover biscuits from the day before, and Bob didn't think he'd enjoyed a finer meal in years, hunger proving once again to be the best of seasonings. That was a lesson Bob had learned long ago, during the War of the Northern Aggression, but he had forgotten it since—until that morning.

"Ask you a question?" Evans asked around a mouthful of biscuit. Bob nodded assent. "You sure were quick to jump on this here deal. Quicker'n a man whose only problem is an empty wallet, you don't mind my saying so. Something else going on?"

"Don't know as I'm wanting to talk about that," Bob replied.

"We're partners," Evans pointed out. "Partners should know what's drivin' each other. Especially when there's gold at stake."

Bob thought that over. "All right," he said, adding "you first."

"Well, you probably noticed the cough, right?"

"Sure."

"Got some kind of problem with my lungs. A cancer, the sawbones in Elko said. Add to that the problem that my Pa had a bum heart, and he passed it on. So, I need doctoring, and that costs money. Figured this to be my best shot at getting some big Frisco doc to look me over."

"Make sense," Bob agreed.

"So, what about you?"

Bob finished chewing a forkful of tender venison. "Wife kicked me off my place west of Carson City."

"Figured you had some kind of woman troubles," Evans observed. "Seen the look on men before. So, you're figuring on buying your way back into her bed?"

"I ain't like that," Bob objected.

Evans said nothing, just raised a questioning eyebrow.

Seized by a sudden need to talk about it—to someone, to anyone, as he had talked about it with no one for over six months—Bob spilled out a torrent of words.

"I ain't never had a lot of money, sure," he explained. "But she never seemed to mind all that much. She showed up in Carson City one day and took up a room above the dry-goods store where she was working. I did a fair amount of trading in there and realized one day that I reckoned her to be the sweetest, prettiest gal I'd ever run across, and I ain't exactly a young man n'more. So, we courted for a while, then got married last May. Was a cold, rainy day, that day we got hitched, but neither of us cared. Brought her out to my place out on Clear Creek. Got forty acres, had a couple horses, a stretch plowed up for truck crops, keep a few pigs and chickens. No place to get rich off of, but enough to keep a family eating, you know?"

"Sure," Evans said. "Grew up on a place like that in Virginny."

"Me too," Bob went on. "So, we were *happy*, you know? First year went just fine. I thought so, anyway. Then a year after we got married, she just up and tosses me out. Said to me, she said, 'Robert Allen, you got to get away. You need to get off this place for a while. You ain't hardly set foot off the place in a year, and you are getting' stale. Write to me here, let me know what you're doing, I'll want to know, but you need to get out for a spell.'"

"That's hard," Evans observed.

"Tell me about it," Bob said. "She told me that once I had some time away, to come back and see if things ain't different. Figured if I went back with a pocketful of greenbacks, well, that'd sure go a long way to ease my way in, you know?"

"She's that fine a woman?"

"None finer. Stuff she used to say, back when times was good… I can't hardly tell you none of the best stuff. Can't hardly remember myself, anymore. All I know is I want to be back on my own place with Isis—that's her name, Isis—again, and if this here venture gets me back there again, then by God, that's what I'll do."

They finished eating in silence. *Damn*, Bob thought to himself as he cleaned up his tin plate and cup in the creek, *but I never thought I'd spill my guts like that—least of all to that sawed-off little bastard. To a preacher man, maybe.*

When that was done, the two conferred again.

"I'll head off to the north," Bob said, remembering what Evans had said about his health; the north slope looked like rougher country. "You go to the south. Check out cliffs, overhangs, anything that might hide a cave, right?"

Evans nodded. "Indian said it was in a cave, covered with a big flat rock."

Bob remembered his Bible. "Has a familiar sound to it, all right. Well then—let's saddle up. See you back here around sunset."

He rode through the morning without anything interesting coming up. Noon found him inspecting a stretch of rock outcrops with no result, so he ate a biscuit and a chunk of venison, and turned back.

Then, in a spot he had overlooked before, there was a small, flat face of rock, set back in a small box canyon. Bob rode up for a closer look, and then…

"Sure as hell," he breathed. There, in the rock face, was a large, flat boulder, leaned against the face; around the edges, Bob could see gaps. Overhead, a small creek spilled down the cliff face, over the boulder, into a small pool; the freezing weather had had its effect.

Bob dismounted and walked over for a closer look. The water wasn't flowing any more, not in the cold, but the flat boulder was encased in a good six inches of clear ice, hard as granite. Through the ice Bob could see the faint form of a cross, crudely etched into the flat rock.

He looked up the cliff, down at the frozen pool – really no more than a puddle – then at the ice encasing the flat rock.

"God damn it," he spat.

November 22, 1886—Pyramid Peak

Got back to our camp way after dark to find Evans sitting there by the fire. He didn't look so good—face was all red, like. He was smoking a cigarette, like always, and coughing, again like always. Told him what I'd found, and he just perked right on up, saying that had to be it, was just like the Indian he talked to described it. Now I'd been thinking he put an awful lot of stock in the word of some old Indian whose name he didn't even seem to know, but sure as hell if that description didn't fit, except for that God damned ice covering the whole thing. Told him about that, and he just went to the packs laying on the ground near where the pack animals were picketed and pulled out an axe. "We'll build a fire under the ice," he said to me, "and then knock it loose with this." I didn't have any better ideas that didn't involve coming back in the spring, so told him we may as well try it.

— From the diary of Robert "Cairo Bob" Allen, 1841-1928

November 23, 1886

During the night, the weather worsened.

Bob awoke with just the hint of lightening in the sky. He shivered in his bedroll. The fire had died down, but once in a while the remaining coals would flare up as the wind ripped across the land. The crude brush lean-to was shaking in the wind. Bob sat up and felt a pellet of sleet hit his cheek.

"Oh, hell," he heard Evans swearing. The short man sat up. "This sure as hell don't look good."

"Let's see if we can get the fire built up." Bob stretched and reached for his old canteen to rinse out his mouth, but the water was frozen solid. He shrugged and climbed out of his bedroll and, shivering, pulled on his old trooper boots and his overcoat.

Evans was guddling around in the remains of the fire. He added some kindling that he had wisely kept dry under his bedroll, but the wind wouldn't allow anything to catch.

"Hell with this," Bob said. "Let's saddle up, load the pack horses, and move up to the tomb. It's in a box canyon, maybe sheltered enough to get a fire going there."

"Fuck," Evans spat. "Sure do hope our luck ain't turned bad."

Bob scowled. "Don't talk like that. Doesn't help anything."

"All right." Evans lapsed into another coughing fit, a bad one, one that bent him double. He spat blood and stood up, face red, gasping. "All right," he managed to gasp out. "I'll see to the pack horses."

They were an hour getting ready, during which time the wind picked up and the sleet turned to a hard, driving snow. The temperature had dropped noticeably by the time they climbed into their saddles.

"Hope to hell we don't freeze to death," Bob said, teeth chattering.

"Let's get on the way," Evans snapped. "Sooner we get there, sooner we can get a big old fire built."

The day before Bob had spent four hours in the saddle returning to the camp from the tomb. Today, riding into the face of a growing blizzard, it took eight to reverse the route. Bob led them by mistake into two smaller side canyons he hadn't noticed the day before, which made Evans angrier.

Finally, as the dull gray sky was beginning to grow dark, they arrived at the tomb.

Remembering an old trick from a winter campaign during the War of the Northern Aggression, Bob cut brush and built a small reflector to block the wind, another small lean-to barely big enough for the two bedrolls, and finally managed to get a fire going. All the while, Evans was glumly examining the apparent entry to the tomb.

"Goddamned if there ain't six, eight inches of ice on that son of a bitch," he groused, returning to the fire. "It's like we weren't meant to get in there."

"I told you, don't talk like that. You'll jinx us, damn it."

"Fine, fine." Evans huddled close to the fire. "I think we ought to take turns sleeping. Fella who's awake can keep the fire up, so we don't freeze to death."

"Sensible," Bob said with a shiver. He dug in his saddlebag. "Here," he said, handing Evans a venison steak cooked the night before. "Put 'er on a rock by the fire. At least we can eat something halfway warm. No water, so no coffee, I guess."

"Fill the coffee pot with snow," Evans suggested, "And put 'er on the fire."

Bob slapped his forehead in annoyance and reached for the pot. A short while later, they had coffee perking.

"Ahh," Evans said after his first long drink of hot coffee. "That's better. That's much better."

"How much gold and so on you suppose is in there?" Bob motioned towards the tomb.

"I got no idea," Evans admitted. "But bound to be a good

amount. And, you know, I been thinking. A few years back I was in this place in San Francisco, fella there was talking about building a place to house and show off all sorts of antiquities and so forth—a 'museum,' was the word he used. I bet if we brought that Spaniard's bones out, and whatever armor or gear might be in there, that would fetch a pretty fair price too."

"Something to think about, anyway," Bob agreed. He was starting to feel slightly less miserable with a belly full of tepid venison and hot coffee.

Suddenly a thought occurred to him: *How come he never mentioned that museum or whatever before now? Maybe he's full of shit about the gold? Maybe the old Indian or whoever never said anything about that, and that's why nobody's ever got in there before?*

Across the fire, Evans was coughing again.

No point in worrying about this now, Bob reminded himself. *We're here. The tomb is here. Tomorrow—tomorrow we'll see what's what. Long as we don't freeze to death first. Damn, and I thought northern Virginia was cold in the winter! This surely is a God-forsaken land.*

"You want to sleep first?" Evans asked.

"Don't mind if I do," Bob replied. "If I can sleep in this damn cold." It had gotten good and dark now, and in the guttering firelight Bob could see snow, driven sideways by the wind. Evans tossed a few more sticks into the dull blaze and piled some more brush to dry off near the low flames.

A thought: "Evans, you got a watch?"

"Yeah." He pulled out a cheap pocket watch. "I make it six-thirty. Two-hour watches?"

"Spoken like an old soldier," Bob agreed. "Very well, then, Colonel, wake me at eight-thirty."

"Count on it, General," Evans said with a faint chuckle.

Bob had thought he wouldn't be able to sleep, but exhaustion claimed him before his heart beat a hundred times.

November 24, 1886 – The Tomb

Wasn't any damn way a fire was going to work in that weather. I thought it might be a good idea to make a camp in some sheltered place, wait out that weather, but Evans, he wasn't having any of that. Got right upset and started shouting. "We've come all this way," he yelled, "and I'm running low on time and patience. No, we'll get in there, and we'll get in there right the hell now," he said, and as I was feeling a bit anxious to have this damn thing over with, I decided to go along with him. Sure ain't any way we're building fire here, though, with that wind screaming along the cliff face. I will add just this—Evans, he still isn't looking so good. Face was almost purple when he was yelling.

— From the diary of Robert "Cairo Bob" Allen, 1841-1928

November 24, 1886

Bob packed his diary away in his saddlebag. They had been waiting, hoping for a break in the storm, but the weather, if anything, was worse. He checked his own watch. "Damn near two o'clock," he said. "Time to fish or cut bait. We can't get a fire going. I still say we should back off, find a more sheltered place, build up and wait out this storm. Should be some better shelter in that stand of spruce off south of us."

The snow had fallen all night, and a foot-deep drift had gathered in front of the tomb and in the lee of the tiny lean-to, which was considerably the worse for wear from the wind. The snow, at least, had stopped for the moment, but the wind was howling louder and harder than ever.

"No," Evans said. He picked up the axe and swung it into the sheet of ice blocking the tomb, knocking off a few small chips. "I'm not waiting. I can't wait. Got to get into this frozen bastard." He swung the axe again, and again, until his face turned almost blue.

"Let me spell you," Bob said. He took the axe. *At least it will keep me warm*, he told himself.

Every swing of the axe removed a few chips of ice. After an hour, maybe a hands-breadth of ice was removed from the edge of the boulder.

"This will take a while," Bob predicted.

"Let me take a turn," Evans said. He swung again and again, his strength fueled by frustration, his face growing dark with effort.

"Wish we had some dynamite," Bob said.

"Wish you'd have thought of that back in Boise," Evans grunted.

"Me too," Bob said. He went to the dying fire, looking around for some reasonably dry wood to try to keep it going. "But you're the one with the plan, you know. If anyone should have thought of dynamite, you're the one."

"Fair enough," Evans said, and swung the axe again. The wind gusted again, stronger.

The two men took turns hacking away at the ice into the night. At midnight Bob wanted to stop to sleep. "Sleep if you want," Evans said. "I'll keep at it."

"Fine," Bob snapped. "Wake me in two hours. I'll spell you. And then, Evans, you goddamn well will sleep, or I'll knock you out. Dropping down from exhaustion don't help either of us."

"All right," Evans said. He swung the axe again. "I'll wake you. Go on, sleep."

When Evans woke him, Bob looked at his watch. "Damn you,"

he said, "It's half past five. Dawn in an hour or so. Why the hell didn't you wake me earlier?"

"Didn't think of it," Evans gasped. He looked like hell. He coughed and coughed, spat blood into the snow. His face was brick-red. "I been working on that bastard and keeping the fire up. Go on, take a look at her, but first look up."

Bob suddenly realized the howling wind was gone. He looked up to see a billion ice-flake stars shining down. "I'll be damned," he marveled, "the weather broke."

"And that damn ice faces east," Evans said, "into the morning sun. Might help some."

"Let me check the horses."

Bob examined all four animals carefully. They were miserable but in reasonably good shape; they had been picketed for the night in a stand of tall, dry grass, of which they had eaten almost all within their reach. As the sky started to brighten, Bob poured the last corn into feedbags for the animals. *Maybe one day's worth of oats left*, he told himself on examining the inventory of fodder. *Then it's dry grass unless we can find some more grain. Hope they live. Hell, hope we live.*

"Let me spell you on the axe," Bob said. Evans had stopped swinging the axe and was standing, staring at the two-foot-wide bite taken out of the ice.

"Evans?" Bob said. "Sam?"

Evans turned slowly. He dropped the axe. His face was purple, and his lips blue. "Oh, hell," he managed to gasp, and fell on his face.

Bob leaped to the fallen man's side. He turned him over, and saw Evan's eyes staring, silently, upward. A final rattle escaped the man.

Bob had seen death all too many times during the War of the Northern Aggression. Now, after all these years, it was like an old, hated friend, returning to pay him a call.

"Guess I can't hardly bury you, Sam," he told the corpse. "Ground is froze hard as a Yankee's head. Sure as hell hope you was telling the truth about your heart, or your lungs, or whatever. Hope you ain't passed on whatever kilt you. And, you son of a bitch, you brought me out here, and now you've up and died on me. What am I going to do now?"

Bob went over and sat by the fire. The blaze was going a little better now with the gale blown out, and after a while, the sun came up and cast a watery light over the box canyon, warming things up a little.

Can't hardly stop now, Bob told himself. *Besides which, sun's coming out. Damn you, Sam Evans, but maybe your plan might just work after all. Spruce trees over on that slope to the south, there should be some branches under the trees still pretty dry, and spruce burns hot and fast. Yeah, worth a try.*

He dragged Evan's body away from the tomb and, frowning, placed the corpse under the lean-to on the dead man's bedroll. He wrapped the bedroll around the body, thinking, *he'll be froze hard as a carp in a couple of hours. Got to figure what to do. Can't leave him here for the wolves. Wouldn't be decent.*

Bob turned and looked at the tomb. He had the beginnings of an idea, but it was an idea that still involved getting through that ice face. *Got to go on*, he thought, *what can I do now but go on?*

There was still Isis, back there in Nevada, in the cabin on Clear Creek. *Got to get through this. Got to get home. Got to live. All of it means getting through that ice.*

He went over to the tomb, picked up the axe and set off towards the stand of dark spruce, about a half-mile away.

November 25, 1886 – The Tomb

Sam's dead as a doornail, and here at the tomb, it's just me. But at least the weather broke. Still cold as hell,

*but the sun's out and the wind died down. I made one trip
on foot over to the spruce and brought back some pieces of
dry wood, then got a bright idea and took both pack horses
over, loaded them up with spruce branches and some bark
off a dead tree for kindling. There's plenty of rock about, and
with the axe I managed to pry out enough flat rock to make
a flat fireplace about five feet by three feet, off the ice and
snow, right at the base of the entrance to the tomb. By noon I
had a roaring, big fire going, and the ice was starting to rot.
I took one of the horses over for another load of firewood,
and when I got back, the ice was melting away fast. I let the
horse rest and took up the axe.*

    — *From the diary of Robert "Cairo Bob" Allen, 1841-1928*

November 25, 1886

Bob sat, watching the ice melt. He had attacked the ice with
the axe on and off through the day, but it was apparent that the fire
was doing most of the work. As the ice melted, he could see the
flat boulder enclosing the tomb more clearly.

That's a damn heavy rock, he thought, peering through the
smoke and flames. *Going to have to wait until the fire's gone out,
maybe hitch one or both of the pack horses to it, pull it over.*

The sun was growing low in the sky again. Bob dragged Evans'
body away from the fire and away from the lean-to and piled some
loose brush over him; he had no desire to sleep next to a corpse.

Bob slept well that night, with the campfire and the roaring
blaze at the tomb entry to keep him warm. He got up several times
through the night to feed both fires, but otherwise passed the first
reasonably comfortable night he had spent at the tomb.

In the morning, in the first light of the weak winter sun, he let the fire at the tomb die down. *Most of the ice is gone*, he noted. With the axe, he chopped away the remaining fragments.

Bob touched the flat stone barrier. It was still warm to the touch, but not hot enough to hurt. He put on his leather gauntlets, grabbed the top of the boulder, and pulled. The rock did not budge.

Should have known that wouldn't work, he reminded himself. *All right, then, I'll try the other way.*

The pack horses had no collars for pulling, but Bob managed to loop a length of rope around a small projection at the top of the flat boulder and made the ends of the rope fast to the pack saddles, hoping that would be enough.

It was. Bob walked around to the animal's heads, took hold of their bridles, one in each hand. "All right," he said, "Git 'er up. Come on," he said, pulling the bridles.

The horses drew the rope taut, straining a little. The flat rock shifted, sank a little into the wet earth, then slowly—ever so slowly, at first, then suddenly—fell over.

"Good," Bob said, patting each horse's nose in turn. He suddenly remembered something he had seen among Evan's gear, went looking in the man's saddlebags—yes, there were some cubes of sugar. He gave a couple to each horse before untying the rope. He picketed both horses in a new stand of dry grass.

Then, Bob went back to the tomb.

Well, he thought, *this is it, sure as hell.*

He looked inside the open tomb, but it was too dark to see. A brand from the campfire did for that, and finally, at long last, Bob entered the Spaniard's tomb.

The chamber was small, maybe eight feet deep, six feet across, and five feet high; Bob had to crouch a little to go in. The floor of the tomb was dusty and dry.

There was nothing on the floor. In the back of the tomb, there was a hole, partially obscured with what was left of some kind of wooden cover.

Bob stepped to the hole and pushed the cover out of the way. He held the brand so he could see down into the hole.

There were a few scattered bones and scraps of cloth. A man's skull looked up at him out of sightless eyes.

No gold. No jewels. No silver. No nothing. Just some dry bones and scraps of cloth.

"Son of a bitch," Bob muttered.

Feeling a little ghoulish, he moved the skull aside. Nothing. He rooted through the scattered bones, through the scraps of cloth that disintegrated almost on touch.

"Nothing," he said. "God damn it."

Bob went back outside. He looked at the campfire, at the makeshift shelter, and then at Evans' wrapped body, not far away. Cursing softly, he picked up the coffee pot, packed it full of snow, and set it on the fire.

He squatted morosely by the fire, waiting for the coffee to boil. His eyes kept drifting back to Evans' body.

Well, Bob thought, *he's dead. My Ma would have cut a switch and took a lick out of me if I'd have spoke ill of the dead, and I suppose she had a point. But damned if he didn't leave me in a hell of a spot. All the way up here in Canada, probably illegal to boot, and no damn gold or nothing.*

I suppose he thought he was doing me a good turn. But damned if it ended up that way. I'm no closer to getting Isis back than I was before I set out.

Then he looked up, at the pack horses and Evans' saddle horse, at Evans' traps laying near the lean-to, the rifle leaning on Evan's saddle under the lean-to. He remembered Evans had a little Smith & Wesson sixgun in one of his coat pockets. *I didn't even ask him if he had any kin,* Bob realized. *Wonder if he has anything in his pockets, might give some clue. If he has any folks, they'd probably care to know what happened to him.*

Damned if I know what I was thinking, leaving Carson City to chase this here wild goose. One thing, at least—spare as things is, I'm coming out of it better than Evans, and that's for sure and for certain.

The coffee boiled. Bob set about putting some venison on the fire to warm up, tossed in a little bacon to give it some heft. He looked around again. *Might come out of this a tad better than broke,* he realized, *presuming I make it back to Boise.*

Reckon I'll spend the night here, he thought. *Sleep a bit warmer just inside that tomb, anyway, with a fire at the entrance. Then tomorrow I'll load everything up, light out for the border. Snuck two of us up here past the Mounties, reckon I can sneak back by myself.*

November 27, 1886 –The Tomb

Nothing, God damn it all, nothing. Not so much as a damn bauble. No Spaniard coins, doubloons or whatever, not so much as a copper penny. Just some old dry bones and scraps of cloth that fell apart when I touched them. Not sure what the hell I'm supposed to do now, but I guess I need to do something with Sam Evans. Never did tell me whether he had any kin anywhere, back in West Virginia or anywhere else. Hell, I don't even know if that's his real name. I went through his pockets, just to see if he had any letters or anything that might give me a clue but didn't find anything but his sixgun, a twenty-dollar gold piece, and a silver half-dollar, all of which I kept, as he ain't got any use for it anymore. Taking his rifle, too, and the rest of his traps. Figure he owes me something anyway, dragging me all the way out here for nothing, and I have to say, if this place ain't

*about five steps from Hell, I'm a Yankee. Leastways I reckon
I know now what to do about Sam's remains. After that, I'm
going to quit this place. I am going home.*

— From the diary of Robert "Cairo Bob" Allen, 1841-1928

November 27, 1886

The last morning broke cloudy but warmer. Some of the ice
above the tomb entrance was dripping. *Figures*, Bob told himself
as he lay in his bedroll, looking up at the drips of water. *All that
work breaking in here, and the damn thing starts to melt now.
Speaking of which…*

He got up, poked up the coals in the small fire he had placed at
the entrance to the tomb, added some dry sticks and got the coffee
going. With that done, he walked over to examine Sam Evans'
body.

Well. No use putting it off.

He grabbed the ends of the bedroll and dragged the body
into the tomb. Evans was frozen pretty solid, but Bob managed to
squeeze his frozen corpse into the grave, atop the scattered bones
of the Spaniard. The wooden cover wasn't much of a lid, but it
was all there was, so Bob placed it carefully atop the grave of the
man he knew nothing about, other than his health issues and his
misguided quest for Spanish gold.

"Well," he said out loud. Removing his hat, he bowed his head.

"Well," he repeated. He wasn't sure what to say, but felt he
needed to say something. "Lord," he went on at last, "I know I ain't
talked to you much these last years, not since the war, really. Ain't
seen the reason to, and that's the truth. But there ain't nobody to
speak for this fella in the ground here but me, so here I am. He
told me his name was Sam Evans, and Lord, I reckon you'll know
him, whether that's his real name or not. I didn't know him well.
I could easily hold a grudge against him for dragging me all the

way out here for nothing, but he's dead, and grudges don't do no one no good, 'specially not when the fella you're begrudging is dead, so I won't. All I'll say is this: I don't think what he did was out of any malice, I think he was just misguided, and misguided me into it along with him. He didn't seem like a bad fella. He was good enough company on the trail here these last few days. If he's there with you, Lord, if you could just pass that on to him, maybe it will make the dying easier. And if he is, please tell him I'll see him again, someday, walking the streets of Glory."

He opened his eyes and looked down at the wooden grave lid. "Amen," he said. He put his hat back on and walked outside to see to the horses.

By mid-morning he was on the way south. Riding one horse and leading three others slowed him some, and his choice of moving through the rougher country of the low foothills made it slower, but within two days he figured was near the border. After an hour spent on a low rise looking over the country, he made his way south, keeping to low ground until he figured he had to be back in Idaho Territory. Late that day he ran into two Indians out hunting deer who confirmed that information.

Good, he thought. *One less damn thing to worry about.*

Two days later he was in Boise. After taking up the same room in the Monarch Boarding House for a night, he went back to Colonel Appleton's stable and sold the two pack horses and their packsaddles and assorted tack. Evans' saddle horse he kept for a spare. A hardware store on the same street as the boarding house bought Evans' revolver and his '66 Winchester. The balance of Evans' traps he kept, against the odd chance any of the dead man's kin might come around looking for him.

That evening, dressed in clean clothes, bathed, with eighty-two dollars in his pocket, Bob felt finer than he had in some time. The drummer from his first night in Boise was gone, replaced by a skinny old man who was a traveling salesman for a piano company. The other faces around the table were more or less familiar.

Mrs. Dalby came in with a huge cauldron of beef stew. Her boy followed, with a big platter bearing fresh, hot bread. Bob spooned up stew until his bowl like to overflowed. As seemed to be the way with Mrs. Dalby, the stew was long on potatoes and short on beef, but the bread was hot, there was fresh butter, and there was plenty of hot coffee.

"How are you finding the stew, Mr. Allen?" Mrs. Dalby asked, impressed at the speed with which Bob was shoveling it in.

Bob stopped eating long enough to grin and reply. "Mighty fine, ma'am," he said. "*Mighty* fine."

What the hell, he thought to himself as he ate. *I'm on my way home, I ain't dead, and I ain't broke. Things could have been a whole lot worse than this.*

After he ate, he thanked Mrs. Dalby again, then went to his room. The bed was narrow and hard, but the sheets were clean. Bob undressed, collapsed into the bed, and slept until almost a half-hour after sunup the next morning.

In the morning, after a huge plate of Mrs. Dalby's biscuits and sausage gravy and more coffee, Bob gave the widow lady an extra dollar by way of thanks. He saddled his horse and, leading Evans' horse—no, now his spare horse—he set off to the south, thinking as he went.

Funny how just a few days can make a difference. Lends a fella perspective, it does. Had some hard times there on that trail, hard as I've had since the war, but here I am, headed home. Didn't come out of it so bad. Won't be taking Isis any gold or precious stones, but I'll be taking her me.

She said I had to get out for a while. Well, I did 'er. She said I was getting stale. Well, I ain't stale no more, not hardly. Reckon I'll make a proper husband, now.

The day was turning fine for the end of November. *1st of*

December tomorrow, Bob remembered. *If I make good time, I'll prove Evans right—I'll be home by the 4th.*

I'll go right out to the place. Tell Isis I love her. That's all. Just that I love her, and I'm ready to come home.

Don't rightly see how she can argue with that.

December 4, 1886—Carson City, Nevada

Funny how a fella goes from here to there. I rode into Carson City real late last night, and it would have taken another couple hours to ride out to the place. Horses were tired, I was tired, and so damned if I didn't pass the night just like I had been doing before I took off looking for Spanish gold—sleeping in the stable stall with my horses. Could have took a room at the hotel or above the Dollar saloon, but figured I'd save my money. Slept plenty of worse places, and that's the truth. The straw was fresh enough and the stable warm enough that I passed the night all right. Now it's early morning. Still an hour before sunup, I bet, but I was antsy, couldn't sleep any more. Just walked over to Miller's Café—they open early—and got something to eat. Now I'm about to saddle my horse, ride out to the place, and see Isis. It's damn well long past time.

— From the diary of Robert "Cairo Bob" Allen, 1841-1928

December 4, 1886

A bird flew in front of Bob, making his horse shy up for a moment. "Come on, you goddamn stupid beast," he said, but good-naturedly; the horse was, after all, just being a horse.

There were a few patches of snow on the ground along the trail west out of Carson City here and there, in sheltered spots. Bob had heard tell that the blizzard that hit Pyramid Peak up in Canada had just been a snowfall here, and the weather had turned mild since. Now, with the morning sun rising behind him, Bob felt like there was a fine day coming on.

Going home, he thought for the hundredth time that day. The idea that Isis might not welcome him back had occurred to him, but he dismissed it—somehow, he knew that this was the right time to go back.

And the wad of bills in his wallet surely wouldn't hurt, either.

As was his habit, he thought as he rode.

Never did understand how a woman can have such a hold on a man, he mused. *Not just by his pecker, neither. Isis, she's got a hold of my heart. And my head. And my life.*

Wonder, did she know just what she was doing when she sent me away?

Up the trail towards him came a farm wagon pulled by two mules. Bob recognized the couple on the wagon. "Mister Henderson," he greeted them, "Missus Henderson."

"Why, Bob Allen," Chuck Henderson said, eyes wide. He pulled the mules to a stop. "Haven't seen you in some time, figured you'd moved on. Are you back home now?"

Bob reined in his horse. If his old neighbors—*Neighbors, hell, they live four miles away,* he remembered—but if they wanted to talk, Bob figured he could spare a few minutes.

"Fixing to be home a while, yes," Bob said.

"We see your wife now and then," Elmira Henderson added. "She's done a pretty fair job of keeping the place up. I hear tell some of the younger local men have come around a time or two, looking to shine her up, but she's sent them all away right smartly."

Bob chuckled. "Sounds like her, all right."

"Where you been?"

Bob considered Chuck Henderson's question for a moment. "Was gone up north," he said, deciding to go with the truth—or most of it. "Had a job of work to do up Canada way. It's done now, so I'm heading home."

"I'm sure you'll be glad to be home," Elmira said with a smile. "Well, Charles, we'd best be off—need to move on, if we're to get our trading in town done and back before evening chores."

"You're right," Chuck agreed. "Well, Bob, welcome home. Glad to have you back." Bob tipped his hat as Chuck Henderson snapped the reins to get the mules moving again.

Bob looked up the trail. It wasn't far now.

Another mile, and he came to the crest of a ridge overlooking the Clear Creek valley. Below, a mile and a half away, he could make out the outline of his cabin and his truck field in the morning sun. He thought he saw someone moving, in the meadow by the creek.

A cavalry scout's spyglass resided in one of his saddlebags, so Bob pulled it out, snapped it open with an ease borne of long experience, and looked.

And there she was. Isis was walking back from the creek through the lush meadow. *Right there where the creek floods that flat every spring*, Bob realized, *and where all the wildflowers come up when it drains dry. Prettiest spot on the homestead. Fitting I'd see her there, even if everything is brown and dead right now.*

He rode down the hill towards home. As he approached, the morning sun caught on the cabin's glass windows. That glazing was one of the few luxuries Bob had on the place, and now it caught the morning sun and sent it back at him as he rode, dazzling, blinding, there and gone, there and gone.

Bob didn't care. He was going home.

At the bottom of the hill the trail went through a small stand of poplars. When Bob had ridden through them, the cabin and fields lay before him—and there was Isis.

Her hands were dirty. She had clearly been up and working for a while, but sleep was still in her eyes; her long, black hair was still rumpled. She was wearing her old dress, the one she kept for choring.

Prettiest damn thing I've seen in the last eight months, Bob said to himself, *and that's for sure and for certain.*

He rounded the last bend. Isis heard the hooves approaching as she was walking towards the cabin with a bucket of water from the creek. She stopped and looked towards the road.

Yep, Bob realized, *she still has that same hold on me she always did. Strong enough to send me into the teeth of a blizzard chasing an impossible thing, just on the chance she'd take me back. And hell, I still don't know if she even will!*

"Shit," he said, quietly.

He booted his horse and rode on in.

December 4, 1886—Clear Creek Valley, Nevada

Something's going to happen here in a few moments, so I stopped to organize my thoughts, like, before riding on ahead. I can see her there, standing on the edge of the truck garden. Looks like she's seen me and is waiting. Morning sun's behind me, so I reckon all she sees is outline of a horse and rider. It's almost like when we were courting, I'm all nervous, like. She looks like she's been out pulling up the last potatoes. Place looks good. She looks good, dirty hands and all. Reckon I'll ride on ahead.

— From the diary of Robert "Cairo Bob" Allen, 1841-1928

December 4, 1886

Bob put the pencil in his diary, closed it and stuffed it in his jacket pocket. He picked up the reins and clucked to the horse.

The moment's stop to jot down his thoughts had managed to let his heart slow back down, if not quite to normal.

He rode up the trail, into the lane, and up to the cabin, where Isis had walked to greet him.

"Bob," she smiled at him. "Where have you been?"

"Around," Bob said, still on his horse, suddenly tongue-tied. "Here and there. Carson City, Boise, was up in Canada a spell."

"Canada?"

"Yup," Bob confirmed.

Isis narrowed her gaze at him. "Something's happened to you. You're... different."

"That's what you sent me away for, I reckon," Bob replied. "And you're right. Reckon I am different. Changed. Not as much as the war changed me, not as much as Egypt changed me, but hell, everything a body does changes 'em in one way or another."

"Different good? Or different... bad?" Isis was frowning.

"Different, different, I guess. I ain't turned mean if that's what you're after."

"So, you were gone a while. What happened?"

And then the whole story spilled out. Bob talked for a good half-hour, still on the back of his horse: The idle months in Carson City, drinking more than was good for him, sleeping in the stable and sometimes in the gutter. Then the rumor, the ride north, and finding Sam Evans. Sneaking across the border, the blizzard, the tomb, Sam's death. The disappointment, the ice, the cold that crept into a man's soul. Then, finally, the long ride home, and the growing warmth along the way, until that morning, when he arrived, there in the lane, in the morning sun.

"And that's how she went," Bob concluded at last.

He noticed that the horses, having grown bored, were cropping at the grass alongside the lane. Embarrassed at his own uncharacteristic loquacity, Bob dismounted. "And here I am. Come home."

"Come home," Isis repeated. She stepped closer, looked into Bob's eyes. He flushed. She smelled like creek water, dirt, and fresh bread, somehow all mixed up together. "You *have* changed," she observed. A slow smile spread across her face. "You ain't stale anymore. Makes sense, what you been through."

"Reckon I ain't," Bob said. "Oh," he said, remembering, "and I ain't come home skint, either." He pulled out his wallet, displayed the bills. "Did manage something out of that trip north. Little over eighty dollars here. Ain't a fortune, but it ain't nothing."

"That's good, but Bob, none of this was about money."

"I know," Bob said, "but hell, money never hurt nothing, either. Cabin could use another room, couldn't it? And with two horses, maybe I can break another field, grow some truck for sale, actually get us ahead a little."

Isis nodded. She looked thoughtful. "Well," she said, "Come on inside. There's coffee, and I'll fry you up some bacon." She smiled. "It is your house, after all."

When Bob had a cup of coffee and a plate of pork and biscuits in front of him, Isis excused herself—"got to clean up from morning chores," she said, and disappeared into the cabin's tiny bedroom. As Bob ate, he heard the water pitcher clanking against the basin they used for washing.

Home at last, he thought as he chewed. *Home at last. Wonder if she'll turn me out again? Don't hardly seem like she's of a mind to.*

Outside, he could hear chickens clucking. Out behind the homestead's small shed, in the pen, he could faintly hear the pigs grunting as they worked through their morning ration.

He finished up. Of a mind to help, he stuck his plate and cup in the cabin's tiny tin sink and poured some water out of the bucket into them to soak.

Maybe could get a well drilled, he thought. *Hate to have to go to the creek every morning and evening for water. Make everything easier to just have a pump handle here. Should take a look at the door on that shed, too, damn thing never was set quite right. Ought to have a proper barn, instead of just a corral and lean-to for the horses.*

He smiled at himself. *Thinking like a homesteader again,* he realized, *almost like a proper husband. Careful, Cairo Bob, you're in peril of turnin' respectable.*

"Bob," he heard her voice. He turned.

Isis had brushed out her long, black hair and put on the deep blue linen dress she'd worn the day they were married. Bob suddenly remembered the cold rain that had fallen that day, and then he remembered other things.

"Sorry," Isis said. "Takes a while, to do myself up proper."

"You look fine," Bob breathed. "But..." He still had that last, nagging trace of doubt.

"Are you going to stay, Bob?" Isis asked. "You are gonna stay, right?"

Bob grinned. "If you want me to," he said. "Hell yes!"

Isis smiled, and held out her hand.

May 5, 1924 –Clear Creek Valley, Nevada

Haven't written anything in this here diary since the day I got home in December of 1886, as I read it here, but today I reckoned it time to do so. Isis passed away yesterday. A year and a day short of our fortieth anniversary. She was eighty-one, and with me eighty-four this year, don't reckon I'll be long after her. Our son Robert is here—no "Bob" for him, him having gone to West Point and all, even going to France with Blackjack Pershing in the Great War. Yankee army these days wears brown, not blue, so that's something. Robert lives up in Elko now, reading law, with his wife Betty and their five kids. All of them here today, come down from

Elko in Robert's new motorcar. Isis sure did get a kick out of the grandkids. Wish she could have seen all of them growed up. Wish I could, too, but don't reckon that I'll last that long. I ain't sad about that. It will be good, to be with Isis again, to see her smile, one more time.

> — *From the diary of Robert "Cairo Bob" Allen, 1841-1928*

May 5, 1924

"You doing all right, Dad?" Robert Edward Allen asked his father. *Not Pa, like I would have said*, Bob mused. *Dad. Times change.*

Bob shifted in his chair. He could see out the window of the screen porch he had built twenty-some years before, to where a line of willows marked the progress of Clear Creek. "I'm all right," he said. "As good as can be, with your Ma gone." In the house's tiny parlor, which had once been the main room when the house was just a cabin, stood a coffin, with the mortal remains of Bob's wife inside. The funeral was to be the next day.

"Your Ma asked to be buried under the big willow out back, you know," Bob said to his son.

"I know, Dad. It's all arranged."

"Time comes, you'll put me right there with her, won't you?"

"I will, Dad. That's a promise. You and Mom were together long enough in life, figure you'd want to spend eternity together as well."

"I reckon so," Bob whispered.

Robert sat down in the chair opposite his father. "I still remember when this house wasn't much more than a cabin. I remember being about ten years old, and you had me fetching wood, nails, and shingles to help build the bedrooms on to the south, and this screen porch here, just a couple of years later."

"Was just a cabin, when I first come to be here," Bob said. "Just a cabin. Cabin, couple of horses, some pigs and chickens, and a truck garden. Not much, but enough. Those were some fine days."

"You've been here a long time," Robert said.

"Long time," Bob agreed. "Of course, I wasn't here the whole time."

"Huh?" Robert's eyes widened. "What do you mean, you weren't here the whole time?"

"Reckon you never heard tell," Bob said, and described the trip up into Canada—leaving out the fact that he had been prompted by Isis kicking him out. Bob figured the boy didn't need to know that about his mother, not now, not with her freshly dead, and the shock still new in their hearts, blossoming like a black flower.

"Before all that," Bob explained, "I wasn't a young man, but, well, I wasn't a serious man. Figured four years of war and ten years of Egypt would have burned that young man's foolishness right out of me, wouldn't you? But maybe I just needed that last little shove. Anyway, I come south out of Canada with no treasure except what I'd learned about myself by almost freezing to death. I was a better man after that, son, and that's a fact."

Robert nodded. He'd seen his own share of death and horror in the trenches, Over There. The boy carried a scar on his shoulder from a shell fragment. He knew about mud and blood and lice and rats, about artillery and machine guns. He hadn't told his father about those things. He didn't have to. He knew his father understood.

Then Robert's wife came in from the kitchen. Betty Allen was a petite, vivacious girl with a head full of blonde curls. Bob approved of her, and Isis had, too. After her poured in the grandchildren, three boys and two girls, aged fifteen to four. Bob managed a smile for the little ones. He had the strength for that.

The funeral was the next day. Bob stood there in a black suit smelling of mothballs, not listening to the droning of the Carson City preacher Robert had fetched out. *I'll see you soon enough, Isis,* he thought. *What the hell, maybe I'll see that bastard Sam Evans up there, too. Not sure if I'll shake his hand or bust his nose. Don't suppose God cottons to fighting on the streets of Glory, so...*

He looked at the closed coffin. Isis had long since insisted that there would be no viewings. "I want my family to remember *me*," she said, "not some waxworks figure in a pine box." She was right.

Isis, he thought. *There was something magical about you. About us. Hell with Canada—if I'd have gone back to Cairo, sooner or later, I'd have crawled on my hands and knees through busted glass to get back to you.*

Reckon you know that, don't you?

You drove me a little bit crazy at times. Suppose I did the same to you. But that's life, and we had a hell of a good one, after all. Lord, I remember the day we wed. That cold rain, that young preacher just out of seminary—he just said the words for you here, just now. He's an old man now, just like I'm an old man now, but if I had the chance, I'd give everything I own in the world just to see you now, like you were on that day, in that blue dress, smiling at me even with that cold rain coming down.

I'll see you soon, Isis, he thought. He stepped forward, laid a hand on the pine box. *I'll see you soon.*

Legionnaire
Inspired by
Bob Dylan's "Shelter From The Storm."

Marseilles, France - 1911

The old man sat in a chair, at a table, with a glass of red wine in front of him. His trousers were old and patched. His shoes were scuffed. On the lapel of his threadbare jacket, he wore a brass device, the grenade emblem of the French Foreign Legion.

He looked up at the midday sun. It was a bright, warm day, as summer days in Marseilles generally were. He closed his eyes and smiled. He had little money, but he had enough for his one-room flat on the *Rue Jean Galland*, enough to feed himself, enough to enjoy a few glasses of wine now and then—or maybe a little more often than that. That was all that mattered. After all, he had no one but himself to please.

"Come a long damn way from South Carolina," he muttered.

When he called for another glass of wine, he spoke French, with the accent of Marseilles. His first tutor in French, many years ago, had been a profane French Army sergeant, who was followed by his total immersion into a world where his soft South Carolina English was unheard. But his personal mutter, in English, had not gone unnoticed; a young man passing by on the sidewalk stopped and stared at the old man.

The old man, feeling the younger's scrutiny, looked up. "*Comment puis-je vous aider?*" he asked.

"I heard you just now," the young man replied. In English. With the accent of Virginia. "You an American?"

"Well," the old man replied, again in English, "that's a right good question. I suppose part of me still is. I was a Confederate, last time I was in the New World. Been a long time since then."

"What brings you here?" The young man nodded towards the empty chair opposite the old man and, receiving nodded assent, sat down.

"Son, that's a long story. First, why don't you tell me what you're doing in Marseilles?"

"Looking for something to do. I come from a small farm a way west of Portsmouth. Old man grows cotton and some truck. Didn't really want to live my life looking at the south end of a northbound mule, so I left. Now I'm looking for some excitement, I guess. Been working my way across Europe."

"Now that rings a bell," the old man said. "What's your name?"

"Philip McGraw," the younger answered. "And you?"

"Caleb Pettigrew. Once of the Army of Northern Virginia. Later, the *Légion étrangère*. That's the French Foreign Legion." He tapped the brass device on his lapel. "Now? Just an old fart drinking wine in Marseilles."

"The Foreign Legion? Now *that* sounds interesting. Can you tell me about it?"

Caleb pointed to his now-empty wine glass. "Tell you what, sonny—grab us a bottle of wine, and I'll yarn on as long as you care to listen. When it comes to the Legion, I could tell stories all day. The Legion was my home, for a long damn time. Could be I could tell you about the War of the Northern Aggression, too, if you like."

"Heard plenty about that from my Grandpaw. He was in Stuart's cavalry. But I'd like to hear about the Legion." The young man's French was rudimentary, but he managed to flag the waiter, requested a bottle of wine and a plate of bread and cheese.

"OK," Philip McGraw said once they were served. "How'd you come to join the Legion in the first place?"

"Now that," Caleb said, "that's a good question."

Northern Virginia, April 12, 1865

Two Confederate soldiers—former Confederates, now—stood, talking. Both were scrawny, both were lousy, and both knew all too well the recent sting of defeat. But Marse Bob had given the order, stack arms and quit, and so they had done so.

"Well," Caleb Pettigrew said sadly, "That's it. We're whipped. Handed in my musket. Now we just have to figure what comes next. What are you gonna do now?"

"Hear tell Egypt is looking for soldiers," Caleb's friend Bob Allen answered. "Might head that way. Don't rightly know if I can stay here, not with the Yankees runnin' everything."

"Ha!" Caleb slapped his old friend on the back. "Not a bad idea, but I think I may head somewhere a might cooler. Europe, maybe. They're always scrapping over there, bound to be a place for a man who's good with a musket."

"Same in Egypt, I reckon," Bob replied.

"Too hot for me. Well, old buddy—I got my back pay, I got the clothes on my back, and not a damn thing else. Guess I'll head for Norfolk, see if I can brag my way onto a ship for Europe. What about you?"

"Hear tell of recruiters for Egypt working out of Charleston. Yankee soldiers were talking about it. Figure I'll check that out."

"I can see it now." He laughed. "Hell, they'll be calling you Cairo Bob for the rest of your born days."

"Likely. And you? What will they call you?"

"S'pose I'll find out when I get to wherever I'm going."

"All right."

The two old friends shook hands. "See you in Hell, Bob," Caleb said.

"See you in Hell, Caleb," Bob replied.

The two soldiers looked at each other one last time, then turned and walked away.

It took five days for Caleb to walk to Norfolk. The roads were crowded with downcast men in tattered gray, heading home. He heard rumors—that the cause was not lost, that out west General Smith was still fighting, that President Davis and a core of loyal followers were fleeing to Mexico, to try to find a way to continue the fight.

Caleb digested the rumors and kept on. He had made up his mind.

He arrived in Norfolk with his shoes disintegrating and his belly empty. Making his way to the waterfront, he finally discarded the remains of his shoes, and walked in bare feet down a row of ships with everything he owned—a pocketful of worthless Confederate banknotes, the remains of his gray uniform, a tattered kepi, and a cheap clasp knife in one pocket. One ship caught his eye. The aging barkentine flew the flag of France, and a loutish man in loose trousers and a stained tunic lounged at the foot of the gangplank.

"Pardon me, friend," Caleb asked the man. "Wouldn't happen to be looking for any help here, would you? I'll work for passage."

"*Il est possible,*" the man replied. His face scrunched up, like a cheap ham actor trying to register Deep Thought. "*Pardon,*" he said at last. "My Eenglish, she is not so good. Can you work?"

"I can work. I can fight. I can cook. I can do damn near anything."

"An' you wan' go to France?"

"I want to go anywhere away from here. In case you ain't been watching the news, friend, we-uns just got our asses kicked. I want to get out while the gettin's good."

"You ever sail the ship before?"

"Nothing this big. Rowboats a lot. Sailed in my uncles' little sailboat in Charleston harbor a few times."

"Well, that is not nothing," the Frenchman mused. "Come along. I take you see the Captain. You convince him, it may be that he let you work for passage. And maybe, just maybe, for some shoes."

"Thanks," Caleb said. A thought occurred to him. "What port are we bound for?"

"Marseilles. Come along, now."

The Frenchman led the way up the gangplank. Caleb shrugged and followed.

Marseilles, France - 1911

"So, I found myself in Marseille," Caleb Pettigrew said, slapping the table. "Right here in this city. I didn't speak French. Not a word. I didn't have any way to earn a living. Oh, that ship captain, he gave me some shoes that didn't fit and a couple of changes of clothes. Henri, the guy I told you about at the dock in Norfolk, he told me they came from a guy who died of a fever on the trip over, and they'd just been sitting around since. Captain also gave me a few francs to tide me over, which was more generous than I expected him to be."

"Point is, I had nothing, and no prospects. I wasn't even in France legal; officially, I'd jumped ship. So, I spent a few nights sleeping in the sand under a dock—trust me, I'd slept plenty worse places during the fighting. Then I found an abandoned shack I could sleep in. But I was out of money—my belly button was rubbin' up against my backbone. And then I heard tell of the Legion. That's where I first met her."

"Her, eh?" Philip MacGraw grinned. "Now it gets interesting."

Marseilles, France, October 1865

"Aubagne?" Caleb asked the policeman, who by a stroke of luck, spoke some English. "How far is that?"

A Gallic shrug. "Thirty kilometers," the policeman said. "A bit more. A bit less."

"And I have to go there to apply to join this, what did you call it?"

"The *Légion étrangère*. You would say, the Foreign Legion."

The policeman had stopped Caleb as he was mooching along a Marseille sidewalk in the early morning, hoping to stumble across some breakfast, trying to decide what to do next. Fortunately, the *flic* seemed a kind-hearted sort; he was giving Caleb some advice, rather than just running him in for vagrancy, and had not (yet) asked for Caleb's non-existent passport.

"And were you in this here Foreign Legion?"

"*Non.*" The *flic* shook his head. "Me, I was regular French Army. The Legion, it is foreign, you know? For the not-French. You go there, if they take you, you will be fed, housed, clothed, can learn French, even earn the... *La citoyenneté*. That's good, *oui?*"

"I reckon." Caleb looked around. "Which way to Aubagne?"

"East," the policeman gestured. "In that direction. Thirty kilometers, maybe."

I wonder what that is in miles. "All right," Caleb said. "Guess I'll start walking. Thanks, by the way—uh, *merci.*" He had learned that much.

His good deed for the day—or perhaps the month—done, the policeman nodded and sauntered off down the street.

"Well," Caleb said to no one. The conversation with the policeman was the longest exchange he had carried out with another human since leaving the ship in Marseille harbor; not being able to speak the language had badly hampered Caleb's normally gregarious tendencies.

The abandoned shack where he had hidden his few

possessions was only a block away, so it took only moments to go there, pick up the old knapsack where his clothes and other effects resided, and start walking.

Fortunately, the last few years had put Caleb in good shape for walking. *At least no damn heavy musket to tote along now*, he thought, smiling to himself. *'Course I can't hardly talk to anyone, either.* He looked down at his sleeve of his gray shirt—the last remnant of his time with the Army of Northern Virginia—his baggy canvas trousers, his cheap canvas shoes that were at least a size too big. *Well, I been on many a forced march in worse than this.*

He set out in the direction the *flic* had pointed. When he came to a fork in the road at the edge of town, he waited until an old man leading a donkey laden with firewood happened along. "Aubagne?" Caleb asked, eyebrows raised in query.

The old man pointed. "*Là-bas.*"

"*Merci,*" Caleb nodded and set off down the road.

The day grew warm as Caleb walked steadily on. The road wound through farmland, past a few places with what Caleb assumed were grapevines, through several small villages. In one village, an old woman hailed him.

"*Où allez-vous?*" she asked

Caleb replied with one of the few phrases he had memorized. "*Je ne parle pas français. Je suis Américain.*"

The old woman shook her head sadly. "*Viens de la guerre,*" she said. Caleb shrugged, not understanding a word. The old woman held up a finger, then pointed down. That was clear enough: *Wait here.* Caleb waited as the old woman went into her little cottage and emerged again, bearing a chunk of coarse bread and a small wedge of cheese.

"*Por vou,*" she said.

Caleb felt genuinely touched, for the first time in a long time. He bowed. "Thank you kindly, ma'am," he said, then, remembering, "*Merci.*" The old woman nodded, then went back inside. Munching on the bread, Caleb walked on. When he finished the gifted meal, a stream running along the road supplied water. As the day grew warm, and the sun shone down, Caleb felt the lack of his old Confederate kepi, lost somewhere in the Atlantic, but all in all he was as comfortable as could be.

He arrived in Aubagne late in the day. The town didn't look much different than Marseille—no port, but otherwise, just another town where he had no place to stay and couldn't talk to anyone or read anything. But as the evening drew into night, Caleb located a military-looking compound; one doorway had a sign over it bearing the legend *Légion étrangère.* Caleb remembered, back in Marseille, the policeman's advice. "Looks like this is the place," he said to himself.

The office was shuttered for the night. But that was all right; Caleb set down his knapsack, extracted an old, tattered sailor's jacket, shrugged it on and settled down against the wall next to the door to wait out the night.

Caleb was awakened by a harsh voice, shouting at him in French. He opened his eyes and looked up, to see a tall, lean man in what was presumably a French Army uniform, leaning over him.

"English?" Caleb asked as he climbed to his feet.

"Yes," the soldier snapped back. "I speak some English. What is it you are doing, sleeping in front of our doorway?"

"Policeman in Marseille sent me this way. I wanted to talk to someone about joining up. I've been soldiering all over Virginia, Maryland, and Pennsylvania for the last four years. Figure on keeping on doing what I know."

"Ah," the soldier said. He looked Caleb over with a critical eye, evaluating his lean, hardened frame, the look in his eyes, the way he carried himself. "So, you come from the American *guerre civile,* then? And which side? The losing one, I presume, else why would you be here?"

"That's right," Caleb said bitterly. "The losing side. Not so much that we *lost*, mind, as much as we were just outnumbered."

"God always favors the side with the most battalions," the Frenchman observed, sounding oddly like he was quoting someone. Caleb shrugged.

"Well. Come inside. We will talk. I will have coffee and croissant brought in if you like. You will tell me about your war, I will tell you about the Legion, it may be that we can allow you to join." He unlocked the door, then looked over his shoulder at Caleb.

"I do not suppose you would have… eh, *le passeport*?"

Caleb was able to figure that out. "No," he said, a sheepish smile on his face. "It, uh, got lost. Somewhere along the way."

"*Assurément*," the soldier said. "Well. Come in. You may call me *Adjudant sous-officier* LeClaire. And you are?"

"Caleb Pettigrew, Corporal, Army of Northern Virginia, as was."

"*Bon*. Come in, then, *Caporal* Pettigrew."

Marseilles, France - 1911

"One thing that surprised me when I joined up," Caleb Pettigrew said after a pause to moisten his throat with some red wine, "what the rule of *anonymat*." You join under an assumed name, you see? It's like your past, your time before the Legion, it doesn't exist. Well, I figured, what the hell, my past was pretty messed up anyway. By the time I talked to LeClaire, I was exhausted, I was hungry, I'd been rained on, snowed on, hailed on, shot at with everything from revolvers to cannon, and I'd marched out at least five pairs of shoes going up and down from South Carolina all the way to Gettysburg and back."

"So, to join the Legion, you have to pick a new name?" Philip McGraw sounded like he didn't much like the idea.

"Yup."

"So, what name did you pick?"

Caleb grinned. "Well, I'll tell you. There was a lot of the War of the Northern Aggression I was happy to leave behind. But one of our corps commanders, well, if he hadn't gotten himself killed, he just might have turned things around. So, I took *his* name. For thirty years in the Legion, I called myself Tom Jackson."

"After Stonewall Jackson?"

"The very same. That's how I joined the Legion. Coming like I did from the Army of Northern Virginia, after four years of fighting, I didn't find the training to be too tough. And I was eating regular and sleeping well. I sure wasn't counting on what happened a few years later—1870, it was."

Sidi Bel Abbès, Algeria – August 1870

Sunday morning. Caleb Pettigrew woke slowly. As was usual in summer, the blistering heat of northern Algeria was already scorching in through the windows of the barracks. His head hurt; he had begun the evening around a card table with three other legionnaires, the game fortified by several bottles of red wine. He had ended the evening in the company of a rather talented Italian prostitute in a discreet little brothel in the center of the dusty little Algerian town that was the location of the 117 officers and 2,400 or so men of the Foreign Regiment.

Leastway's it's Sunday, Caleb thought to himself. In the privacy of his own thoughts, he still considered himself Caleb Pettigrew, even as his fellow legionnaires knew him as Tom Jackson. *No training exercises. No officers or sergeants comin' in hollering at us. Guess I'd better get up and find something to eat.* His head was pounding from the cheap, vinegary red wine his friend and fellow legionnaire had scrounged up. That worthy, a Spaniard who styled himself as Charles Sebastian Diego y Sanchez but whom Caleb simply called Charlie, was snoring away in a nearby bunk.

Caleb sat up. He picked up his canteen off the floor and sloshed it around; at least half-full. He removed the cap, drank down the tepid, nasty-tasting water, and then tossed the canteen at the sleeping Spaniard.

"Charlie," he called. "Wake up."

Sanchez stirred and muttered a few Spanish obscenities. His eyes opened, blinking at the morning light. He looked over at Caleb.

"*Por qué?*" he asked. He went on, in his usual mishmash of French and Spanish: "It's Sunday, *amigo*. We don' have to get up. And my head hurts."

"So does mine. Blame that shitty wine you came up with."

Sanchez sighed, resigning himself to being awake. He rotated himself on the narrow bunk, sat up, placed his long, narrow bare feet on the planked floor. "*Si*," he admitted, "the wine, it was not so good. But you must admit, *amigo*, it was better than no wine at all."

"I'd give my left nut for a bottle of decent sipping whiskey," Caleb grumped. Whiskey of any sort didn't seem to be available anywhere in North Africa, much less decent whiskey.

"You left the game early last night," Sanchez grinned. "You go to town, *si*? You go to see Marissa again?"

"You know damn well I did." Caleb's appetite for the buxom Italian prostitute was well-known.

"Tomas, you may end up ensnared, if you are not careful. The Legion, she does not wish us to have entanglements."

"I'm not getting entangled," Caleb assured his friend. "That's the last thing I need. Just having a little fun, that's all. Marissa's a girl with some substance, you know?" He mimed fondling two ample breasts, which made Sanchez grin broadly. "I like that. And if the Legion objected to us visiting a whorehouse, do you think they'd let this one keep operating, so close to the base?"

"It could be that you are right," Sanchez admitted. "And I have no intent of forgoing visits of my own."

At that moment a human hurricane burst into the room, an Englishman who bore the unfortunate (to Caleb's thinking) name of Grant Edward Smythe-Carstairs, and whom Caleb insisted on calling 'Eddie.' He was capable of pouring down wine, cognac, brandy, or any other alcoholic beverage endlessly with no ill effect; he was short, scrawny, loud, profane, and insisted repeatedly he came from a wealthy family of "bloody boring Cornwall landowners" and had joined the Legion "as a bit of a lark."

"Here, you lazy sods," he proclaimed, producing a canvas satchel. While he spoke French, as the Legion insisted upon, he necessarily rendered some terms in English— "the Queen's English," he loudly insisted at every opportunity. "Some bloody awful rolls from the mess hall. They had coffee, but I had nothing to carry it in. You'll have to go get that yourself." He opened the satchel and tossed rolls at his comrades, then took one himself and stuffed it into his mouth. "You all hear the news?" he asked, masticating noisily.

"What news?" Sanchez asked. He regarded the roll suspiciously, took a small bite and grimaced.

Caleb's stomach did a slow roll at the thought of eating. He set the roll aside. "Yeah, Eddie," he said. "What news?"

"The Army of the Rhine is defeated. The Prussians rolled right over them, just earlier this month. The Emperor, good old Napoleon III, he handed over command of the Army to Marshal Bazaine, and they are forming a second army, under the command of Marshal MacMahon."

"MacMahon?" Caleb asked. "That doesn't sound French. Sounds Irish."

"He is, old sod, he is," Eddie affirmed. "One of us, in fact; he came from the Legion, left in 1845 for the regulars."

"Will we be sent to France?" Sanchez asked.

"No poop on that yet, I'm afraid." Smythe-Carstairs sat down on his own bunk, extracted another roll from the satchel, took an enormous bite.

Caleb looked over at the rack of breech-loading Chassepot rifles. "Legion isn't allowed to fight in France, right? As I understand, they can't send us to Europe."

"Needs must when the Devil vomits on your pillow, old man," Smyth-Carstairs pointed out. "If His Imperial Majesty Napoleon III decides he needs the Foreign Regiment in France, then to France we shall go."

Caleb couldn't find a counter to that, so remained silent.

Over the next few weeks, the news from Europe just got worse. In September, Napoleon III was captured by the Prussians, and Marshal MacMahon surrendered the Army of Châlons to the forces of *Feld*marschall Helmuth von Moltke.

Two days after that news broke, the commander of the Foreign Regiment, Colonel Deplanque, announced that two regiments of the Foreign Legion would be sent to France, to fight for the new Republic.

"Hoo boy," Caleb Pettigrew muttered when he and his comrades received the news. It was early evening, after the evening meal, and the three legionnaires were once more relaxing in their barracks. "Was bad enough having Yankees shoot at me with muzzle-loaders." He looked again at the rack of the Chassepot breechloaders with their long, shining bayonets. "Gonna be a whole lot more bullets flying now."

"The Colonel," Sanchez pointed out, "he said, they are only taking volunteers."

"Yeah, and you know damn well anyone who stays behind— besides being stuck here with every German in the Legion, as they aren't taking them—will be branded as yellow, and never be promoted, not if he stays in the Legion until Judgement Day. No, no man will call me yellow. I'll go. Reckon you will too, right, Charlie?"

Sanchez nodded. "*Si*. It's why I joined—to fight."

"Eddie?" Caleb asked the Englishman.

"Too right, old man," Smythe-Carstairs agreed. "I'm in. Hope it doesn't prove to be a cock-up."

Caleb wasn't familiar with the English term 'cock-up,' but the meaning was pretty clear. "Well," he said, "I saw plenty of cock-ups in the War of the Northern Aggression. I lived through that. Reckon I can live through this. You two, follow my lead when it gets thick, you got that?" The other two nodded; Caleb was the only one among them who had seen actual combat, and he had seen plenty of it. "Follow my lead, and with a bit of luck, we'll get back to Sidi Bel Abbès in one piece."

"And you'll get back to Marissa," Sanchez said slyly.

"Yep." Caleb mimed fondling two large breasts again. All three of them laughed.

Marseilles, France – 1911

The plate of cheese and bread was exhausted, and the two Americans were on their second bottle of wine. Caleb Pettigrew, lost in his memories, was still holding forth.

"So, us volunteers, we were organized as the 5th Battalion, and assigned to General de La Motte Rouge's 15th Army Corps. We made it to Orléans on the tenth of October. They tossed us into the defense of the city. On the tenth and eleventh, we fought for that city, and we sure as hell fought. I thought the Yankees were tough—hell, the Yankees were tough—but those Prussians, they were something else. They just wouldn't quit."

"How did it all end up?"

Caleb emptied his wine glass, then looked at the empty wine bottle and frowned. He waved for the waiter. "I'll get this one, son," he said, and laid down a few coins. "Now where was I? Oh, yeah, Orléans. What a mess that was. We were outnumbered—but hell, anyone who followed Marse Bob Lee around for four years was used to that. Only advantage we had was a better rifle. The Chassepot was a damn sight more accurate and reliable than what the Germans were using—a "needle gun," they called it. One of our guys, a little Belgian called Féront, he killed eighty Prussian soldiers with his rifle, one at a time; little fucker just couldn't seem to miss. Then, late that day, our commander, Major Arago, was killed, and the French regulars passed down the signal to retreat."

Orléans, France, October 1870

The streets surrounding the large open square in the Bannier quarter of Orléans were obscured, partly by long, late-afternoon shadows, mostly by the thick clouds of gunpowder smoke that hung in the air. Caleb Pettigrew—Caporal Tom Jackson to his fellow legionnaires, Caleb having been promoted and placed in charge of a squad—crouched behind an overturned wagon, peering through the smoke, watching for the advancing Prussians.

Private Charles Sebastian Diego y Sanchez was lying on the ground beside Caleb. Private Grant Edward Smythe-Carstairs crouched a few feet away, covering behind the wreckage of a wall. The Englishman looked up. "Did you bastards hear that? The French regulars are sounding the retreat."

"Fuck that," Caleb said. "They won't be taking this square away from us."

"*Amigo*," Sanchez said, "We wait a few moments longer, we may no longer have anything to say about it."

The little dago's right, Caleb thought bitterly to himself. They were badly outnumbered; the streets were littered with the bodies of dead legionnaires and French regulars. Down the street, a figure wearing the light-blue uniform of the Bavarian *Jägers* peered around the corner of a wrecked building. A French Chassepot boomed from the second floor of a building to the left, and the Bavarian collapsed in a boneless heap. "That little Belgian Féront again, I'll wager," Eddie Smythe-Carstairs observed.

"Very likely." Caleb watched down the street, thinking hard. From somewhere in the rear, a bugle call, *Retreat.*

"Fuck it," he said in English, prompting a grin from Smythe-Carstairs and a confused look from Sanchez. Caleb switched back to his Legionnaire's French. "How many men do we have here?"

"Looks like about thirty," Smythe-Carstairs said, looking around. "Some from the first company, some from the third. We're all mixed up, old man."

"Any officers?"

"None that I can see."

"Sergeants? None of them, either? Who the hell is in charge of this mess?"

"Looks like you are, *amigo*," Sanchez said.

Caleb heard a voice, high-pitched in fear, shouting from their rear: *"The Prussians have closed ranks behind us! We are surrounded!"*

Well, shit. Come on, Caleb old boy. Think. What would Stonewall have done?

He remembered First Manassas. Sure as hell.

Caleb checked his ammo pouches. He had three rounds left, which he handed to the Spaniard. He laid his empty rifle down. A dead Legion lieutenant lay nearby. Caleb slid over to the dead officer, picked up the man's sword and his Lefaucheux revolver. He quickly checked the revolver and found it to be fully loaded.

He stayed in his crouch behind the improvised barricade. "Men of the Fifth Battalion," he bellowed, as loud as he could. *"Fix bayonets!"*

Around him came the rattle of bayonets being affixed to the men's Chassepot rifles. Down the street, a large body of Prussian and Bavarian soldiers were forming. *They are going to storm our positions.*

"We will charge," Caleb shouted. "And when you charge, yell. Yell like Furies!" *Why not,* he thought. *Sure scared the hell out of the Yankees.*

Caleb paused. He took a deep breath. Down the street, he could hear a Prussian officer shouting orders. *We need to get to them before they get to us*, Caleb realized. He leaped to the top of the barricade, sword in his right hand, revolver in his left. He pointed with his confiscated sword. A Prussian bullet went past his head, trailing a slight sound, *wheat.*

"Fifth Battalion!" Caleb roared. "*Forward!*"

The Legion charged.

Caleb ran in front of the men. The Prussians and Bavarians were frantically forming a line, maybe a hundred meters away. It seemed to take a century to reach them. Bullets whizzed past, missing Caleb only by what was surely a series of miracles. He ran, boots pounding, pointing with the sword, screaming the Rebel yell. Around him, legionnaires ran, copying the wild call. Caleb felt himself filled with an unreasonable, impossible joy. *The boys of the Army of Northern Virginia couldn't have done it any better.*

They lost a third of their number just reaching the Prussians. Caleb, out of the corner of one eye, saw Smythe-Carstairs go down, but there wasn't time to worry about his friend. He led the Legion crashing into the half-formed German lines. He slashed with the sword. A German private swung his Dreyse rifle around; Caleb pointed the revolver, awkwardly in his left hand, and put a bullet between the man's eyes. Around him, the men of the Legion fought like demons, until, at last, there was no point in going on. The Prussians were too many; the Legion, too few.

"Cease fire!" Caleb shouted in English. He shook his head;

drops of blood flew from his beard, but at least the blood wasn't his. "*Capituler!*" he shouted in French. "Surrender! *Déposer les armes!*" Caleb looked around; there were only eight men left to do so.

The Prussians, seeing the dropped rifles and raised hands, stepped forward to take the men of the Legion prisoner. Caleb laid down his revolver and looked around; there was Sanchez, hands held high. And there, supported by two of their fellows, was Smythe-Carstairs, a blood-soaked bandage wrapped around his leg. Caleb nodded.

A Prussian officer approached Caleb. Caleb looked at the man's insignia; a major. Caleb held out his sword. The Prussian major nodded and accepted it. "Corporal," the man said, in fair French, "I am told that you led this charge."

"I did," Caleb replied.

"I should like to shake your hand," the Prussian said. "You and your men are to be congratulated. That was one of the finest acts of courage I have ever witnessed."

Caleb shook the man's hand. "Thank you," he said.

The Prussian noted Caleb's accent. "You are not French," he said. "You are not from the Continent at all, I think."

"I'm an American," Caleb said.

"Ah. These are the men of the Legion, then."

"We are."

Then, impossibly, a volley of bullets crashed into the Prussian's flank. The Prussian major clutched at his chest and fell. Caleb and his comrades hit the ground, scrabbling for their abandoned weapons, but the volley had hit the Prussians and Bavarians. "Men of the Legion!" Caleb heard a voice shouting from a side street. "This way! Run!" Another volley; the Prussians were reforming, their prisoners, for the moment, forgotten. The men of the Legion disappeared into the growing shadows of the narrow street.

A few minutes later, Caleb came face-to-face with their savior;

a lieutenant of the Legion, Kara George. The man was short, swarthy, and impossibly, had a bedraggled flower stuck in the pocket of his uniform tunic. "Did you men not hear the retreat?" he demanded.

"Can't say as we did, sir," Caleb said. "Must have been too much shooting going on."

The lieutenant glared at Caleb. "I should ask your name," he said, "but I saw your charge. It is only good we were able to save you from captivity. I will be bringing this to the attention of the General, of course."

Caleb felt his stomach lurch. "Of course."

Five days later, Caleb was surprised to hear of his promotion to Sergeant, "in recognition of conspicuous gallantry."

Well, Stonewall, he thought after receiving the news. *I hope I did you proud.*

Marseilles, France – 1911

"I didn't see Eddie again after that. Two of the guys carried him out, but I heard later that they took his leg off below the knee, so I would think he went back home. And that lieutenant, Kara George? Would you believe he was a prince? Guy was crowned Peter I, King of Serbia, what, eight or nine years ago. Couldn't believe it was the same guy when I saw it in the newspaper, but sure as hell, it was him. Probably won't hear much more about it—when was the last time you even heard of anything anybody from Serbia ever did, anyway?"

"I couldn't even tell you where Serbia is," Philip McGraw replied.

"Out east," Caleb Pettigrew said helpfully, "south of Austro-Hungary. Not that anyone but the Serbians much care about Serbia."

"Probably. So, what happened after the battle?"

"That," Caleb said, "well, now, that got right interesting there for a while. See, losing a war to the Prussians, turns out it wasn't so hot for old Napoleon III. And some folks decided they could do better. Some of those folks were Communards, and they weren't about to wait to be voted in. They just tried grabbing with both hands, and the whole city of Paris went up like a tar barrel. People were screaming for soldiers to come bang heads together. Next thing you know, we were in Paris."

Paris, France – June 1871

Caleb Pettigrew—*Sergent* Tom Jackson to his fellows—and *Caporal* Charles Sebastian Diego y Sanchez walked cautiously down the streets of Paris. Both had their Chassepot rifles loaded. Caleb had found a knife that would have made Jim Bowie proud, and now he wore it conspicuously on his belt. He knew his Spaniard compatriot had at least three small blades concealed about his person. The two men of the Legion walked cautiously, their heads constantly swiveling about. The *Semaine Sanglante*— the Bloody Week—had seen the Communard rebellion crushed at last.

The Paris Commune was suppressed, twenty thousand Communards killed and many more captured, at the cost of seven hundred and fifty French regulars and men of the Legion. But the city was still tense, and nobody was yet quite sure who was in charge. The men of the Legion walked as cautiously as barefoot men walking through broken glass.

"I wonder when we will be sent back to Sidi Bel Abbès," the Spaniard mused aloud.

"Who knows? And why worry about it? I don't mind staying in Paris, long as things stay peaceful." Caleb had taken a minor wound, no more than a scratch, while storming a Communard barricade. Sanchez had come through untouched; the Spaniard seemed to live a charmed life.

"I would not mind either, *mi amigo,* but the law, she is not changed. The Legion is not supposed to be in France. Now that the emergency is over, one wonders when we will be sent home."

Caleb chewed on that a moment. "I suppose."

"Besides," the Spaniard continued, grinning, "there is always *tu dulce niña*, yes, my friend?"

Caleb smirked. He took his right hand off his rifle and mimed fondling an ample breast. "Well, sure, Charlie, there is that. And it's not like you've never been to that house your own self."

"*Si*, but I prefer variety. You, it is always Marissa."

"If you have a horse, you ride it." Caleb grimaced a little at the inaptness of the comparison. Marissa was many things, but horse-like was not one of them.

When the two legionnaires finished their patrol, they arrived back in the temporary camp on the outskirts of the city to find their fellows buzzing with the news: "Back to Algeria," was the word. Within the week, the Legion took ship at Marseille, bound for Oran.

"We will have to march from Oran to Sidi Bel Abbès," Caleb's Spanish friend observed as they filed onto a rather battered old two-master.

"Count on it," Caleb replied. "What the hell. Have to be alive to march. Plenty of men are dead."

"*Si.*" Sanchez shook his head sadly. "And the people of France, they are angry. Angry at the Prussians and Bavarians for parading through Paris. They will want revenge on the Germans, my friend, you wait and see—we may be done fighting them now, but we are not done fighting them for good."

"You forgot one other thing the people of France are angry at," Caleb said.

"What is that?"

"They're angry at us. The French regulars, the Zouaves, the Legion, all of us who fought and lost. Heard plenty of that when I was walking from Appomattox to Norfolk. Folks don't like being whipped. And just you watch, they'll blame us for it."

"Maybe. Maybe not. Napoleon III is gone, removed from his throne. France is a Republic now. Maybe things will be different."

"And maybe not. Well, we're going home at any rate."

When the ship finally got under way, Caleb remained on deck, leaning on the railing, listening to the shouts of the sailors as they scrambled up the masts and made sail, and enjoying the calm Mediterranean winds and the clear blue Mediterranean sky. He remembered his own brief stint as a sailor. *Never really did get the hang of it*, he reminded himself. *Guess I'm better at soldiering.*

The passage to Oran was uneventful. The ship docked safely, and the men of the Legion dismounted and formed ranks, under the direction of the surviving officers. Caleb took his place at the head of one of the ranks, due to his new status as *Sergent*, and was surprised to see a round-faced man in the robes of a priest sitting on a spavined old horse at the head of the column of legionnaires.

"This," bellowed a leather-lunged *Sergent-Major*, "...is the Bishop of Oran, His Excellency Jean-Baptiste-Irénée Callot. He will be accompanying us to Sidi Bel Abbès and will be holding holy services morning and evening along the way, for those of you miscreant souls whose confessions have not been heard in some time, as I suspect is the case for most of you. Attend! We will march as soon as all are in formation."

"Don't matter none to me," Caleb muttered, slipping into South Carolina English. "Raised a Baptist my own self. Damned old monkey in fancy robes ain't got nothing for me. Reckon it's the Old Place Down Below for me no matter what happens."

The legionnaire next to him glanced over. He spoke softly in French: "*Sergent*, you do not listen to the Bishop?"

Caleb shook his head. "Not likely. Quiet, now. Orders coming."

The Legion took their time marching home again—three days to cover eighty kilometers, through some rough, dusty country. Caleb, in his mind, translated the distance to fifty miles, musing to himself, *we'd have gone a lot farther and a lot faster if old Stonewall was cracking the whip.*

It was a hot, bright late July afternoon when they arrived at the Legion cantonment in Sidi Bel Abbès. A tall, scrawny, cadaverous *Adjudant* with a patch over one eye appeared in front of them. He extracted, of all things, a bugle, and blew a sharp three-note welcome.

Caleb chuckled. He wasn't the only one.

"Men of the Legion!" the walking cadaver shouted. "Stow your belongings. The refectory remains open until you have all been fed, but do not dally. Welcome home, legionnaires!"

"Welcome home," Caleb muttered. "Hurry up and get yourself fed, or else go hungry until morning." He went looking for his Spanish friend and found him in front of the barracks that they would be re-occupying.

"*Mi amigo,*" Sanchez said, "I am devastated that we will longer be in the same bay."

"Oh. Right." As a result of his promotion, Caleb would be moved into the non-commissioned officer's rooms at the end of one of the barracks.

"We can still be *amigos,* yes?"

"Don't see why not. You figure on heading into town after we eat?"

"*Si.* Like before we go to France, yes? You will be anxious to see Marissa."

"I suppose." Caleb remembered the Italian girl; her ample bosom, her narrow waist, her full lips, her white teeth—and her penchant for biting in the heat of the moment. "Yeah. I suppose I am."

Marseilles, France – 1911

Caleb Pettigrew drained another glass of wine. He looked up; the afternoon sun was moving along, behind the row of buildings. He looked over at Philip McGraw. The boy was hadn't been trying to keep up with Caleb's drinking, but the South Carolinian, after years of practice, had a high tolerance for red wine.

The old soldier went on: "Things were kind of quiet for a while after that. Oh, there was a big old scrap down in southern Algeria, the Battle of Chott Tigri, they called it. I got promoted again after that, and then again in 1880, mostly just because I hung around a long time. My buddy Charlie, he made *Sergent*, and I ended up as *Sergent-Major*. We just kind of kept on soldiering together— buddies, you know? Guys that have ended up facing death together, they end up like brothers, only maybe more so."

"That's what my Grandpaw used to say. He stayed pretty tight with his friends from Stuart's cavalry, letters, reunions, and such, until the day he passed on."

"That's just it. Anyway, other than that one scrap, we mostly just did training, field problems, saying goodbye to old guys getting out, breaking in the new kids coming in. Then, in 1883, boy, did the shit hit the fan. We ended up going half-way around the world, a place called Indochina. And was that ever a mess!"

Indochina, November 1883

"Can you imagine, the nerve of that General de Négrier? 'You, Legionnaires, you are soldiers in order to die, and I'm sending you to where one dies!' No shit, am I right? This is where he sent us to die."

Sergent-Major Caleb Pettigrew—Tom Jackson to the Legion, but after all these years, he still used his given name in the privacy of his own head—scowled at the Canadian upstart who had joined the Legion at Sidi Bel Abbès the year before. Paul Paige, the boy's name was, and the one martial skill he picked up quickly was complaining.

"You would do well to keep quiet," *Sergent* Charles Sebastian Diego y Sanchez admonished the lad. "The trees, they have ears. And those Black Flag *cabrons*, they have been defeated at Palan, but many of them are still in the field."

The legionnaires, sent out in a patrol ten men strong, were moving quietly down a jungle path, their Gras Modèle 1874 rifles held at the ready. The new rifle was pretty much the old Chassepot modified to take a metallic cartridge, but it was far more reliable in the dank conditions of Indochina, which made the men of the Legion fond of the new arm.

"There are too many reports of enemy forces and bandits out here," Pettigrew whispered harshly. "And Charlie's right; some of those bandits are what's left of the Black Flag Army. We hold our base at Hải Dương, but we don't know what's going on out here in these forests, so somebody has to go see. That somebody is us. So shut up and keep your eyes open."

"Yes, *Sergent-Major*," the young Canadian gritted out. He clearly wasn't happy.

The patrol pushed on down a narrow jungle trail.

I don't like this, Caleb thought. *The kid has a point. He's a complaining little asshole, but he has a point. Can't move into the jungle, or we'd spend all day hacking at the undergrowth to go a hundred yards. And this damn trail—it's just made for an ambush. And they sent just ten of us out here?*

They moved in loose order, a couple of meters between each man, close enough to support each other, far enough away so as to make it difficult to hit the entire column with a volley. But at a bend in the trail, the column closed up, just enough...

Caleb had set a Portuguese *Caporal* at the head of the column, a skinny, swarthy little man Caleb thought of as 'that sneaky little dago.' The man proved to not be sneaky enough for the jungle. A musket boomed from a ridge where the trail bent to the left, and the man on point went down hard.

"*To the front*," Caleb shouted, but the warning was late; a volley raked the column from the front, and another from the right. The unseen enemy was in an 'L' formation, a textbook-perfect ambush.

But the enemy was armed only with muzzle-loading muskets. They charged, screeching like animals. The legionnaires fought as only they could, but there were too many of the Black Flag rebels. Caleb fired a shot into a little man in ragged clothes that charged in from the right, then swung his bayonet to impale another. The line came apart. Another *boom* came from the right as one of the rebels managed to reload. Caleb saw his friend Charlie go down with a squawk of pain.

Then, there was an explosion of light and pain, and he knew nothing more.

Caleb came to slowly. He tried to move, then realized his hands and feet were bound. He opened his eyes and could see only a short span of dirt and trampled grass. Nearby, he heard incomprehensible talk and guttural laughter. He bent an elbow and managed to turn face up.

"*Hola, amigo*," he heard Charlie's voice. "I am glad to see you are still with the living."

"Only just," Caleb replied. His head pounded as though a ten-inch cannon shell has struck it. "What's going on?"

"They carried us here," Charlie replied. "That is, you and I. We would seem to be the only survivors. We are in a small village on a hill, maybe ten kilometers from where they struck us."

"Why did they take us prisoner? The Black Flag usually doesn't bother."

"I am not sure these are Black Flag, my friend. They are bandits, yes; if you turn, you will see that they throw dice to see who gets our rifles and gear."

Caleb took a brief self-inventory. "Who got me? Don't feel like I was shot."

"I think one of them struck you with the butt of the musket. I am shot in the leg. They bandaged me, crudely. I was awake when they carried us here. I do now know what they intend to do."

"I'm afraid I have a pretty good idea."

The bandits were gathered around a small fire in the center of the village, divvying up the clothing, weapons, and gear of the legionnaires. Hearing the murmured conversation of the survivors, one of them got up, walked over to where Caleb and Charlie lay bound on the ground, and grinned at them.

"I am Huy Phan," he said, in passable French. "I lead the Golden Hand." He waved at the ragged band of thugs, as though they were a respectable force. "We were with Lưu Vĩnh Phúc's Black Flag Army, until he allowed himself to be pushed out of Upper Tonkin. We are of Tonkin, not from China, as are the Black Flag Army, so we stay here, we fight the foreign devil invaders. You are the French Army, are you not? Tell me your names and your battalion."

"Go fuck yourself," Caleb said companionably.

The Tonkin laughed. He hauled off and kicked Caleb in the ribs, then squatted beside him and pulled out a small, wicked-looking little knife. "You will tell me," he said. "You will tell me everything about your battalion, how many men, where they are. You will tell me all this and I will kill you quickly. If you do not, I will give you to my men. Then your death will not be quick."

"Kiss my ass."

Beside Caleb, Charlie let loose a torrent of Spanish; his long association with the Spaniard allowed Caleb to understand that the *Sergent* was discussing Huy Phan's ancestry, his sexual habits, and his relationship with his mother, in addition to offering up several suggestions that were anatomically impossible. Caleb grinned.

"You should reconsider," the Tonkin bandit said. "If you think my offer to give you to my men is an unpleasant one, you should know there are worse things that could happen to you. I could also give you to our women. It is said that the Tonkin women have ways to make a man die a hundred deaths. It has been known to take four, five days. You do not want that to happen, my friends."

"I don't know what you think you can do, even if we did tell you. The entire French Army is coming this way. We aren't looking for little groups of bandits. We're looking for the Black Flag Army. We're looking to move north. You think we'd bother with you? We won't even notice you unless you make us. And that's what you're doing right now."

"So, then, there is no reason for you not to give me the information."

Caleb scowled. Then he smiled. As the Tonkin man stared, eyes wide, Caleb began to sing:

> *We are a band of brothers and native to the soil,*
> *fighting for the property we gained by honest toil.*
>
> *And when our rights were threatened, the*
> *cry rose near and far, hurrah for the Bonnie*
> *Blue Flag that bears a single star.*
>
> *Hurrah! Hurrah! For Southern rights, hurrah!*
>
> *Hurrah for the Bonnie Blue Flag that bears a single star.*

Huy Phan straightened up. He laughed. Then he pulled an ancient muzzle-loading pistol from under his baggy tunic, aimed, and shot Charlie between the eyes.

Marseilles, France – 1911

"Holy shit," Philip McGraw breathed.

"You have no idea. Charlie had been my best friend for fifteen years. He was the guy I always knew I could count on. Oh, he razzed me about Marissa, back in Sidi Bel Abbès, and I chaffed him right back. That's what old buddies do. But he was a hell of a good man. A better man never lived."

Caleb Pettigrew stopped. He coughed. He pulled a tattered handkerchief out of one pocket and wiped his eyes, then poured out another glass of wine and gulped it down. "Sorry, son," he said. "Charlie's pretty near thirty years dead, and I still miss that damn dago, you know?"

"But what happened next? I mean, after that guy shot Charlie. How the hell did you get out of that one?"

"She came for me," Caleb said cryptically.

"She? Who?"

Indochina, November 1883

The bandits left Caleb Pettigrew alone after that. They gave him no food or water, but left him lying in the dust, bound hand and foot, next to the cooling corpse of his old friend. He lay there through the night, and well into the next morning, before Huy Phan finally approached him again.

"You have had some time to consider your position, I think," the bandit chief said. He squatted next to Caleb and held up his knife. "You can be done with all this. Just tell me…"

Phan was interrupted by one of his men, who came running up and spat out an incomprehensible stream of whatever the Tonkin people spoke. Phan listened, then barked some orders. The bandits roused, started grabbing weapons. The Tonkin leader turned back to Caleb.

"There is a man," the bandit said, "on a ridgeline, some ways to the south. He is on a horse and appears to be looking at the village through a glass. I will send some men that way. Perhaps we can capture him. Then, you will have company, yes?"

Caleb shrugged noncommittally. *I got a pretty good idea what's going on, he said to himself, and it ain't gonna be pretty.* He gave silent thanks that the bandits had left him and Charlie bound at the edge of the village, and not near the morning fire, now burning in the center. The wood-fueled fire sent up a plume of white smoke. *That's going to be the aiming point,* Caleb thought.

Three kilometers to the south, French regulars were wrestling three breech-loading 85mm field guns into position. It took a few moments to place the guns; an officer on horseback, a few meters away on the ridgeline, shouted range and azimuth commands. The artillerymen made their adjustments, loaded the guns, and yanked lanyards.

Caleb heard the whistling sound before the distant *booms* of the guns. He rolled to face away from the village center, closed his eyes tight and opened his mouth just as the pattern of three exploding shells landed across the center of the village.

Screams rose above the thunder of the explosions. Caleb felt himself picked up as though by a giant's hand and slammed back down to the ground. He looked around. Beside him, the bandit leader was on his knees, shaking his head.

Caleb rolled. Ignoring the protests from his muscles after the better part of a day in binding, he pushed off with his arms, kicked, and struck the bandit chieftain in the jaw with both feet. Huy Phan fell to the ground, stunned further. Caleb threw himself across the bandit leader, tossed his legs over the man's head, and tightened his knees around the thug's throat. He squeezed.

Another pattern of three rounds crashed into the village. This time Caleb managed to ignore the impact. He gathered himself, tightened his grip on the bandit, pushed up on his elbows, and threw himself to the side, breaking Huy Phan's neck.

He rolled again and looked around. The 'Golden Hand', at least the ones who were not scattered in pieces or laying broken on the ground, were running into the forest. Caleb scanned the ground nearby; sure enough, there was Huy Phan's wicked little knife. Caleb managed to roll, to get hold of the knife, and cut himself free.

The artillery seemed to have stopped. *Gotta get outta here,* Caleb told himself. *Gotta head south. That's where that artillery came from.* A few paces away, a Gras rifle lay on the ground, and next to it, a cartridge box. Caleb got to his feet, ignoring the cramping in his legs, and grabbed the rifle and ammunition. He paused for a moment next to the body of the Spaniard.

"Goodbye, Charlie," he breathed. "You were a hell of a good man."

He set off to the south at a shambling run. After about a kilometer, he started shouting: "Foreign Legion! Foreign Legion!"

He was greeted in a small clearing by French infantry, moving north. With them:

"Paul Paige," Caleb said in English. "I'll be a son of a bitch. How the hell did you get away?"

The Canadian shook Caleb's hand. "Not on purpose, *Sergent-Major*. I was fighting this big guy in what looked like black pajamas. He knocked me for a loop, but when I came to, in the bushes a way off the trail, I was lying next to him, and my bayonet was in his chest. No idea how that happened. I could hear the Black Flag talking, so I laid low. Presently I saw them carry you and the *Sargent* away to the north, so I snuck out to the south and caught up with the regulars, told them what happened, and led them back up this way."

"Lucky all around, I guess."

Paige looked around. "Where's the *Sargent*?"

Caleb frowned. "He didn't make it."

A *Capitaine* of the French regulars walked up. "*Sergent-Major*," he said, "If you please, your report."

"Yes sir," Caleb replied.

He spent some time detailing all that had happened to the

Regular officer: The position of the ambush, the location of the village—the officer had been the one directing the artillery, and so already had that information—and the composition of the bandit group.

"They aren't Black Flag," he concluded. "Not anymore, anyway. Just a very ambitious bunch of thieves."

"*Bon.*" The *Capitaine* regarded Caleb critically. "You look frightful, *Sergent-Major*. Take your man, Paige, he is to escort you to the south. A kilometer, maybe two, you will find the baggage train. There is a surgeon there. Have him look you over, clean your wounds, and by my order, you are to rest there for no less than twenty-four hours. Then, I will see you are returned to your unit. You are Foreign Legion, yes?"

"Yes, sir."

"Today, *Sergent-Major*, I am certain the Legion is proud of you. All of France is proud of you. You found yourself in an impossible situation, and yet you escaped. You now live to fight another day. I extend my hand," the officer said, and did so.

Caleb took the proffered hand and shook it. "Thank you, sir." There didn't seem to be anything else to say.

He looked around. There was Private Paige. "Come on, Paige," Caleb said. "Let's go."

On the walk south, he said nothing. Things seemed somehow different. He couldn't shake the image of Charlie, laying there in the dirt, a red round hole between his eyes.

Damn it, Charlie, he thought. *You had to go and die on me, you damn shifty dago. You were the one man I could always depend on. You always had my back. Even more than Paul Allen back in the Army of Northern Virginia, more than that damned Englishman Smythe-Carstairs, more than anyone I ever knew. I guess I got too used to having you around.*

He remembered his arrival at Sidi Bel Abbès, on a hot, dusty morning. He remembered being shown to a barracks and taking an empty cot next to an inert figure, snoring, and breathing out cognac fumes. When the man finally roused, he looked up blearily at Caleb. Caleb remembered it as though it were yesterday:

"Good morning," he said. He stood up, assumed the position of attention, and saluted. "My name," he said formally, "is Charles Sebastian Diego y Sanchez, and I am very, very drunk."

"You damn dago," Caleb breathed as he walked south. "I'd say damn you for leaving me alone, but I know what you'd say about that. You'd say, 'but you are not alone, *amigo*. You have the Legion.'"

Marseilles, France – 1911

"Charlie was right," Caleb Pettigrew told the young man who sat across the table. "I had the Legion. So, I went on. We ended up fighting the Chinese in that Indochina mess, but we managed to 'pacify' Tonkin, if you'll accept 'killing a whole bunch of people' as 'pacifying.'"

"They made a desert, and called it peace," Philip McGraw quoted.

"Something like that. Anyway, the whole shebang ended up being put together as something called French Indochina, although why France wanted that place is anyone's guess."

"So you went back to Algeria, then, after that?"

"For a while." Caleb finished off another glass of wine. He yawned and looked around. The shadows were growing long. Time to finish the story.

"Oh, there was more fighting. In Sudan, in Dahomey, plenty of hot, dusty places. But most of my job by that point was breaking in the new troops, making sure they didn't get kilt in their first engagement. Then, in 1895, the Legion was tasked to go to Madagascar, of all places, and I decided I'd had enough of fighting in God-forsaken hellholes. I had enough put by to get out and live the rest of my life peaceably, so I did. Hell," he chuckled, "Some of what I had put by even came from my Legion pay. And, of all the damn things, I decided to stay in France."

Sidi Bel Abbès, Algeria – July 1895

"So, what will you do?"

Sergent-Major Tom Jackson—Caleb Pettigrew, to himself alone—walked across the dusty parade ground with his commander, *Colonel* Victor Duchenne.

Caleb looked ahead at where his Regiment was gathered—at least, those of the men that had net yet embarked for Madagascar. "To be honest, sir," he said, "I was thinking of going to Marseille. I have not seen a lot of that city, but what I saw, well, was congenial. Good food, good wine, good weather."

"Marseille is a beautiful city, that is true, although I confess to some surprise that you would make Marseille yours. You are an American, no? You do not want to go to your home?"

"No, sir, and I have given that a lot of thought. It's been a long time since I was in Carolina. Long time and a lot of water under that bridge. The Legion offered me French citizenship, and I accepted. I was born an American, but it hasn't been my home for a long time. So, Marseille—and my real name back."

"Ah – of course, *anonymat.* You did not apply to regain your name after a year? The Legion allows it, as you must know, for those few who are not complete scoundrels and may want their own names."

"I knew. Just didn't seem all that important. The Legion knew me as Tom Jackson. Simpler to keep it that way."

Colonel Duchenne looked at the retiring *Sargent-Major.* "And the name to which you will return, if I may ask?"

"Caleb Pettigrew, at your service," Caleb said, a wistful smile on his face. It was no secret; he had already given that name to the clerks completing his discharge papers. "Corporal, as was, Army of Northern Virginia." It was the first time he had spoken his real name out loud in thirty years; the whole thing sounded strange to him after so long.

They were approaching the review stand. "Well, then, *Monsieur* Pettigrew, let us see you officially discharged."

Normally discharges were handled administratively; the Legionnaire being released was simply handed his discharge papers and sent unceremoniously on his way. But *Sergent-Major* Jackson was a special case, made so because of his long service, dedication to the Legion and unquestioned courage in battle. So, the Regiment Caleb served in was turned out, to stand in the afternoon sun of Sidi Bel Abbès and see the senior man off. *Colonel* Duchenne and Caleb stood at the review stand; the *Colonel* handed Caleb his discharge papers. Caleb saluted; the *Colonel* gravely returned the salute. The officer turned to the Regiment and spoke:

"Men of the Legion! One of our own leaves us today, to spend the balance of his life in peace. Let us congratulate *Sergent-Major* Jackson, thank him for his long and faithful service, for his long membership in the brotherhood of the Legion, and wish him well in his new life. *Sergent-Major*." The officer stepped back, indicated the assembled men. "Would you care to say a few words?"

Caleb knew he was expected to say something. He had spent the previous night trying to think of what to tell the younger men, but even as he stepped forward, he was still at a loss for words. *Best then to keep it simple*, he finally decided.

"Legionnaires. Men. Friends. Brothers. I leave you all now, but a part of me will always be with you. A part of me will always be with the Legion. Stand in closed ranks together. Stand together, and when you face the enemy, as one day you will, again," he suddenly remembered Stonewall at First Manassas, "...give them the bayonet!"

The Regiment roared.

An hour was spent passing among the men, shaking hands, laughing, telling scraps of old stories. A young man, new to the Legion, came to Caleb as the supper hour approached: "*Monsieur*," he told Caleb, "I am Legionnaire Hopewell. A horse has been laid on for you to ride to Oran, tomorrow, to the port. I will ride with you, to lead your horse back."

Caleb slapped the young pup on the back. "Good enough."

He ate in the mess that night, surrounded by comrades. He would spend his last night in his Spartan non-commissioned officer's quarters, but before he slept, he had one piece of business yet to conclude in Sidi Bel Abbès, so after the evening meal he managed to evade his fellows and slipped quietly into town, where he knocked on the door he had so often knocked on over the past thirty years. The door opened to reveal a woman who showed signs of a hard life, but who had nevertheless kept the soft edges Caleb had enjoyed so often.

"*Signore* Jackson," Marissa smiled. "You are here to conclude your part of this business, then?"

"I am."

"Step into the office, then."

Caleb followed Marissa—now to be the sole owner of the house. In the office, she handed Caleb a fat envelope. "It was not easy," she said, "for me to do this. It took many sacrifices on my part, you must know. But now," she indicated the envelope, "I have amassed enough to buy your half of the House. Would you like to count the money?"

"No," Caleb said. He smiled at the buxom Italian woman, seeing her as the girl she had been, so long ago. "After all this time, Marissa? No. I think you would not try to trick me, after all we have been to each other."

"I will miss you, *Signore* Jackson."

"I will miss you, Marissa. Or shall I say, *Madame*." He smiled.

Marissa leaned forward and kissed him. Caleb hugged her and, tossing the fat envelope casually into the knapsack he had brought with him, left the place for the last time.

Marseilles, France – 1911

"That's it. The tale's told." Caleb stood up. He reached in a pocket, mined a few coins, and dropped them on the table. "Have another bottle on me, youngster. If you join up, it will be your last one for a while."

"If," McGraw said. "Yeah. If. I'm inclined to join up, to tell you the truth. You said I can do that in Aubagne?"

"Yup." Caleb pointed east. "That way. Thirty kilometers. A bit more, a bit less." He shrugged, as Gallic through long practice as any Frenchman, and grinned. "Good luck. Keep your head down. Sooner or later, France will get involved in another damn war. Sooner or later, the Legion will go fight again. But not me. Not anymore. I was a Legionnaire. Now I'm a tired old man who needs his sleep. Take care, son." He shook Philip's hand and turned to stroll into the Marseille evening; Philip noted that, old man as Caleb may be, his stance and stride were still soldierly.

"Wait," the boy called as Caleb walked away. "The lady. The one you always said, the one who sheltered you—who was she? Was it Marissa? Someone else? Who?"

Caleb stopped. He turned, looked back, and smiled.

"Ain't you figured it out yet, son?" he asked. "You should have worked it out by now. She was the Legion. She was always the Legion. The life I lived, whenever it went bad, the Legion was there. For thirty years, the Legion was always there. When I was hurt, the Legion cared for me. When I was sick, the Legion got me better. When I was low, the Legion helped me up. And when I was captured, the Legion came for me. I owe her my life. I owe her everything. Thirty years in the Legion, and had I the chance, I'd do it all over again—even the bad parts. And one day soon, you'll find out why I say that."

The old man turned and walked off, through the darkening streets of Marseilles.

Season of Ice

Beretan, summer

Hengist crouched in the brush, overlooking the small farm. A young man was working in the field, digging yams. As Hengist watched, a young woman left the small farmhouse, bringing the young man something. They smiled at each other, shared an embrace, after which the young woman went back into the house.

She's a beauty, Hengist, thought, suddenly feeling the lack of a woman in his own life.

Hengist was, like most of the Northmen of the nation of Ikslund, tall, fair, with a broad, ruddy face, a nose that had obviously been broken several times, and ice-chip eyes. His long blonde hair was braided into three queues, and his dangling mustaches were likewise braided. He was a big man even for an Ikslunder, broad-shouldered, with a barrel chest, and fists like hammers. Hengist also had a head for tactics and a knack for leadership, making him an ideal leader of the summer raiding parties for which Ikslund was notorious; every summer the longboats of the northern nation would fan out, to Beretan, to Ashlands, to Howa's Bane and Tiramon, raiding, taking slaves, raping, and looting.

And that was Hengist's purpose today, on a typical warm, sunny, late-summer Beretanian afternoon. To the right and left, the twelve men of Hengist's raiding party were spread out in the line of brush, hidden, waiting for his orders. After a season of raiding in Beretan, his group of hardened Northmen were a well-oiled team; it had been a good summer season, and they were making their way back to the coast where their longboat was hidden. The men were laden with heavy bundles of loot, a few slaves, and a shortage of foodstuffs for the journey back to Ikslund. Thus, the decision to raid the small farm, which looked prosperous. Now the loot was hidden in the brush, the slaves bound and gagged so as not to warn the farmers.

Hengist's second in command, Jorgunn, crouch-walked over next to him. "Everyone is in position," he whispered.

"Good. Have Egmund take out the farmer first, then we all go in. I'll take the house. The rest of you fan out through the outbuildings, kill anyone you find, gather grain, fruits, goats, anything good for forage on the ship home."

"Nobody but that girl in the house," Jorgunn grinned.

"That's as may be," Hengist replied sharply. "Which is why I'm content to be going in alone."

"As you wish, Chief," Jorgunn agreed cheerfully. He moved off to give the archer his order.

A moment later, an arrow shot across the short distance from the tree line to the field, to take the young farmer in the throat. He dropped silently into the field, kicked a few times, and lay still. The raiders moved swiftly and quietly in.

Hengist sprinted ahead of his men, covering the mostly harvested yam patch at a sprint, drawing his short sword as he went. He reached the door and, without pause, put his shoulder to the wood panels and smashed through.

Inside, it was dark, dusty, crowded. Hengist's practice gaze took in all the details at a moment. The house was small. Rashers of pork hung from the rafters, and casks of vegetables crowded the space. A small table and two chairs stood in the center of the room, and a ladder led to a loft overhead, presumably the sleeping quarters.

And the girl. Hengist spotted her as she spun away from a

small window, where she had obviously witnessed the killing of the farmer—her husband?

She was prettier than Hengist had thought from the brief look he had gotten earlier; tall, long-legged, with a substantial bosom, and long brown hair. Her eyes flashed as she spun to face the door as Hengist crashed in; brown eyes that flashed for a moment in a luminous blue.

Magic user, Hengist thought. He held his sword in front of him, the flat facing the girl, his off hand on the end of the blade. The blade had a mild, cheap enchantment to deflect magic attacks; he hoped it would be enough.

She crouched. Her eyes flashed again, and her hands fluttered. Hengist braced as a bolt of ice shot across the room. He blocked it easily, sending the bolt into the rafters, and moved in.

The girl's hands fluttered a second time, sending a stream of horrendous cold at Hengist. He took the blast on the flat of his sword, which quickly turned almost too cold to grip...

...but just as quickly, the seasoned raider stepped forward, into the blast, and slammed the pommel of the sword into the girl's jaw.

She staggered away, stunned. Hengist dropped his sword, grabbed her up by the waist. His hand shot into a jacket pocket, came out bearing an iron choker with a catch bearing a round agate; he placed it around the girl's neck, snapped the catch closed and sealed it by snapping three catches in just a certain order and then placing his thumbprint on the stone.

The girl's eyes fluttered open. She raised a hand, fingers arched in a spell configuration, but nothing happened.

"A binding collar," Hengist explained to her. "I got it from a mage in my own land. We carry them on raiding parties, for dealing with magic users."

The girl didn't reply, but that mattered little; Hengist had other intentions for her now. He dragged her to the table, threw her stunned form on the square surface. She resisted, but feebly, still dazed; to the hardened raider it was as though a child was trying to push his hands away. He threw up her knee-length skirts. She started thrashing her legs; Hengist pulled her legs straight and tore off her underdrawers. She kicked at him once, only to receive the iron-hard flat of his hand to the side of her head. Hengist unfastened his trousers, let them drop to the floor, spat on himself. Grabbing her legs, he raised them over his shoulders and, standing at the edge of the table, forced himself into her.

The girl cried out once, twice, but Hengist ignored her. He thrust hard, reaching to fondle her soft breasts through the woven hemp cloth of her dress. Hengist had been without a woman for long and long, and so took only a few moments to finish.

When he was spent, he pulled up his trousers, refastened them, and was just re-sheathing his sword when Jorgunn entered the farmhouse. The girl lay on the table, crying softly, her legs hanging from the table's edge, arms over her head.

"Only the girl in here, then?" Jorgunn was grinning widely. "She is a pretty one, eh?" He took a step towards the table, only to be halted by Hengist's sharp command:

"No. Mine."

"As you wish," Jorgunn replied easily. He had taken a female slave himself on this summer's excursion, and so was not terribly put out. His captive more closely resembled a Beretanian yam than the long-legged, generously figured beauty Hengist had just taken, but she was still a girl…and when Jorgunn was home, she would fetch a decent price in the markets of Ikslund.

Jorgunn turned to his chief. "The men have gathered a few goats, a few sacks of grain, some yams, some dried fruits. Should see us home all right. We found a donkey and cart, with that to move our loot and foodstuff we should be able to march quickly, get to the ship by nightfall and be under way."

"Good. Pack everything up. Take some of the pork hanging in

here, it's cured, and we can eat it even at sea without a cooking fire."

"As you say, Chief."

"I should expect the Beretanian provincial guards are no more than a day or two behind us now, so the sooner we're at sea with the rest of the raiding fleet, the better off we'll be. Where is this cart?" Hengist demanded.

"Lugann and his idiot brother should be pulling it up in front of the house in a moment."

"Well done. Let's be on our way, then." Hengist looked around, quickly spotting what he was looking for, a spool of woven cord. He walked to the table, swiftly bound his captive's wrists and ankles. That done, he gathered up the sobbing girl, slung her over his shoulder and went outside.

Next morning

Loading the longboat, seeing to the settling of supplies, and making away from the coast by nightfall had consumed Hengist's attention since he and his men had reached the sea. He had only attended his captive twice, and then only to untie her wrists and ankles long enough to enable her to use a pisspot, after which he had bound her again and left her against the side of the boat near the steering-tiller at the stern, where she keenly felt his eyes on her.

At mid-morning Jorgunn spelled Hengist at the tiller. With a few spare moments and the rest of the raiding fleet in sight on the horizon, Hengist breathed a long sigh of relief and finally went to speak to his captive.

"I am Hengist," he told her, in passable Beretanian. "Henceforth, you are mine. Do you understand?"

"Your slave, you mean," the girl snarled, replying in Hengist's

own tongue. In the night, her fear and shock had obviously turned
to anger.

"If you like. Worry not that I will sell you to the slave traders,
even though a pretty one like you would fetch a good price. No,
you are mine, and mine you will stay. I have no woman to tend my
house and fire. You should do nicely."

Suddenly he produced a knife and cut her bonds. She tensed,
as though to spring at him.

Hengist chuckled. He tossed the knife at her feet. "Go on," he
said. "Pick it up. Try to stab me. I won't resist."

She picked up the knife but found it quite impossible to move
towards him with it.

"I told you, I put on you a binding collar. You may do me
no harm, not while the collar is on you, by magic or mundane
means. You may use no magic at all, for any reason. And only I can
remove it. So, get used to that fact."

"I suppose I can look forward to more rape."

"I would have you serve me as a woman in all ways," Hengist
replied. "I prefer you do so willingly, and I will treat you gently if
you only would. But willing or not, you will tend my house and
warm my bed. I am not a rich man, but I have a comfortable house
on a lake in the northlands. My fields are fertile, the forests around
them are rich with game and furs, and my lake has many fish. I
promise you this; you will never know hunger."

"Given that I have no choice, what can I do but submit?"

"You are a smart one," Hengist allowed. "Now then: What is
your name?"

The girl scowled for a moment, as though reluctant to give
even that small bit of information; but after a moment, her face
showed resignation. "My name is Mabinne. Mabinne Madone."

"Well met, Mabinne," Hengist bowed his head formally. "I am
sure that, once you get to know me, we will get along well enough."

"I suppose we'll find out," Mabinne said, and to herself, *I am sure you think so, but I will never, ever forgive the murderer of my husband.*

"Make yourself as comfortable as you can, then," Hengist ordered. "We will be with the rest of the summer fleet by nightfall, and in ten days we'll be at Port Stronghold in Ikslund. There I will reclaim my horses and wagon from the boarding stable, and in four more days you'll see your new home. And now, my sweet, if you will excuse me, I have a ship to run." He nodded at her and moved off.

The ten-days at sea seemed to pass like summer lightning. At night, Hengist came to her with a heavy fur robe and spread it to cover them both, sleeping beside her. Through the first night Mabinne lay rigidly awake, expecting another rape, but Hengist simply fell, pulled her close, wrapped the fur around them both, and quickly fell to snoring. This pattern held for the next nine nights, whether due to the Ikslunder wishing her to accept his presence or simply his unwillingness to perform for his men in the open longboat, she never knew. By the third night she managed to sleep the night through, and by the tenth, as the longboat moved into the frigid Never-Summer Sea, she was beginning to appreciate the big Northman's warmth.

On the morning of the eleventh day in the longboat, the summer fleet hove into view of the massive fortifications guarding the entry of Ikslund's principal harbor, Port Stronghold.

Mabinne was seated in the longboat near where Hengist was manning the steering-tiller. She had heard of the great trading port of the north but could have hardly imagined the narrow inlet passing though great cliffs, enclosed further with massive stone walls; armed men stood atop the walls, manning siege weapons intended to stand off any hostile seafarers.

Mabinne was wrapped in the huge fur robe, which Hengist had explained was taken from a great bison of the northern interior's taiga; he had given her the fur as a gift. "You'll appreciate it," he informed her, adding "summer it may be, but the nights in Ikslund are cold even now."

Hengist had discovered he enjoyed watching Mabinne. She had regained her composure, cleaned herself up as best as possible in the longboat, and even borrowed a hair-pick from Hengist to comb the tangles out of her long brown hair. She was looking forward now, staring in amazement at the massive stone walls enclosing the only entry into Port Stronghold; as the summer fleet approached, horns were blown in a prearranged signal, and the great chain across the harbor mouth was lowered into the water to allow passage. Sails were furled and the fleet's men took over oars to move the ships into shelter. A stiff breeze was blowing across the gate, making Mabinne's hair whip out like the battle flag on an Ashlands trireme. Her eyes were wide, her mouth, with its full lips, slightly open…

…Hengist felt himself growing hard inside his leather trousers. *I must get her home soon*, he thought to himself.

The fleet entered the harbor. Hengist turned for a moment to watch the chain being drawn slowly back into place after the last of the summer raider longboats passed, and then turned his attention to his own boat.

"On to the oars." Hengist ordered. "Medium cadence, you lot. We're home."

He looked down from the tiller to see Mabinne looking his way. "We'll stay here in Port Stronghold tonight, perhaps tomorrow," he told her. "I have booty to sell, and I must get my horses and wagon out of the boarding stable. Then we'll be away to my home."

Mabinne simply nodded, expressionless.

Port Stronghold was the only real city in the far north and was a major trading center for traffic passing through the Never-Summer Sea on their way to the western domains of Mondria and Juteland. Mabinne had known this, but the knowledge didn't prepare her for the bustling docks and marketplaces of the northern city. Everywhere was activity—shouting, cursing, the banging of oars against wooden longboat hulls, the scraping of boats against the stone jetties as they tied up, the happy shouts of men setting foot on solid ground for the first time in several days.

When Hengist's longboat docked, young roustabouts swarmed aboard. Hengist grabbed three of them, pressed a gold coin into each youth's hand. "My wares," he told them, indicating his three large leather bags of spoils. "Take them to Kal Gunderson's shop on the canal. Not a bit of booty goes missing, you young whelps, do you hear?"

"Have not a care, Chief," the oldest of the three replied, sketching a rough salute with one finger against his eyebrow. "One piece missing, me and mine, we starve—word of thieves gets around fast here, eh? Don't worry, we'll get it all there, every piece. Come on, brothers, we've work." The three gathered up Hengist's loot and scampered ashore, the weight of the booty seeming to inconvenience them not at all. On Hengist's longboat and the others, similar arrangements were being made by the other raiders—clearly it was going to be a profitable trip.

As Mabinne was pondering the irony of Hengist's worries about the thieving of his stolen loot, she was mildly startled when the man himself suddenly spoke to her.

"Come," he said gently, extending a hand to help her to her feet. "There's an inn. It's not far. We'll stay there tonight, maybe two nights, while I conduct my business here."

She examined the extended hand for a moment. Then she looked up at the man. His face was carefully neutral, but there was no threat in his pose and no anger or lust in his eyes, only a strange, speculative look. She took the hand.

Hengist looked her up and down. Mabinne was still wearing the simple dress and ankle-high shoes she was wearing when captured; the only addition to her wardrobe had been the heavy bison robe. Her Beretanian clothes were clearly the worse for wear. "You need some new clothes," Hengist decided. "Warm clothes. A coat, new boots. We'll take care of that one the way to the inn."

He proved a man of his word. First, he bought four skewers of cooked venison from a street vendor; Mabinne ate hers slowly, carefully, while Hengist wolfed his three portions in half the time she took with one.

Then he led her down a side street and into a large square that seemed to be taken up entirely with clothing vendors, all shouting, protesting, haggling, calling to passerby.

Hengist quickly singled out one merchant, and after a great deal of shouting, cursing, haggling, thinly veiled threats and, finally, an agreement, Mabinne had five sets of new clothing:

> Three sets of stout leather leggings paired with hip-length tunics, an attire that would have been mildly scandalous in Beretan but, from Mabinne's observation, seemed to be something of a uniform for the women of Ikslund.

> Two new ankle-length dresses of a thick, rich wool, one died a deep dark red, the other a brilliant blue; Mabinne raised an eyebrow at that expense until Hengist explained: "For receiving visitors, holidays, trips into the city and so forth. I'm not a poor man, and fine clothes show you are valued, respected." Mabinne raised a sardonic eyebrow at that, which Hengist ignored.

> Two pairs of boots, one stout pair of heavy bull hide for everyday use and outdoor work and travel; the second of finely worked, butter-soft calfskin, to go with the fine dresses.

> A long, heavy coat, that came down to well past Mabinne's knees; heavy leather lined with sheepskin, it seemed stout enough to withstand an Ikslund blizzard, and Mabinne had no doubt it was intended for precisely that eventuality.

Along with the clothes, Hengist insisted that Mabinne select what undergarments and foot wraps suited her.

Burdened with this, and with evening drawing near, they proceeded to the inn. The proprietor was an old friend of Hengist's, which entitled the raider to a large room at the top of a narrow set of stairs—with a door that locked from without. The room was big, with a round table and two chairs, a fireplace with a fire already cheerfully crackling away, and large bed covered with heavy quilts.

Mabinne entered the room with some apprehension about spending her first night alone with the big Northman, but Hengist simply ushered her into the room, placed her clothing parcels on the bed, then stood apologetically in the doorway.

"It is tradition," he said, "to spend the evening drinking and feasting with my men. I feel sure you would like an evening alone, to compose yourself. I will have Fals downstairs bring you some supper. I apologize for the need to lock the door, but even in the inn, this city is not always safe for a woman alone—I'm sure you understand."

I understand you don't want me trying to escape, Mabinne thought. *I understand you don't want my trying to find a magic user to get this collar off my neck.*

Still—he is trying to be considerate, or what passes for it among his people.

"So, I must be off. I will be back quite late, I'm afraid. I will try not to disturb you."

I wonder if that means he won't rape me again until tomorrow night?

Hengist made no indication he knew what Mabinne was thinking. He simply blinked twice, reached into his long coat, and extracted one more parcel. "Here," he said. "You may open this after I've gone, if you like." He nodded and stepped out, closing the door behind him; Mabinne heard the clicking of the key in the lock.

She examined the door briefly. It was heavy, of stout oak framed with iron straps; she doubted even Hengist could break it open. The windows looked out on the street but were too narrow to crawl out of and too high to drop down from in any case. The room was clearly meant to imprison; it was a comfortable prison, but a prison all the same.

She remembered the parcel. She retrieved it from the table where she had dropped it to examine the room.

Undoing the leather ties, she unwrapped the cheap leather enclosing what felt like another article of clothing, but she was not prepared for what she found—a knee-length, sleeveless nightgown of rich, deep blue, beautifully embroidered with red and black patterns.

The implications of that gift made her shudder for a moment—Hengist clearly meant her to wear it to bed with him—but at the same time she could not help to wonder, *what sort of a man dresses a slave so richly? What does he want of me?*

Port Stronghold

As the sky outside the narrow windows were going dark, the innkeeper brought Mabinne her supper as promised—a thick stew of vegetables and the flesh of some bird or another, accompanied by a small bowl of nuts warmed in the oven, and a bronze mug of coarse ale. Mabinne ate and drank, enjoying the best meal she had eaten since her capture.

She added some wood to the fireplace, then yawned hugely; she was exhausted. She looked at the bed, then at the nightgown; she was not yet willing to wear it, knowing how Hengist was liable to react if he returned and found her wearing it. Instead, she used the pot hanging on the fireplace to heat some water from the jug and basin with which the room was supplied. She undressed, washed from head to toe for the first time in days, combed out her long brown hair, put on one of the new tunics and leggings outfits Hengist had bought her, padded in bare feet to the bed and lay down.

Then a thought occurred to her. She got up again, picked up her Beretan clothes. The dress was badly soiled and torn; her old undergarments were not salvageable. The leather shoes were still serviceable—barely—but seemed unlikely footwear for the cold North. Bundling her old clothes and her old life up, she pitched the bundle into the fireplace, then lay back down. It was wonderful to finally be clean, in clean clothes; she relaxed completely for the first time since the Northman had broken into her farmhouse. Sleep came quickly.

It was pitch-dark in the room when she heard the key turn in the lock.

Mabinne sat up suddenly in the darkness. The door creaked open, slowly, and in staggered Hengist, more than a little unsteady. The strong odor of ale preceded him. He held a clearly empty flagon in one hand, a guttering candle-lamp in the other. Grunting, he closed the door behind him and slumped to the floor, back against the heavy door panel.

Mabinne looked at the big raider, so clearly drunk, but was surprised to see no threat in him. He looked somewhat downcast.

"Mabinne," he said, "M'sweet. I'm…sorry. Sorry I dragged you into all this business. You seem a fine woman. Deserve better."

"You could take me home," she said softly.

"No," Hengist shook his head vigorously. "Can' do that. Wouldn't do. Men would think 'm goin' soft, for one. Won't follow a soft raid leader. And tha's not all. Wan' you stay with me. In time, maybe, you come to care for me, maybe jus' a little."

Doubtful, she thought, but said nothing.

Hengist set the candle on the floor. He looked up blearily at her, then around the room once. His head sagged. He snored.

Mabinne slowly, quietly, picked up the candle lamp. She looked once at the door, the big Northman snoring away in front of it, and the jacket he wore that surely contained the door's key somewhere in a pocket.

Outside she could hear the bustle of Port Stronghold, even at the late hour—a strange city, a foreign city, where she knew no one, about which she knew nothing.

She shook her head. Turning back to the bed, she blew out the candle, wrapped up in one of the quilts and went peacefully to sleep.

She was wakened by the sound of the key in the lock. She stretched and yawned, sat up and looked around. Hengist was gone, but the round table bore a wooden platter holding a couple of skewers of meat, still steaming from the stove, and a mug of some aromatic tea. She got up, combed her hair out again, breakfasted—the tea seemed to contain some combination of sage leaves and juniper—and then, with nothing better to do, sat by one of the windows and watched the people on the street below.

Outside, it looked to be a fine, sunny day. Mabinne was mildly surprised at the variety of people on the street below; not just the tall, fair Ikslunders but also short, swarthy Jutelanders, ruddy, black-haired Mondrians, even a couple of dark, curly-haired Ashlanders. Clearly the reputation of the great northern city as a center of trade had spread far.

The time wore on slowly. Midday was approaching by the time Mabinne heard the key turn in the lock again; she turned to see Hengist burst into the room, a broad grin on his face.

The big Ikslunder shook a huge leather purse at her. Mabinne heard the distinctive dull clink of gold coins, apparently a good many of them. Hengist laughed. "It's been a fine, profitable summer, my sweet," he said. Since the previous evening, "Sweet" seemed to have become his chosen name for her. "Trade hereabouts is brisk this year. Come, now, get on your traveling boots and gather up your things—here, I brought you a satchel for your new clothes." He tossed her a heavy leather pack with a single strap. "My horses and wagon are out front. I've already bought provisions for the trip home. Pack up, and we'll be off."

The sight of Hengist's transport lent some credence to his claims of being well-off. The horses were a fine matched pair of dapple-gray geldings, large, heavy-footed, and shaggy, as most of the northern horses seemed to be. The wagon was stout, if not fancy, made of fine, close-grained wood, four-wheeled, with a heavy leather tarp stretched over wooden bows covering the cargo area and the bench where the driver and passenger were to sit.

As they climbed into the wagon, Hengist gestured at the beasts. "The one on the left, Toothbreaker, he's a lively one; I have him saddle-broken as well as to the cart, but he's feisty and can be difficult even for me. Buttercup, the fellow on the right, now he's gentle as a sheep." He gathered up the reins, shook them and clucked. The horses started off at a walk.

"Do you ride?" Hengist asked, gesturing at the horses.

"No," Mabinne answered.

"I'll teach you. You'll enjoy it. Perhaps you'd enjoy a hunt in the fall. We hunt elk, bison, sometimes a mammoth. It's very exciting."

"I'm sure it is." Hengist seemed oddly anxious to interest her in something. *An odd man, that feels some need to please a slave*, she reflected.

The sheer size of Port Stronghold, along with the many people on the streets, meant that it took most of the morning just to get to one of the city's western gates. A farm girl by birth and inclination, Mabinne had trouble adjusting to the stench of a city and was glad to pass through the gates in the massive wall into the clean air of the countryside.

Hengist seemed content to let the afternoon pass in silence. Not long after leaving the city he handed the reins to Mabinne with a murmured "if you would, sweet, just for a moment." He disappeared into the back of the wagon and returned bearing two small pies, with thick golden crusts and rich fillings of meat, gravy, and vegetables. He took the reins back and ate heartily—and silently.

Mabinne tried her pie and was surprised to find it delicious, savory, with just enough salt and some other, unidentifiable spice to add to the flavor of the meat without overwhelming it; she hadn't expected culinary subtlety from Ikslund.

As the afternoon moved on towards evening, Mabinne began to grow nervous. Hengist remained uncharacteristically silent, but she noticed him watching her with a speculative air—and she hadn't failed to notice the bundles of furs in the back of the covered wagon that clearly served as a bed.

Well, I suppose it must happen sometime. He's made no bones about his intention.

She giggled suddenly at her own silent innuendo. Hengist looked at her with a raised eyebrow, but she just shook her head.

As the sun was growing low in the sky, Hengist pointed to a grassy meadow with a lone of trees along one edge. "There's a creek there," he said. "Good clean water nearby, level ground and a fire pit. Far enough from the road to be out of the dust. We'll stay there tonight."

"As you wish" Mabinne said in a low voice.

Building the fire and eating their evening meal—some kind of coarse, unleavened bread and cured pork—seemed to take only moments. And then, Hengist suddenly stood, still brushing crumbs from his beard, and motioned towards the wagon. "To bed, sweet," he said, his tone gentle but still somehow conveying an order. "I want an early start tomorrow."

Mabinne nodded. Hengist extended a hand to help her into

the wagon, but she grasped the tailboard and climbed aboard herself. Hengist shrugged and followed.

Inside the covered portion of the wagon, it was already good and dark. Hengist removed his boots, so Mabinne did likewise.

Hengist spread out a rough pad made of coarse cloth that seemed to be stuffed with grass, then laid a spread made of wolf pelts over it. He lay down on it and pulled up another huge bison robe as a cover.

"Here, sweet," he murmured, motioning at the space next to him.

There was nothing else for it. Before climbing into the wagon, Mabinne had gone into the trees on the pretext of making water before sleep; she had left loose the drawstring that held her leggings about her waist.

She lay down, her back to the Northman. Hengist drew the bison robe over them both, then moved close, an arm around Mabinne's waist.

He lay still for a moment. Mabinne could feel part of him moving, at least; he was rising, growing hard against her backside.

With a silent sigh, she pulled her leggings off, arched her back against Hengist and opened her legs to allow him.

Hengist entered her slowly from behind, thrusting slowly at first, then more rapidly; he reached under her tunic to fondle her breasts.

Tolerate it, Mabinne told herself. *My own husband even used to...no, no! Don't think of him. Not now.*

Hengist seemed to go on forever, but finally he shuddered and came.

"You see, my sweet," he breathed into her ear. "Not so bad. You'll grow to enjoy me as I do you, I'm sure of it." He rolled onto his back and quickly began to snore.

Mabinne wiped herself with a rag that lay in the wagon, replaced her leggings, and rolled over to sleep. The big Northman hadn't kindled even a spark of feeling in her. She hadn't expected he would.

On the Trail

The two remaining days in the journey followed much the same pattern; arise in the morning, wash in cold water. Hengist would hitch the horses and the pair would set off, walking the horses through the day.

The second night found them camping in high pines along a small, bubbling brook. On the third day Hengist took a road branching off the main thoroughfare, bound more or less north into low hills. In the late afternoon they came to a low hill overlooking a lake to the east, forest to the north and a vast sweep of grassland to the west. On this hill sat Hengist's house.

The house was larger than Mabinne had expected; a long, low, rambling U-shaped structure with connected barns for stock, and a stone-paved trail from the courtyard, enclosed by the U, to a small dock on the lake. The house looked warm; it was built of native stone up to window height, with heavy squared logs on up to the high-peaked roof. Four chimneys emitted pale woodsmoke. Whoever had built the house clearly intended it to be sturdy and warm.

The windows, Mabinne was surprised to see, were glass; an expensive commodity in Beretan, Mabinne had never thought glass-crafters worked in what she had always thought of as a barbarian land.

Mabinne also noted stock; a flock of white ducks was scattered about the place, and behind the house she heard the distinctive lowing of a milk cow. *He wasn't just bragging,* she thought. *This isn't the home of a poor man. It's more estate than homestead.*

As they approached, the door to the house opened and an odd-looking youth emerged. He was short, shorter even than

Mabinne, but squat, and something about his head wasn't quite right; it was misshapen, somehow, as though his skull had been somehow compressed. He had large eyes set a little too far apart, and his jaw was set slightly off-center to the left. But his eyes were bright, and his smile radiant when he saw Hengist.

"Gerd!" Hengist called to the boy as he brought the wagon to a halt in front of the house. "All is well, I presume?"

Gerd nodded vigorously. He made a series of gestures with his hands; Mabinne half expected some magic to emerge from the gesturing, but instead an entirely different sort of wizardry was in play. *The boy can't speak*, she realized. *This is how he communicates.*

"Good, then," Hengist answered. Obviously, he understood the boy's gesturing, which meant nothing to Mabinne. "How is your father? Your mother?"

More gestures.

"Good." Hengist dismounted. From a small pouch on his belt, he counted out ten gold coins, which he handed to the boy. "For your summer's work. The place looks fine. Well done."

As the boy disappeared back into the house, clinking the coins happily in his hand, Hengist turned to Mabinne. "My sister's son," he explained. "Something went wrong with his birthing, and as you can see, he isn't quite normal. Never make a raider or farmer out of him, but he is able to look after my place in summers while I'm away and take care of the stock and so forth." Hengist walked around the horses, patting their noses and stroking manes as he went.

"I see," Mabinne replied.

Hengist continued to explain as he walked. "His father lost an arm several summers past. Good man but farming to feed my sister and their children is about all he can manage. They count on Gerd's coins every summer. I help them with elk and bear meat now and then, as I can. Family, eh? Not always easy." The big Ikslunder offered Mabinne a hand to help her down from the wagon.

"I'm sure they appreciate the help," Mabinne agreed. She took Hengist's hand and climbed down. This was another surprise; the prevailing wisdom in Beretan was that the big Northmen were savages. She hadn't expected the kind of compassion Hengist showed towards his sister's family.

A thought occurred to her. "You have much room here," she asked, "wouldn't your sister's family be better off staying here with you?"

Hengist smiled down at her. "You haven't been around us long, my sweet," he explained. "We Ikslunders, we're a proud folk, and my sister and her husband no less than any. They won't accept not being able to keep their own farm, their own home. And I can't blame them. My brother-in-law, he would roundly be seen as something less than a man, were he to do so. I'd gladly have them, but, well, that's how things are here in Ikslund. So, I give them what help they will accept. In fact, since I can't be arsed to grow vegetables—I hate grubbing in the dirt—I buy from them all they can spare, which again helps them get by. Farming turnips, carrots, and beets is something a one-armed man can do well enough."

Mabinne didn't comment. She stood, looking all around; she had to admit, the homestead was set in a lovely location, and Hengist hadn't been just bragging when he spoke of his prosperity. She had to remind herself that a good part of it came from raiding and banditry.

"I'll be some time putting the horses up. Go inside, sweet, and look around. This will be your home henceforth. I want you to be comfortable. If you don't like the way anything is arranged, let me know and we'll set it to rights."

"As you wish," Mabinne said softly. She headed for the front door.

Mabinne went in the front door and found herself in a small entry room. She saw Gerd's shoes placed on a rack to one side, so she removed her shoes and went inside in her linen foot-wraps.

Inside, the house was spacious and airy. Even in the mild, sunny late-summer day there was a small fire crackling merrily away in the large hearth on one side of the room. The floor was covered in rugs, the walls with cloth hangings; the house looked as though it would stand through any winter and still stay warm.

Gerd emerged from a back room, evidently a sleeping room. He was carrying a cloth sack over one shoulder; he grinned at Mabinne as he passed on his way outside. Mabinne heard him shuffling about in the anteroom with his shoes, then the outer door; she could just make out the muffled tones of Hengist's voice speaking with the lad.

So, this is home now, she thought. *It's not a poor home. I wish I could forget where much of this came from.*

She walked slowly around the big main room, looking at some of the odds and ends that decorated the place. The wall-hangings were embroidered, and there were small decorations on shelves on the walls and the tables alongside the big, well-upholstered chairs—bits of agate, polished stones, carvings of bone and ivory.

A thought occurred to her: *No man living alone put this place together. A woman did this.*

That, she felt certain, was a story that Hengist wasn't about to tell her. At least not yet.

Mabinne spent some time wandering about the house. One wing housed a small bedroom that looked long unused and a large, well-stocked pantry. The other...

Hengist found her examining the main bedroom in the second wing. He walked silently up behind her as she was examining the bed; it was huge, with a large spread of wolf furs, and large, well-stuffed pillows. She had laid back the cover to find sheets made of a dark, smooth, incredibly fine cloth... She recognized it; the same material made up the nightgown Hengist had given her.

"Silk," Hengist explained softly. "It comes from the land of the Manchin, far to the east. Trade comes in across the Northern Ocean. I've never been there, but I've heard tales. Great cities of yellow sandstone, a great wall to the south that protects the Manchin from their unfriendly neighbors, whose name I forget... Anyway. I bought two sets of silk bedsheets for... well, it was a long time ago now."

"I've never felt anything like them," Mabinne admitted.

Hengist shrugged. "Gerd has set off for home. Did you see the trap door in the floor of the pantry? It leads down into a small cavelet in the stone on which the house sits; there is ice in there, all year long. I've brought up some bison meat to cut up for stew."

"Do you have some yams? Carrots? Onions?" Mabinne asked. Hengist's implication, she thought, was obvious.

"*We* have carrots and onions," Hengist replied, stressing the first word just enough for Mabinne to notice. "No yams, but there are some turnips and leeks from my sister's garden."

"I'll get started," Mabinne said softly.

They ate just after sunset. The stew turned out better than Mabinne had hoped; the bison meat was fatty and rich, and the vegetables were of fine quality. There was no bread, as she would have had in Beretan, and when she inquired about wheat or barley, Hengist just shook his head. "What barley we grow hereabouts goes into making ale. I'll see if I can get you a sack or two when next we go to the trading post. Yes, there is a small town and trading center about a half-day's horseback ride from here, a day if we take the wagon. I'll take you there before the cold weather comes."

When the time came for bed, Hengist went to one of the two large wooden wardrobes in the bedroom. He opened the door briefly; Mabinne caught a glimpse of what were plainly a woman's clothing within. He extracted a warm-looking woolen nightgown and handed it to her.

"Whose...?" She began.

Hengist just shook his head. "Not now, sweet."

Hengist made no demands on her that night. She slept soundly.

Autumn

One morning at breakfast, as the leaves on the trees around the homestead were growing golden, Hengist announced a trip to the trading post he had mentioned. "It's along the Black River," he told Mabinne, "About a day's trip south by wagon, assuming the road is good. There's a pass through some low mountains we'll have to go through, but it's early enough in the year we should have no trouble. We'll want to make the trip in a single day, though, so we'll rise early tomorrow morning and set out. I'll set up the wagon and our gear today, so in the morning all I'll have to do is hitch up the horses and we're away."

"We'll be spending at least a night there, then?" Mabinne wanted to know.

"Yes," Hengist nodded. "There's an inn. I know the innkeeper, as it happens. He serves up some of the best food I've tasted; it's an Ashlander couple does the cooking, their food is spicy but very tasty. I think you'll like it. Think, then, today, on anything you'll want by way of supplies for the winter, and we'll fill the list."

They set out before sunrise the next morning and took the trail south. Mabinne wore one of the tunic-and-legging outfits she had worn almost continually since coming to Hengist's home along with her heavy lined coat, but in her pack, she placed the blue wool dress Hengist had bought her in Port Stronghold.

The horses' breath sent plumes of mist into the chilly air;

Hengist and Mabinne's breath did likewise. As the sun rose, Mabinne watched as the landscape rolled past.

Through the morning, the road (Mabinne thought it was being a bit overly generous to call a pair of wheel-ruts half-buried in grass and weeds a "road," but she kept her silence) climbed into some low hills that eventually gave way to taller ones; a tad before midday they crested a final rise on a saddle between two large, rocky mounts to see a wide gentle valley below.

As they descended into the valley one change made itself manifest very quickly. "It's warmer," Mabinne noted. In fact, she was growing uncomfortably warm in her heavy sheepskin-lined coat, and so removed it and placed it in the wagon behind her.

"It is warmer," Hengist agreed. "As we drop down towards the river, it will grow warmer still. We're on the south side of the peninsula on which Port Stronghold sits, you see; on that northern side, the ocean is near the northern ice and is cold but here, a current from the south swings by and keeps the weather milder. The hills back there, they block most of that weather from moving north but here, one can feel the full effect. Nice, isn't it?"

"It is. It's a wonder anyone would choose to live in the north with this land looking so agreeable. And there don't seem to be many people about."

Hengist shrugged. "Home is home, eh? Besides, not too long ago, in my father's time, war swept through here. The land and the people haven't fully recovered yet."

"War? With whom?"

"Jutland. Mondria." He looked at her. "And Beretan."

"When I was in the magic-user academy," Mabinne said soberly, "they taught that Ikslund declared war and began by raiding on our coasts. Beretan allied with Mondria and Jutland to drive the invaders out."

"Sweet," Hengist said gently, "the town we are heading for was occupied by Beretanian troops for three years. Beretan invaded the south side of this peninsula, along with Mondria, while the Jutlanders came at us from the west. Port Stronghold held out, but the invaders swept over most of the countryside. Towns, villages, farms were burned, whole families taken into slavery. This academy you speak of, it's on the south end of Beretan near the coast, yes?"

"On a cliff overlooking the ocean, yes."

"And many of the workers, the cooks, stable-men, drovers and so on are Ikslunders, yes?"

"Why, yes," Mabinne replied in some confusion; she had noted that as a girl in the academy, but had never given it any thought; the tall, fair Ikslunders were just servants and workers, surely?

"Slaves," Hengist said. He looked ahead; his expression was now carefully neutral. "Many such were taken when Beretan, Mondria and Jutland occupied southern Ikslund. Many more taken on their raids into the north, even to the approaches of Port Stronghold. They took their slaves with them when King Harald Iron-Jaw finally raised an army of Northmen from Ikslund; they and our allies from the Ashlands drove them out. My father fought in King Harald's army when I was just a boy. He took an arrow in the chest at the final battle in the Auburn Hills and died only three years later, leaving me his home. While he lived, he often told me of his cousins who lived here in the south, who were taken. Many families lost members to the slave-traders in the south. When we get to the town, ask any of the folk there, they will be able to tell you."

"And so, you raid Beretan now…"

"To get a little of our own back," Hengist finished for her. "And in the hopes of finding some lost relatives. Every year, the raiding parties bring a few Ikslunders home. Too few."

They rode on in silence for some time after that. Hengist was brooding; Mabinne thought it best to say nothing. At length, Hengist spoke again.

"I've grown very fond of you, sweet," he said at last. "I may well grow to love you one day. But I am an Ikslunder. I cannot forgive Beretan for what has happened to my land. I hope you can grow to understand that."

Mabinne just nodded. Everything she had thought about the matters between Beretan and Ikslund seemed to be wrong; the shape of her world had just gone topsy-turvy.

Sometime later, she felt the need to break the silence. "Hengist," she said, using his name for the first time, "your mother?"

"Died," he said simply. "Birthing me." He looked at her and smiled sadly. "So, you see, while my father died at the hands of Beretan, my mother's death, well, that was my fault."

"It wasn't your fault," Mabinne objected. "You were a baby."

"That's as my father always said." He gave Mabinne a wry smile. "Somehow, you know, it never made me feel any better about it."

They rode on in silence for some time after that; Hengist continued his uncharacteristic brooding. Mabinne dithered; she had grown accustomed to the big Ikslunder's usual cheerful good nature and wasn't sure how to bring him out of the brown study that had captured him.

Finally, late in the afternoon, they crested a low rise to see a bend in a large river, and alongside it a town of good size. The trading village of Tillgatt sat on a bluff overlooking the Black River, on the outside of a shallow curve in the river. Lower ground on the upstream and downside gave access to the river, while the bluff protected the town from floods; it was an ideal situation.

Hengist had described Tillgatt as a village, but it seemed to Mabinne to be a good-sized town. It was nearing nightfall when they arrived at an inn on the edge of the main marketplace. The building was clearly old; the huge wooden beams of the walls were black from soot and exposure. The big main hall was framed by two large wings of what Mabinne guessed were sleeping quarters. The sound of horses and rattling of tack gave hint of a stable behind the main building.

"Go on inside," Hengist said as he brought the wagon to a stop in front of the inn. "I'll see to the horses and join you as quickly as I can." He smiled at her. "I'm sorry about my ill humor earlier, sweet," he said. "Brooding on past injustices does a man's spleen no good, eh? I'll make it up to you with a good dinner and a warm sleep in a soft bed, what do you say?"

Mabinne nodded and clambered down from the big farm wagon. "It's warmer here, but the chill still comes on quick in the evening. I'll meet you inside."

"Give the innkeeper my name," Hengist called. "You'll know him when you see him, big fellow, thick beard. Tell him Hengist Jorgenson seeks a hot dinner and a warm bed, he'll know how best to answer." Chuckling softly to himself, he snapped the reins and drove the big horses off towards the stable.

Mabinne pushed in through the big double doors. The main hall wasn't too different than those of inns in Beretan, although it was larger; but then, the typical Ikslunder was larger than most any Beretanian, so that wasn't much of a surprise. On opposite sides of the room, fires crackled merrily in identical stone fireplaces; a couple of barmaids carried platters of food and mugs of drink around to the several small tables occupied by men and women. Larger tables sat along the back walls, mostly occupied by families; the chattering of children lay as an overtone to the mutter of conversation and the occasional burst of laughter.

In the center of the room stood a small counter and, on a stool behind that counter, the fattest man Mabinne had ever seen. He was easily as tall as Hengist, and as wide as he was tall; he was chatting with a customer, and pale blue eyes sparkled merrily over a huge, gray-streaked beard. He gestured as he spoke, revealing broad hands with fingers like bloated sausages.

This was, presumably, the innkeeper.

Mabinne walked over to the counter. The fat man's eyes swung over her, at first in appreciation, then in speculation.

"Evening, lass," he said. "Outlander, aren't you? Beretan?" His eyes no longer sparkled. Mabinne suddenly remembered Hengist's stories of the occupation of the town.

"I was of Beretan," she replied easily. "Now I live in Ikslund. Hengist Jorgenson sends his regards, and says I am to ask you for a dinner and a bed. He is putting up his horses in your stable even now."

"Is he now?" The fat man peered at Mabinne for a moment in silence. Then his broad face opened in a wide grin, and the sparkle returned to his eyes. "And so, how is that young bastard? Haven't seen him in two, three years—what brings him to Tillgatt now?"

"Supplies, grains, spices, wax for candles," Mabinne answered, "stuff we can only obtain in trade."

"We?"

Mabinne found herself blushing. "Yes. I share Hengist's household."

"And his bed, no doubt. Well, good enough. I am Bjorn; Hengist is my cousin, which is how that presumptuous young lout thinks he can just assume I'll keep a place for him. I do have a room, as it happens; it even faces the morning sun, as I know he prefers."

Mabinne had by now been in Ikslund long enough to know that the term "cousin" was generally used to imply "someone I've known a long time," not necessarily a blood relation.

Just then Hengist burst in through a back door. "Bjorn!" he shouted. He strode through the dining room to grasp Bjorn's fat hand. "You old bastard. How do things swing for you?"

"Well enough." Bjorn slapped Hengist on the shoulder. "And your traveling companion, I must say—you always did like the pretty ones."

"Indeed," Hengist chuckled. "What to eat?"

"Bison stew, baked ducks, pickled beets. Cold ale if you want it, hot tea if you'd prefer."

"I'll have the lot!" Hengist roared, "and a round of ale for the house!" A roar of approval shook the rafters at that remark. Hengist took a pouch of gold coins from his jacket and tossed them to Bjorn. "And whatever my sweet might want, bring it to her!"

They took a small round table pulled up cozily to one of the fireplaces. Hengist ate like a man starved, while Mabinne was satisfied with a leg of baked duck and a small dish of pickled beets, of whose tart flavor she was fond. The duck was delicious, having been marinated in savory Ashlander spices before roasting. Hengist was certainly right about the food.

When at last he finished, Hengist drained the dregs of his last mug, belched companionably, and smiled. "Let's be off to bed," he announced. "We'll do our trading tomorrow. Here," he found another small leather purse that clinked heavily and handed it across to Mabinne. "In the morning, I have some business to tend to, and I'll be off to the market to fill our list of foodstuffs—I'll get you that grain and yeasts for your bread, as you mentioned. To the east of the inn are the fine goods stores, clothing, jewels, the like. Anything you want, anything you need, you buy it, yes? If you run out of coin, come find me. We won't be able to come back for maybe a year, so buy accordingly."

"I will," Mabinne agreed. *Is he really going to leave me on my own? But then, why not? Where would I go? Who here, in a town that was occupied by Beretanian soldiers, who here would help me?*

"Good. Let's be off to bed, then."

Tillgatt

Hengist was gone when Mabinne awoke; he had a way of arising, dressing, and slipping out without disturbing her. She dressed quickly, donning the heavy blue dress, and wrapping a warm shawl about her neck and shoulders. She found the purse of coin and left the inn, walking east on the crowded street. The shopping area was an Hengist described; vendors of clothing, jewelry and other luxury goods shouted and haggled all about. But Mabinne was looking for something in particular.

After a half-hour of exploring, she found what she was seeking. Mabinne was glad to see that the practice for identifying a magic shop was the same in Ikslund as in Beretan; a simple placard on the door bearing a distinctive pattern of waving lines. She hesitated for a moment, then shook her head and went inside.

A small chime jangled as the door closed behind her. From behind a curtain came a woman, clearly an Ashlander, short, swarthy, and smiling. "Hello, my dear," she said. Then she looked closer at Mabinne, and her expression grew guarded and her accent more pronounced. "Beretanian, then, are ye?" It wasn't the first time in the trading village that someone had looked at Mabinne with suspicion.

"I am Beretanian," Mabinne assured the woman, "My name is Mabinne. But I live here now, in Ikslund, with a man of Ikslund, on a homestead north of the hills."

"As you say," the Ashlander said. "I suppose you would hardly be here otherwise, after all that happened… Well, never mind. I am Duress. What can I do for you?"

Mabinne moved closer to the store's small counter. She unwrapped the shawl she wore about her neck to reveal the binding collar. "Can you remove this?"

Duress leaned forward and examined the collar. "No," she said. "In the first place, it's strictly against guild rules. I presume whoever put that on you—your Ikslunder man, perhaps? Then he had good reason to do so, and I won't interfere. In the second place, even if I wanted to, I couldn't. It's keyed to the user, and no one else can remove it. Only he can do that, and love, if he dies, it stays on you until *you* die."

"I thought as much," Mabinne said. "He may remove it, one day…In the meantime, may I look at your wares?"

Duress nodded. She extracted a long Ashlander pipe from a robe pocket, stuffed some foul-smelling weed in it, lit it, and proceeded to puff out clouds of smoke.

Mabinne presumed the smoke was intended to make the air unpleasant and so to cause her to leave faster, but she ignored it. Most of the shop's content was typical, herbs, potions, poultices. But in one basket…

"What are these?" Mabinne picked up a small black crystal on a silver chain. In the basket lay another identical crystal and chain. They were like nothing Mabinne had seen before, black with a hint of purple, about as long as her middle finger.

"Soul crystals," Duress said. "They can greatly amplify a magic-user's power for a brief time. Using them destroys them, but the results can be impressive. Mind you, they don't contain a person's soul; that's just a story to scare children. But they do work. But love, your magic is useless to you while you wear that collar. Amplifying nothing still gives you nothing."

Mabinne ignored that comment. "How much?"

"Six gold each. Eleven gets you both."

Mabinne picked up the other gem. "Will you sell them to me?"

Duress looked at her, exhaling another cloud of thick smoke. "Why not? Few magic-users about, and the Ikslunder magic users consider those naught but Ashlander superstition. Stupid. I suppose you can't use them, so what's the harm?"

"I'll give you seven for both."

"Nine, love, no less. I'm no fool."

"If you're no fool, then why did you already admit to me that no one hereabouts is interested in these? Eight."

Duress scowled. "Damn me for a big mouth," she said. Then she smiled. "Well haggled, love. Very well. Eight it is."

Mabinne handed over the coins and tucked the gems into her pouch. She'd tell Hengist they were jewelry. And, as long as she wore the collar, that's all they would be.

She went back out into the chilly morning. She bought a few heavy shawls, a warm fur hood for Hengist, and made her way back to the inn to find Hengist seated in the main hall, swilling an ale, and telling Bjorn a story of a bear hunt in the mountains.

"Ah, my sweet," he greeted Mabinne. "I have what you asked— Ashlander yeast, five sacks of wheat, two of barley, salt and spices. We'll eat well this winter, eh?"

"We will. Here," she said, handing Hengist the fur hood. "I know the winters here are cold. It's important to keep your head covered."

Hengist looked from her to the hood, then back; he broke out in a grin. "I thank you, sweet," he breathed. Clearly a gift was the last thing he expected.

And honestly, Mabinne mused, *I'm not sure...I don't know why, but his pleasure...pleases me.*

Why?

The next morning, wagon loaded, they set off for home.

The autumn brought cooler weather during the day, and downright cold weather at night; Mabinne grew to appreciate the several large hearths in the house, even if feeding them required her to help Hengist in cutting, splitting, and stacking wood. For a few days Gerd came over to help. Hengist quietly explained that Gerd couldn't handle an axe, but that he was good at carrying the split wood to the overhanging shed attached to the house and stacking it within.

Then Gerd had to go back to help his parents with harvesting, and Mabinne was left to carry wood, as Hengist chopped and split. He seemed to relish the task, whirling the axe expertly around his head, and working bare-chested even in the chill autumn air.

On one particularly bright, sunny day, Mabinne took note of the several ugly scars that Hengist's back and chest were adorned with. He had never mentioned being injured, but surely the life of a raider was a hard one—and several of those blows must have come close to killing him.

And where would I be, she wondered, *if one of them had? Back in Beretan, certainly.*

The thought came as something of a surprise, but not as surprising as realizing she hadn't thought of Beretan or her dead husband in some time.

Am I actually coming to accept this life? Hengist may have taken her in a raid, may have raped her in her own house and ordered the murder of her husband—but here, in this place, he treated her with deference, even kindness. He had encouraged her to order his house, kitchen, and furnishings as best suited her, and hurried to carry out her wishes in the slightest regard where those things were concerned. She had noted another thing; over the weeks he had stopped referring to the place as "my house," and instead as "our house."

He was good to his family, going out of his way to accommodate a nephew who clearly was damaged in some way.

And at night, in the bed, he strove to be gentle and considerate, even tender.

It was a perplexing contradiction, the two sides to this man; Mabinne wondered if she'd ever understand it.

Meanwhile, there was wood to be carried. Hengist had stopped chopping for a moment and was watching her. She picked up several chunks of cordwood, more than she had been carrying. Then she tried for one more; with her load balanced, she straightened up, took a step—and stumbled over a rough patch of earth, spilling the wood onto the ground.

Hengist let out a shout of laughter. "Careful, sweet," he chided her. "Ambition suits you, but if you try to carry all this at once, we'll be out here into the night."

Mabinne looked at the wood on the ground. She looked at Hengist, who was still chuckling merrily. She looked back at the wood, then back at Hengist.

Then, for the first time, she smiled at him. Hengist's face broke out in a huge grin.

At the homestead

A hands-span of days after Hengist reckoned they had enough firewood—and indeed, the shed was full to overflowing—the first snow came. Mabinne awoke in the night to a strange luminosity from the window. She got up, even though the bedroom had grown chill with the fire burned down to coals and looked out through the glass.

The snow was already at least ankle-deep, and more was falling in great, silent flakes.

She heard Hengist rouse, but stayed at the window, watching. It rarely snowed in Beretan, and then only wet, spitting pellets— miserable stuff; she had never seen this kind of snow, the great, crystalline flakes floating gently down.

She gently fingered the binding collar, still on her neck. She had once commanded the cold; now she could only watch it.

Hengist had tossed another log onto the bedroom's guttering fire. Now he came to stand behind her, looking over her shoulder out the window.

"It's beautiful," she said.

"It is, sweet," Hengist agreed. "And so are you. But it's cold, here by the glass. Let's be back under the furs."

It *was* cold. Hengist had his hand extended. With a small sigh, she took it, and allowed him to lead her back to bed.

Two days later, early in the morning, two men showed up on horseback. They knocked on the front door as Hengist and Mabinne were just sitting down to bowls of hot boiled groats with chunks of beef, Hengist's favored breakfast.

Hengist looked up at the knock. Mabinne was still standing, so went to the door and opened it to find two men she had not seen before; Ikslunders, clearly, like Hengist, but older, their dark blonde hair and beards shot through with gray. They were thickly clothed in heavy leather and wolf furs. Behind them, their horses breathed plumes of mist into the cold air. Large lances were carried upright in leather holsters on the saddle, one on each side, each with a long iron blade on the end.

"Jordvir, Engvar!" Hengist called. "Come in! Will you eat?"

The two men said they would, and came in, kicking their snowy boots off in the anteroom.

"Taken a new wife, have you Hengist?" the one called Engvar asked in a gravelly voice. "A pretty one, she is."

"This is Mabinne," Hengist answered simply. "My sweet, this is Jordvir and Engvar, they are brothers with a big place up north on the edge of the steppe. They are mammoth hunters." Mabinne's eyebrows rose; Hengist had not corrected Engvar's use of the word *wife*. She opened her mouth to object, but at the last moment, chose not to.

"We are farmers," Jordvir chuckled. "But, yes, in the winter, we hunt mammoths, for the meat, the fur, and the fat."

"We are low on rendered mammoth lard," Hengist mused. Mabinne had noted that to Hengist only the day before. "I wouldn't mind some mammoth meat, either. Sweet, you've never tasted the like; rich, fatty, smooth. A mammoth roast is a feast all on its own."

"He speaks true," Engvar agreed.

"Putting a party together, are you?"

Jordvir drained a cup of tea. "We are," he replied. "Thought you might be interested."

"Usual split?"

"Yes," Jordvir said. "The tusks to the man who strikes the fatal blow. Equal shares of meat for all in the party. Pelts likewise divided."

Hengist looked at Mabinne. "I would go with them, sweet, if you've no objection. I'd be gone three, maybe four days. I can ask Gerd to come stay with you if you wish."

"There's plenty of wood and plenty to eat," Mabinne said. "I'll be fine."

"As you wish. Boys, let's finish eating, and I'll get my gear together."

They rode off at mid-morning, Hengist on the more spirited of his two horses, lances like the others bore framing him as Mabinne watched him ride away through the snow.

The next few days passed slowly. The house seemed strangely quiet without the big Northman's bustling presence, and the big bed seemed to take an inordinate amount of time to warm up. Mabinne found she had to stoke the bedroom hearth-fire up more to sleep warm; she hadn't realized how much warmth Hengist's presence generated under the furs.

Chores occupied most of her days. Hengist normally cared for the milk cow and the ducks, all of which required attention morning and evening, but Mabinne had grown up on a farm, and had lived on one after her marriage, so none of the chores were new to her.

And even on her own, the big estate's requirements left her with idle time during the day. She had only herself to cook for and she ate relatively little, so even meal preparation didn't take up much time.

On the second afternoon, she walked down to the lake.

The sun was already growing low in the sky, setting the western horizon glowing orange behind a few scudding clouds. Mabinne walked out onto the small dock and looked out on the cold waters.

She felt the weight of the binding collar on her neck. She stuck an index finger under the collar and wiggled it, but there was almost no play in the device; it fit well.

Taking a deep breath, she closed her eyes and concentrated. Her hands rose, making the sign for an ice-bolt. She bore down, mentally, forming the signs in her head and with her hands for the spell, but nothing happened save for the binding collar growing warm.

She tried a wind spell. Bearing down again, mentally, and physically, she thought she felt the slightest response, but then the collar began to grow uncomfortably hot. She let the spell drop.

I wonder if that's how it's supposed to work, she mused. *If I start being able to work some magic, the collar grows hot and burns.*

I wonder if I could overpower it, freeze it out before it grows hot enough to kill me.

There didn't seem to be any way out short of Hengist removing the collar. Meanwhile, it was growing dark; with a small sigh, Mabinne walked back to the house.

Five days later, in the morning, the hunting group returned.

Mabinne was in the back of the house feeding the ducks, who set up such a gabble while she was scattering grain that she didn't hear the horses approaching. Her first warning was when the mammoth hunter Engvar walked around the house and hailed her.

"Mabinne," he called. "You'd better come along. Hengist has been hurt."

She felt her heart suddenly skip a beat. *Why*? She wondered briefly but hurried to follow the big Northman.

In front of the house, several men and horses were assembled. Hengist's big gelding, Toothbreaker, was drawing a travois made of two long mammoth tusks; as she drew near, Mabinne saw Hengist lying on the travois.

She broke into a run. As she stopped beside the travois, Hengist looked up at her; his face was pale, drawn up in pain, but he managed to smile.

"Sorry, my sweet," he breathed. "I'm afraid I didn't dodge in time." He coughed once and faded into unconsciousness. Mabinne saw blood on his lips.

"Help me get him inside," she told the others.

Once Hengist was bundled inside, changed into a nightshirt, and laid to sleep in the main bedroom the main body of the hunters left. Jordvir and Engvar put up Hengist's gelding, stacked the mammoth tusks up against the front of the house, and spent some time transferring a large quantity of mammoth meat and fat tightly wrapped in mammoth hide into the cold cellar beneath the house. With that done at last, Mabinne made hot tea for Engvar and Jordvir, and when that was served and the three were seated at the big dining table, the brothers told Mabinne the story:

"It was morning, the day before yesterday," Jordvir began. "We spotted four cow mammoths, with three youngsters. We were planning how best to move in on them when Hengist sighted the old bull, up on a ridgeline."

"A grown bull is still fine eating," Engvar added, "not quite as good as a young cow, of course, but the tusks are worth a pretty price, either in trade or in workings. Nothing like ivory for handles, jewelry and so on…But forgive me. Jordvir, go on."

"Hengist wanted to go after the bull, so we split the party. The Hardresen brothers went to take one of the cows, while we two and Hengist went for the bull. We had it planned, you see; we two, on horseback, would approach the old fellow from the front, gaining his attention, while Hengist approached on foot from the rear, taking advantage to get in close and strike a deep blow with one of his lances. While we rode into position on the ridge, Hengist tied Toothbreaker to a bush and took up his two lances."

"I was in a better position to see what happened next," Engvar explained, "as I was a bit higher up the hillside. We two rode in about ten paces apart and paused about fifty paces from the old bull. He had seen and scented us, of course, as the wind was from us to him, but old bull mammoths aren't afraid of anything. He trumpeted at us, of course, and shook his tusks at us to warn us off. We each took up a lance in case he came for us, but otherwise we sat still. The old fellow stopped feeding and watched us in turn, which was of course what we wanted."

"Hengist is a brave fellow," Jordvir added. "Coming in on foot like that. Some would say foolhardy, but we've seen him do the like before. The young fellow just doesn't seem to know fear."

"Yes," Mabinne breathed softly. "I have seen that about him."

"Hengist came in from behind and downwind," Engvar continued. "I thought he was moving to hamstring the old fellow, and sure enough, his first blow struck true, breaking the hamstring on the bull's off hind foot. The bull really let out quite a roar, but mammoths can't move much with a hind leg crippled, so that struck him in place. We started forward intending to attack from the front."

"He came around the crippled bull on the downhill side, where I was approaching," Jordvir added. "I intended to strike from the left, as my brother came in to strike from the right, but we rode well clear of the trunk and tusks, you see, so it took us a few moments longer. The bull was making quite a commotion, of course, and Hengist saw a moment, so he ducked low and came in fast, intending to strike for the heart with his second lance. You've seen the lances, dear lady; that's what they are made for, almost a sword on the end of a long pole, meant to strike deep on a large, strong animal, and at such things Hengist excels. But the mammoth, while immobilized, wasn't helpless; as he came in, it sensed him moving, and pivoted on its three good legs. Swinging its head with tusks low, it caught Hengist up on its tusks and threw him."

"The only reason he's alive at all is because of his initial strike," Engvar explained. "When he was struck, he was tossed a good twenty paces down the hill, and were it sound, the bull surely would have followed to trample him or seize him up in its trunk and dash him against the ground. As it was things would have been less dire, but when Hengist landed he struck a large rock."

"We moved in and killed the bull then," Jordvir concluded. "That is the meat and fat you have below, and the bull's tusks at the front of the house. Hengist had sat up and waved at us, so we did not at first understand the extent of his injuries, but once the bull was dead, we went to him and saw blood on his lips."

"One of the Hardresens is good at physicking and takes care of injuries and illnesses for the local folk in their area. He examined Hengist and said he had several broken ribs and had taken a nasty hit on the head. We bound his ribs and bandaged him up, but that night he fell into raving. None of us slept that night, but towards morning Hengist fell into a deep sleep. We had done with our butchering—the Hardresens spooked the cow herd and didn't land a blow there—so that morning we made up the travois, broke camp and brought Hengist to you, traveling through last night to get here."

"The tale is told, then," Engvar said, yawning hugely.

Mabinne looked at the two men, noticing again the gray in their beards. "Traveling through a day and a night, you must be exhausted. Wait here, I'll bring food and some ale. When you've eaten, go into the extra bedroom, just through there, and I'll bring you hot water for washing. You can sleep there as long as you like."

She stood and turned towards the kitchen, then turned back. "And thank you so for bringing Hengist home. I will do my best to care for him. He will be fit for next year's hunt, I promise."

The brothers slept through the balance of the day, rising only in the evening for a meal before immediately heading back for more sleep. Mabinne reminded herself again that they were older men, probably well past their normal limits of exhaustion after the hunt, the butchering, and the overnight journey to get Hengist home. When Engvar and Jordvir finally left the next morning, she had prepared food and drink for them for their journey. She hugged them both as they made to depart. "Thank you again for bringing Hengist home to me," she said. "I'll take care of him. He'll live, and be well as before, I promise you."

"You are a good woman, to care so for him," Engvar said with a sad smile. "Hengist is lucky to have you here. Be well. We'll let his kinfolk know, I feel sure his sister will want to come help you care for him."

He must recover, she added to herself. *Otherwise...*

"Thank you both," Mabinne told the brothers. "I will be glad to have the help of Hengist's kinfolk, if they can spare the time for the journey."

Then the brothers left, and she was alone, with Hengist still unconscious in the big bed.

At the homestead

Hengist slept throughout that day, the night, and through the next day. Mabinne sat by his side, dabbing his head with a wet cloth, cleaning him up when required. On the evening of the second day, he awoke.

Mabinne was dozing in the chair next to the bed when he spoke. "Well, my sweet," he said in a low, pained tone, "I must apologize for putting you to all this trouble. I simply forgot to dodge, you see."

"You are a lot of trouble," she smiled at him. "How do you feel?"

"Well, I've felt better," Hengist admitted. "My head feels as though that mammoth was inside it, banging to get out. My chest hurts as though he was standing on it. I presume Engvar and Jordvir brought me home?"

"They did," Mabinne said. "Traveled through a day and a night to get you here."

"Good men, they are. Did they tell you what happened? I remember ducking around to the downhill side of the bull to stick him, then a flash of his head moving, and then...nothing." He rubbed his head. "Must be that hit on the head I took."

"He hit you with his tusk," Mabinne told him. "Threw you some ways down the hill. You landed on a rock, or so Engvar and Jordvir said." She proceeded to relate the narrative the two brothers had given her.

"I rather think I'm lucky to be alive," Hengist said when that was done.

"You're more than lucky, you reckless, unthinking Northman," Mabinne replied. "Suppose you had been killed?"

"Then, my sweet, you would have had this place all to yourself," Hengist said. He shifted a little in the bed, wincing in pain.

"Fine chance of that," Mabinne snapped. "Your family would move in, or at least would find someone to take it over, and I'd be set out on the road with the clothes I stood in."

"Not so," Hengist smiled tiredly at her. "Not so. When we were in Tillgatt, I swore out a disposition oath to the King's magistrate there. Should I die, all my lands and properties are yours, including my ship. It's law here in Ikslund that a man can do so."

"You...did that?"

"I did." Hengist's eyes were closing. "And now, I'm glad I did. Should I have died—should I die—you will be settled, have a place to lay your head, fields and stock to feed you. I could hardly rest easy, knowing that you lacked for anything. You see, my sweet, I lied to you a little on the road to Tillgatt. In fact, I find I'm already growing to love you, more than a little." His eyes closed, and he snored.

Mabinne sat back in shock. She regarded the sleeping Ikslunder anew. *He did that,* she mused in some amazement, *for me. When he has family living in spare circumstances?*

She sat for another hour, watching Hengist with a troubled mind. Finally, she went off to sleep in the spare bed, but found sleep evasive; she lay staring at the ceiling long into the night.

Hengist slept through the night and most of the next day, arising only to stagger to a chamber pot in the corner of the room. Towards evening he sat up and drank some soup, following which he crashed back into a deep sleep.

On the next day, a blizzard moved through, dumping a heavy snow almost waist deep. Mabinne scarcely noticed until evening, when she went outside to tend to the livestock; the snow forced her to stop and clear paths before feeding the ducks and the milk cow and its calf.

Hengist spent a ten-day recovering. On the afternoon of that tenth day, a warm wind was melting the snow under a bright blue sky. Hengist looked out at the sun. "Sweet," he announced, "I'm going outside."

"If you like," Mabinne replied. "You haven't been out since..."

"I know." He went to the hangers near the door and started pulling on parka, hood, and boots. He looked over his shoulder. "I'd be happy if you'd join me. I was just thinking of walking to the lake."

"Of course."

They walked through the melting snow to the small dock on the lake shore. The previous fall Hengist had built a small bench on the end of the dock, so they sat there in silence until the sun grew low in the sky.

Finally, Mabinne spoke. "How are you feeling?"

"Quite well, my sweet," Hengist said. "My head still hurts a little, and it's still a bit hard to take a deep breath. But all in all, I've been hurt worse."

Mabinne nodded. She'd seen the scars.

"Dark soon," Hengist mused. "Let's get inside."

When they went in, Mabinne removed her outdoor clothing, then went through the house, stoking up the fires in kitchen, sitting room, and bedroom. "I want you to be warm," she explained when Hengist raised his eyebrow at her. "You're not fully recovered yet, you know."

For their evening meal Mabinne made a thick, warming stew with some of the mammoth meat. When they had eaten, she cleared away the dishes and fussed over Hengist, insisting he settle into his favorite chair close by the fire. Then she disappeared.

She was gone for some minutes. Hengist was just considering going to look for her when she reappeared in the doorway to the bedroom.

She had let down and brushed her long brown hair into a mass of shining waves. Hengist's eyes opened wide; it wasn't her hair that made his breath come short.

Mabinne was wearing the blue silk nightgown he had bought her that first evening back in Port Stronghold.

"Gods beneath us," Hengist breathed, "but you're beautiful."

"I was so worried about you," Mabinne confessed. "Damn your oath of disposition; I couldn't live here without you."

Hengist found himself unable to speak, so he just held out his arms. Mabinne swarmed into his lap and, for the first time, kissed him. Hengist found his strength suddenly returned. With Mabinne still in his arms, he stood and carried her into the bedroom.

The days leading up to spring were some of the happiest, most contented days Hengist had ever known, but there was one bone of contention between him and the Beretanian woman he loved and now acknowledged as his wife.

"I don't see why you wouldn't remove this binding collar. You know I can control all manners of cold and ice with my magic. I know it doesn't seem that useful now," Mabinne said one evening as she was clearing away the supper dishes. "But just think, some summer. It gets hot here, yes?"

"It does," Hengist agreed. "Hot and sticky. Not for long, a moon or two; but it does."

"How much of the meat in the cavelet below goes bad?"

"A fair amount, if it's hot," Hengist replied. "I usually dry some meat to keep over the warm months, it keeps better. But, sweet, remember, I won't be here through much of the warm months. Gerd comes and stays, true, but he doesn't cook; he isn't up to handling the stove, and so he eats mostly sausage and dried meats and vegetables."

"And that's another thing," Mabinne insisted. "I still say that I could be of great use to you in your raiding, if I had full use of my magic."

Hengist shook his head. "The men would never accept it, sweet. Only last summer you were taken as a captive. They'd never understand what has happened between us in the winter between. Trust, sweet, is essential in that business."

Mabinne nodded. "Well, I still wish you'd remove the collar, at least here. Have *you* not learned to trust me, at least?"

Hengist just looked uncomfortable. Mabinne let the matter drop; her point was made.

The last few weeks of winter and the first few weeks of spring slid past as the days grew slowly longer and warmer. The drifts of snow around the house shrank, and icicles formed as water dripped from the eaves of house and barn. A few days of warm (well, tepid, to Mabinne's reckoning) rain accelerated the thawing, and in time, grass hidden for months by snow was revealed and started to come up green.

Whenever Hengist was otherwise occupied, Mabinne would walk to the end of the dock and try to push her magic past the binding collar. Each time she failed. Once she pushed to the point where she actually generated some frost on her fingertips, but the collar burned her neck.

Fortunately, Hengist didn't notice the burn or, if he did, chose not to mention it. Mabinne had noticed, with some apprehension, that the big Ikslunder's mood grew more serious as the days warmed. He pulled his leather armor and sword out of the chest he kept them in over the winter and went over it, polishing the leather, adjusting the straps, sharpening his sword. Mabinne wisely said nothing.

At the homestead

One evening as they sat in their chairs in the house's main room, watching a fire burned down to coals, Hengist asked her about the magic academy that lay on the Beretan coast.

"My sweet," he explained, "there are a fair number of Ikslund captives held there. You've remembered that yourself. How difficult for my men and me to take the academy, and free those captives?"

"Impossible," Mabinne replied. "It's not just the students. If it were, you could probably manage. Even one of the instructors, you could probably deal with, one way or another." She remembered all too well how easily Hengist had overpowered her on their first meeting, powers notwithstanding. "But there are at least a dozen instructors. Their specialties run the gamut—fire magic, ice, wind, you name it. But still…"

"What, sweet?"

Mabinne leaned forward in her chair. "You could take one advantage. You see, you know those magic-users are there. You have a fair idea of their powers. They, on the other hand, will see only a horde of raiders with swords and axes, and will suspect they'll be able to handle you with ease."

Hengist knew she spoke truly so far as it went; Ikslunders weren't much for the magical arts.

"But if you took me along," Mabinne continued, "I could immobilize the instructors before they could respond to your attack." A note of pride entered her voice. "I was, after all, a distinguished student; old Master Etienin said I was one of the most powerful ice-magic users she had ever seen. And they won't be expecting me."

"If something went wrong, your own folk wouldn't take kindly to your helping us. You'd be hanged as a traitor, sweet. I don't know as I want to take such a chance."

"I know the risks. I know what would happen in that case. And I'm willing to take that chance. I want to help you, Hengist. I didn't know how much your people had suffered at the hands of Beretan. And nobody deserves to be held in bondage. Not anyone, anywhere."

"As I held you," Hengist said softly.

Mabinne reached out and took Hengist's big, rough, callused hand in her own soft, long fingered one. "That was before," she assured him. "I'm here of my own accord now."

Hengist squeezed her hand gently. "Let me think on it, sweet," he said.

Three days later, a rider came and left a leather message-container in Hengist's hands. Mabinne saw him unroll the message, read it carefully, and give the rider a reply before the young man rode off.

That afternoon, while Mabinne was feeding the ducks, Hengist called to her. "Sweet? Could you come here a moment?"

"Yes?" Mabinne answered. She walked the few feet to where the big Ikslunder stood with a slight smile.

"Hold still a moment." Hengist reached out, tapped the contacts on the binding collar, then placed his thumb on the stone. The collar fell to the ground.

Mabinne felt as though a dagger of ice had entered her chest. She felt the cold swelling within her. Her eyes flared with an awful blue light, as the cold swelled, swelled within her; she had never felt anything like the incredible surge of power. Hengist's eyes grew wide as the temperature dropped suddenly around his Beretan wife.

"I'm sorry," Mabinne said through gritted teeth. "It's been a while...Have to gain control..." Slowly, the cold faded.

Mabinne held up her right hand, looked at it. A slight sheen of frost lingered on her fingertips. "I seem to have gained some power," she said, "while restrained. I wonder how that happened?" She prudently didn't mention all the times she had tried to overpower the binding collar.

"Hengist," she said after a moment, "Walk to the dock with me?"

"Of course, sweet."

They walked to the end of the dock. The lake was open now in the warm spring sunshine, but Mabinne knelt on the end of the dock and put a hand in the water...

The lake froze over almost instantly.

Mabinne withdrew her hand from the glaze of ice. "It will thaw by tomorrow," she guessed. "I only froze the very top. I just wanted to see how much I've gained, and it would seem to be a lot."

Hengist nodded. He was looking at the ice. "Good," he said

after a few moments. "The men are already putting my ship to rights. We'll leave for Port Stronghold day after tomorrow. The raiding season is upon us, and those captives in the academy are waiting for us to come free them."

A ten-day later they were at sea.

Hengist had argued through their first evening in Port Stronghold and through most of the next day to get his men to accept Mabinne's presence. Only after an explanation of the proposed attack on the magic-users academy, after which his second in command Jorgunn gave in and agreed, did most of the men accept her on the crew—all but two who refused to go to sea with a woman on the crew. They left, and Jorgunn recruited three youths to take their place.

Now Mabinne stood in the prow of the ship as it made its way down the coast, her long hair trailing in the wind like a battle flag. She wore all Ikslund garb: Heavy tunic, leggings, stout boots, and the heavy coat Hengist had bought her in Port Stronghold the year before. She looked much like any other member of the crew save that, when she wasn't wearing her heavy coat, her clothing could not quite hide her gently curved figure—or her beautiful (and beardless) face.

"There is a large river," she had told the men the night before sailing, "that empties into the sea a few leagues south of the academy. If we can row up that river there are a number of small villages, and many small farms. They won't be well-protected that far south."

The farms and villages proved to be just as Mabinne predicted. The first village fell almost at a stroke. As the ship approached a cry of alarm went up.

"Get the ship in to the bank, as fast as you can!" Hengist roared at the rowers. "It's a good-sized village, we can't let them get any defense ready!"

They didn't have to wait to hit solid ground. As the rowers

moved the ship close to the bank, Mabinne put her hand in the water and froze the river solid. "Go over the ice," she told the raiders. They did, slipping and sliding over the frozen water, and swarmed into the unprepared settlement.

A magic-user proved to be in the village. One of the raiders was burned to a cinder by her first attack, but Mabinne's long-denied magic proved stronger; she froze the girl's hands together in a block of ice, preventing her from further action. The raiders put a binding collar on her and took her captive, looted, and burned the village, then moved on upriver.

As they rowed upstream, Jorgunn came to sit next to Hengist and Mabinne. "Chief," he said, "that went very well. I never thought of having a magic-user on the crew, but we would have had a deal more trouble in that village without her. That fire witch, she could have burned half of us before someone got to her. Now, she's just another prize that will fetch a good price in the markets at Port Stronghold."

"A practice Ikslund should look at," Hengist agreed. "We have never considered having women among our raiding crews, and most magic-users are women." His eyebrows raised a notch. "Why is that, sweet? We have few magic-users in Ikslund, but the ones I have seen have all been women."

Mabinne considered that; it was a serious question. "At the academy, almost all the students were girls, as were all of the instructors. We were told that women have an affinity for magic that men lack. Now that I think on it, I can probably count the number of male magic-users I've encountered on one hand."

Jorgunn grinned. "Now I'm more inclined than ever to take this magic-users academy. We'll take some good captives, and we have enough collars for quite a few." He tapped a heavy jute bag with the toe of his boot. The bag clanked; there were at least thirty binding collars inside.

On the afternoon of the next day, the ship grounded near a

small farm but the old man who lived there, apparently alone, scrambled on a horse, and rode away to the south before the Northmen could stop him. As evening was approaching, Hengist decided they would butcher a couple of the old man's goats for the evening meal and plan their next move.

"That old man, he'll return with a company of provincial guards within a day, bet on it," Jorgunn said around a mouthful of cooked goat. He, Hengist, Mabinne and two other senior raiders sat around a fire, eating roast goat, and drinking Beretanian ale, which the Northmen reckoned weak stuff but better than no ale at all—and the old farmer had a big barrel full.

"They'll know we are here," Hengist agreed, "if they didn't already. But we've a fair profit already, and I'm not inclined to move farther upriver and give the guards a chance to cut us off. Better, I think, to head down river, to someplace they won't be expecting us."

"The academy," Mabinne said.

"Yes," Hengist said. Jorgunn and the others nodded. "It's time."

"Good." Mabinne leaned forward and scraped a patch of dirt clear with her boot. Most of the raiders would have used a stick to draw in the dirt, but Mabinne extended her hand, and ice congealed into a three-dimensional model of the academy where it sat on a bluff overlooking the sea.

"The problem is approach," she explained. "There is a road coming to the academy from inland, but the two towers you see facing inland are used by the watch; one of the instructors is always on duty in each of those, and we'd be cut up badly before we could even get to the gate, much less breach it. Now, on the back, the academy is open, as the walls only go to the edge of the bluff. There are wards around the edge that would make it impossible to get around there, but there is nothing but gardens and grass behind the academy proper to the edge of the bluff."

"Looks like a hard climb up from the sea," Jorgunn said. He

leaned forward and squinted at the model. "No good place to land the ship there, either."

"No, but there is another way." Mabinne explained for some minutes. "Even now, it won't be easy, but I think I can do it."

By the time she was done, the Ikslunders were all grinning. "Damn me for a fool, Hengist," Jorgunn chortled, "but I was almost persuaded to vote against bringing your girl there along. Thought for sure she'd be bad luck. Gods take me if I wasn't wrong, and I'll be the first to admit it."

"We'll make contact with the raiding fleet first," Hengist said. "Some ships are always laying a way off the coast, planning their next moves. The take from this will be considerable, we'll need several ships for loot and captives."

Everyone agreed. "Good," Hengist said. "Get some sleep. I want us on ship and moving down-river before sunup."

On the river

Moving downstream was, as it always is, much faster than rowing up. On the first afternoon they passed the village they had raided and burned, to find a band of provincial cavalry picking through the ruins. The horsemen rode to the riverbank and loosed arrows at the Northmen's ship, but Mabinne gestured, and a sheet of ice rose from the river, deflecting the arrows. As the ship moved away, its crew untouched, the horsemen made to follow but found their horses' hooves frozen to the ground. When they dismounted, they found their own boots encased in ice as well.

"The horses will be uncomfortable, but they shouldn't be lamed," Mabinne said as the laughing rowers moved the ship down-river, away from the shouting, cursing provincials. Hengist looked at her, one shaggy eyebrow raised. Mabinne shrugged. "It's not the horses' fault who rides it."

Later that day, Mabinne took some water to their sole captive, the fire caster from the village they had sacked. The girl's eyes blazed. Mabinne undid her gag to allow her to drink, which she did, thirstily. Then she spiked Mabinne with a glare.

"You're of Beretan, aren't you?" The girl's Beretanian sounded strange to Mabinne after so many months of speaking Ikslunder. "What are you doing with these…beasts? What made you turn against your own kind?"

"You wouldn't believe me," Mabinne snapped, "if I told you." She regarded the girl. "What's your name?"

"Aalis," the girl replied. "Aalis Pummeroy."

"You'll have been to the academy, then."

"I have."

"You'll remember the Northmen and women there? They did the cooking, cleaning and so on?"

"I do."

"Slaves," Mabinne told her. "How does that sit with you?"

"No less then they deserve, if you ask me," Aalis said, scowling. "A generation raiding our shores, only just we get some back."

"Wait a few days," Mabinne advised. "You may find yourself singing a different tune."

The rest of the trip was uneventful, and three days later they were on the open sea, tied alongside two other ships of the summer fleet.

The raid leaders conferred on Hengist's ship. While they were skeptical at first, Mabinne explained her plan, and Hengist and his second Jorgunn assured the other leaders that Mabinne was sincere. After a detailed description of her actions to date, the plan was agreed to.

That night, just after the moon had set, the three ships anchored at the foot of the cliff under the magic-user academy.

"Sweet," Hengist said, motioning to the water. "It's all up to you now." The crews of all three longboats were in full fighting trim: Iron breastplates, swords, crossbows, and helms.

Mabinne moved to the front of the ship. She extended her hands...

A broad, solid patch of ice appeared and grew, slowly, slowly. Mabinne let out a gasp of effort; Hengist placed his hand on her shoulder, a concerned look on his face, but Mabinne shook her head. "I can do it. Saltwater freezes harder than fresh." She could feel the weight of one of her soul crystals, on a chain around her neck. *No*, she told herself, *I'll need those later*.

"There," she said at last. "Get everybody on the ice."

The raiders scrambled on to the sudden ice flow, cautious of their footing at first, then more confidently when they found Mabinne had managed to texture the surface to make for sure footing. When the last raider was aboard, save the one man each left behind to mind the longboats, Mabinne stepped onto the ice and walked to the forward edge.

"Mind yourselves," she warned the raiders, "and stay away from the edge. This isn't going to be easy."

The men clustered together, but Hengist remained at Mabinne's side. "You can do this, sweet," he said, smiling. "Raiders in a hundred years will sing songs of this day."

"I know," she said, smiling. Then, with an audible gasp, almost of pain, she raised her hands.

The ice floe rose. A column of ice rose from the sea, bearing the raiders aloft—higher and higher, until it reached the top of the cliff.

There was no response from the great stone bulk of the academy building.

"Let's go," Hengist said, his voice little more than a whisper.

Mabinne collapsed into the grass. In spite of the ice, she was physically spent, soaked with sweat from the short but overwhelming effort. When she finally looked up, she could see she was proven correct. There were no guards, no watchers covering the rear of the academy. The raiders swarmed in through the gardens, into several doors, and took the bulk of the students and instructors in their sleep. Mabinne got tiredly to her feet and followed.

One fire-wielder incinerated two raiders in a narrow hallway before Mabinne arrived to encase her in a block of ice hard as granite. She moved to an overlook in the front wall she remembered from her time as a student, and so by the time the raiders got to the front of the building, the watchtowers, and the guards within, were likewise encased in ice.

In the end, sixteen students—all girls—and four instructors, three women and one man, were taken captive. The raid leaders placed binding collars on each of them, and then the sack began.

While the raiders were looting, Mabinne went back outside. The sun was rising. She could see the great round elevator of ice she had made, and remembered, not so long ago, when she couldn't have imagined doing such a thing.

It was that binding collar, she mused, *and more than that, it was that I fought against it. Somehow it made me stronger. As a blacksmith grows powerful through handling iron all his life, as a messenger grows faster from running, somehow, my pushing back against the collar gave me greater magical strength. I wonder what I could do with one of the soul crystals.* She reached into the pouch she wore on her belt; her other soul crystal was inside. It felt faintly warm.

She watched as a pair of laughing Northmen led the captives out of the building. All had hands bound in addition to the binding collars, but Mabinne could see several of them fighting to summon their own particular magics. *I'll have to watch that,* she thought. With the captives came a dozen laughing, liberated Ikslunders, three men and nine women, chattering excitedly, happy to be going home.

Mabinne found lowering the pillar of ice easier than raising it. *All I had to do is release my hold on it,* she mused, realizing in the moment that she hadn't been aware that she had been maintaining the ice by force of will. *No wonder I'm so exhausted.* Her amazement at her new-found strength had not gone away. *It was the months in the binding collar,* she reminded herself. *I wonder what just a few days will do for these captives.*

She climbed into Hengist's ship and watched from his side as the freed Ikslunders and the captives were loaded into the raiding fleet's ships. Then, as the sun was not yet at the zenith, the fleet set sail north for Port Stronghold.

Over the three days the fleet sailed north, Mabinne made a point of circulating among the captives. She described Port Stronghold to them, its markets, the general layout of the city. "Things might go more smoothly if they have some idea what to expect," she told Hengist when he asked her about it. "Also, you know, I have some idea how they are feeling right now. I cannot help but be a little sympathetic, even if things for me did turn out rather better than I expected." She smiled at the big Northman.

"Some of the men may be keeping some of the girls for themselves," Hengist pointed out. "They won't all be going to the markets."

"I have told them that, too," Mabinne said. "I could hardly have forgotten that, you know."

Hengist grinned, nodded and moved off.

Finally, they arrived at Port Stronghold. As the year before, the great chain was lowered to allow the raiding fleet to enter the harbor. As the year before, the sails were furled, and Hengist bellowed at his men to man the oars. And as the year before, the ships of the summer fleet arrived at the docks.

When the ship was tied off, Hengist stood, and started to shout orders. As the year before, young roustabouts swarmed aboard the ship to carry the loot away to the markets.

Mabinne stood up. She leaned over the side of the ship, looked at the water, and extended a hand.

The water around the ships froze.

Hengist stopped his shouting. He looked down at the water, then turned to look at the Beretan woman he now acknowledged as his wife. "Sweet?"

The ice rose swiftly up over the sides of the ships, into the ships, and grew up to encase the Ikslunders—only the Ikslunders—in a hands-breadth cocoon of ice. Tendrils of ice reached out to the captives, encased their binding collars and, with a tap of an ice tendril, shattered them. The mages were loose.

Mabinne had left Hengist's head free. She walked over to look him in the face with a snarl. "Did you think I'd forgotten?" she snapped. "You murdered my husband, raped me, took me as a slave. Didn't you think that one day I'd take my life back from you?"

The ice grew over Hengist's face, sealing him in a solid cocoon.

On the shore, city guards and a host of armed Ikslunders had seen the ice and were rushing towards the docks. Aalis Pummeroy came to stand beside Mabinne, flame dancing around her fingertips. "What do we do? We can't handle all of them."

"I can." Mabinne reached into the pouch on her belt, found the soul crystal, crushed it.

An unbelievable surge of power filled her, overflowing, making the surge she had felt when her binding collar was removed as nothing by comparison. She knew the power would overwhelm her in a moment, and so stepped to the bow of the ship, around the icy coffins of Hengist and his Northmen, and held her hands high, let the icy power flow away…

And all of Port Stronghold was covered in ice. Rock-hard ice, as deep as a big Ikslunder was tall. The mightiest city of the Northlands was laid low in a stroke.

Mabinne stepped back, exhausted. "We'll take two of the ships," she said, softly, to the captives. "Aalis, melt the ice around us. Someone, raise the sails. Any wind mages, take us out to sea."

Over the years that followed, the news spread like fire, warning of an army of magic-users, that preyed on the villages and ports of Ikslund and the Ashlands. The army was led by a Beretan woman, an ice-magic user with long brown hair, who was said to be on the path of revenge. Mabinne the Merciless, as she was known, and no settlement was safe; all Beretanian, Jutlander, or Mondrian captives were freed, those that held them killed, any others that resisted were burned or buried in ice.

Mabinne, at the head of her growing army, often heard of the fear her army inspired, and was amused. But sometimes, late at night, alone in her sleeping furs, she could still hear Hengist's laughter.

Fire and Ice

Port Stronghold

The city lay in ruins.

As the longboats commandeered by Mabinne and her magic-users sailed off to the south, the primary port city of Ikslund lay frozen, covered by ice as deep as a big man was tall. Buildings had collapsed under the weight of the ice; the roads into the city were blocked. People standing in the open were locked into sheathes of ice, freezing and suffocating. Thousands died in a few minutes after Mabinne had crushed the soul crystal, directed the overwhelming flow of power into her ice magic, and locked the city and the port solidly under an instant glacier.

But the late-summer sun still shone on the city. Before Mabinne's commandeered ships were out of sight, water began to drip from the ice.

On the outskirts of the city, the ice ran thinner and thinner as the distance from the port increased. A league from the port, the ice was only a fingers-width thick, and people and stock easily pulled free. Within the hour riders were fanning out, across the countryside, to inform Ikslund of the disaster. One veteran of the King's cavalry saddled his horse and headed for the King's court at Thunder Castle, a day's ride to the east. Within a day, Ikslunders bundled in winter clothing were entering the city, looking for survivors.

Nightfall brought a halt to the searching all too soon, but in the morning more people had gathered. Two men, brothers, tied iron ice-walkers to their boots and penetrated the city as far as the harbor. A horrible sight awaited them.

"It's like whoever did this had a grudge," one of them said.

"Indeed."

Here, by the docks, the layer of ice was not as thick, covering the ground and the wooden docks to a depth of no more than a hands-breadth. Here and there, on the docks and around the nearby offices and warehouses, were strange, upright caskets of ice, ice frozen hard as granite, only now showing signs of thaw as the morning sun strengthened.

And in each casket was an Ikslunder. Most of them had the look of summer raiders, although some of the caskets contained dock workers, merchants and, in several heartbreaking instances, children.

One of the brothers gave voice to both of their thoughts: "It's as though one of the ice giants from the old legends took form and froze the city."

"Look, over there. One of these ice coffins is broken open."

A few paces away one of the caskets was indeed broken. A stout figure, wrapped in a sodden bison-hide jacket, hung from the ice, his head, upper chest, and right arm exposed. The brothers hurried to his side.

"Gods beneath us," one of them exclaimed. "He's still breathing."

"Let's get this ice chipped away. We need to get him to the healers. He may be the only one who can tell everyone what happened here."

Thunder Castle, Ikslund: Two years after the fall of Port Stronghold

King Harald Iron-Jaw was getting on in years, having just seen his sixty-fifth summer. Twenty years earlier, after his successful war against Beretan, Jutland, and Mondria, he had been a great hero to the Ikslunders. Now—now, with the magic-user army of Mabinne the Merciless ravaging their country, he was rather less so.

Harald was a big man, like most Ikslunder men; broad-shouldered, ruddy faced, with thick red hair and a magnificent russet beard, both now streaked with gray. Seated on his mammoth-tusk throne in the castle's great hall, wearing his shaggy mammoth-hide robes of office, he still cut an imposing figure.

But the war was damaging his standing in Ikslund. Unless something changed, he was in danger of facing a Moot, at which the nation of Ikslund would choose a new king.

He was hoping that the man who now stood in front of him could change all that. This was, after all, the sole survivor of the fall of Port Stronghold.

The man was clearly badly damaged by the freezing of Ikslund's major port. He had, Harald had been told, only survived because his great strength had somehow enabled him to move his head back and forth enough to crack the ice over his face, allowing him to breathe—barely—and to eventually work himself free. But on the rest of him, the frost had taken its toll. His left leg was missing below the knee, where a wooden peg now took the place of the missing appendage. His right foot, Harald had been told, was wooden as well, after the amputation of everything below the ankle. His left arm ended just below the elbow, and on that stump, he wore a heavy leather-and-wood appendage that ended in a heavy iron casting, made to look like the head of a blacksmith's hammer. His right hand was missing the fourth and fifth fingers, but Harald understood that the man had, in the months since he had gotten out of the recovery bed, been training himself to cast a heavy lance with his ruined right hand.

The rest of him, at least what was visible under the heavy

bison-skin robes he wore, was badly scarred by severe frostbite. A patch covered his missing left eye. His long, tangled hair and his matted beard were as white as new snow, but he looked strong enough.

It was his expression that impressed the King. He wore a dark scowl, his one blue eye glittered with rage. This was a man bent on vengeance.

"So," Harald said. "You are the man of legend; the man storytellers are singing of. The sole survivor of Port Stronghold."

The man bent his head in a minimal show of respect. "I am, Highness." His ruined voice was that of black water dripping into cold pools in some dark place.

"What do you seek?"

"Revenge, Highness."

"Revenge for yourself? Or revenge for Port Stronghold?"

"Both," the man answered, candidly.

"That may take some time," the King informed him. "Mabinne's army—and navy—is growing day by day."

"Revenge, Highness," the big man rasped, "is patient."

"You know Mabinne the Merciless personally, I am given to understand."

"I do. I took her as a slave on a raid to Beretan, the year before Port Stronghold fell. As I had no woman at my farm, I kept her on, instead of sending her to the slave market. She was mine for a year, and with her magic-users wiles, she found her way into my confidence, and into my affections, which is why I removed her binding collar." He stopped to catch his breath; clearly speaking was not easy for him. "I assure you, Highness, I will make no similar mistake in the future. And, Highness, that makes me ideally suited to bring her to her just end. I *know* the bitch, as no one else does."

"I remember your father," the King mused. "A braver warrior never drew breath. Can you live up to him?"

"I can, Highness. I will."

"Step forward, then, you who was Hengist Jorgenson, now known as Hengist Hammer-Fist."

Hengist limped forward, to just in front of the throne. "I cannot easily kneel, Highness," he apologized.

"Never mind that," Harald said, waving a dismissive hand. "That's not necessary."

Hengist nodded gratefully.

The King extended his hand. "I name you *General* Hengist Hammer-Fist. I have five ships and five hundred men at the port of Greenstead. They are to be yours."

Now the big man bowed, as deeply as his ruined body would allow. "Endless thanks, Highness. I swear, by the scars I bear, by my life, by my blood, by my teeth, by the bones of my father, and by all the gods below, that I will bring Mabinne the Merciless before you, in a binding collar and chains—and nothing else."

"Now *that*," the King said, "I will look forward to." He produced a scroll, handed it to the scarred man. "Your commission. I will order an escort to take you to Greenstead."

"With all my heart, I thank you, Highness. You will not regret this."

"I'm sure I won't. I have another gift for you, Hammer-Fist." The King turned to a nearby servant and made a gesture. The servant nodded and disappeared. "Would you object to magic-users in your army?"

"I would not," Hengist replied. "Indeed, it would help to even the odds."

"Good." The King smiled as two women entered the great hall, escorted by the servant. "I give you the twins—Agneyastra and Kristol Anagsdottir. They are well motivated; they, too, seek revenge against Beretan."

"Fire and ice," Hengist mused. "That would be useful." He

nodded to the twins. "I presume you took your names from your powers?"

"We did." The women each raised their hands, Agneyastra her left, Kristol her right. Agneyastra's hand lit up with a clear, blue flame. Kristol's hand gave off a sparkling haze of ice crystals. "Our magic is substantially more powerful if we are in contact." They joined hands, and both displays strengthened noticeably.

"Interesting. Are you willing to spend months afield or at sea, to fight, to suffer, to eat bad food and suffer cold, heat, seasickness, to see your comrades wounded and killed, to stand the chance of being wounded or killed yourselves?"

"Our parents were killed in a Beretanian raid when we were but six summers," Agneyastra said. "Also, our younger brother. Our older sister was taken as a slave. For all we know she is still enslaved somewhere in Beretan."

"We will suffer anything," Kristol added. "Anything, in the name of vengeance."

"I think we will get on very well," Hengist said. He regarded the twins. They were typical Ikslund women in being tall, long-legged, and fair. They seemed to be about his age; both had pale blue eyes and pale blonde, almost white hair, gathered into two braids that hung over their shoulders. Hengist noted also that they were identically beautiful.

That part of him, at least, was still fully functional.

It will be difficult to tell them apart, Hengist realized. *Never mind. I suppose that will sort itself out.* "Greenstead is a two-day ride away. Have you horses?"

"I will order the stables to provide horses for them," the King interjected.

"Good. Highness, by your leave, we will depart at once."

"Of course. May the gods see to your success."

Hengist nodded to the King. He glanced at the twins, who smiled, nastily, identically, angrily, with narrowed eyes. "I presume you have clothes and so forth to gather. Can you meet me at the front gate in an hour?"

"We will be there," Kristol said.

Far to the west – the Sea of Dreams

Mabinne awoke slowly. She could hear her people moving around outside the large tent that made up her sleeping quarters. A gentle wind rippled the canvas. The morning sun shining through the trees made a shifting pattern of shadows on the tent.

Mabinne the Merciless, she mused. *More like Mabinne the Exhausted.*

Mabinne yawned. She got up from the hard pallet on the canvas floor, used her slops pot, and splashed her face with some water from a basin on a low table next to her pallet. She pulled her nightshirt off over her head, dropped it on the pallet and dressed quickly, donning neither an ankle-length dress as she would have worn in Beretan nor the tunic and leggings she had worn in Ikslund, but instead a light jersey of some off-white Jutlander fabric. The jersey hung to her knees, so she simply added a belt about her waist, pulled on some knee-high, soft leather boots and went outside.

The sun was already well up. Mabinne felt a trifle guilty for sleeping late, as many of her followers were already moving about, but she reminded herself that they were not on campaign at the moment. *You can't worry about everything*, she reminded herself, *and you need sleep as much as anyone, and probably more than most.*

An old rumor voiced by an older Beretanian man in Mabinne's army had led them to sail west, seemingly off the face of the earth, to find the archipelago of islands in the middle of a warm current that ran up from the south. The camp was set on the beach on one of the larger islands, a good way above the tide line in the shade of some scattered trees, close enough to the water to see any ships approaching. That seemed unlikely, since in her year with the seagoing Ikslunders Mabinne had not heard anyone even speak of islands to the west; the appellation of Sea of Dreams had been assigned by Mabinne herself, on first beholding the lovely, green, warm lands contained therein.

A person could build a home here, she thought, not for the first time. *A people could build a society here.* Some of the people had explored inland and found forests of oak and maple farther from the salt water, as well as a rocky spine of mountains in the middle of the island. The forests were full of birds, and there were fish in the sparkling streams that ran down from the mountains, but oddly, nothing with fur lived in the archipelago.

It was a warm morning. Mabinne walked over to the communal cooking area. A large kettle stood on one of the fire-pits. Mabinne found a metal cup, poured some tea, stuck a forefinger in the cup and cooled it until it was near freezing, as she preferred her morning tea cold on warm days.

"Lady Mabinne," a gravelly voice greeted her. Mabinne looked up to see a pale, ice-eyed Jutlander, Andreas Kokko, who led the soldier's contingent of Mabinne's army; that is, the portion of her forces that were not magic-users, but ordinary troops. With his men, Mabinne's 'army' had grown in number to almost five hundred, and that army was now scattered across three nearby islands, fishing, hunting, preserving food, resting, and preparing for the next attack.

"General Kokko," Mabinne greeted the man.

"Lady," the man went on, "we have been on the island a ten-day. My men are becoming restless. When do you anticipate sailing back to the mainland? When do we take the fight to the enemy again?"

"I would like everyone to have another day or two to rest," Mabinne thought out loud. "There is a trading village in Ikslund, south of the mountains, on the Black River. I would like to take that village. There is something there that may prove very useful to my magic-users." She reached into her tunic pocket and brought out the one remaining soul crystal, that she had bought in the magic shop in Tillgatt, the year before. The crystal, hanging on a silver chain, sparkled in the sunlight, black with hints of deep purple. "This," she said. "When held by a magic-user, can enhance their abilities greatly. But I have only the one, and as I understand, they do not last forever; they can be used gradually, or they can be crushed and give the wielder a sudden, overwhelming burst of magical power."

"Ah," Kokko nodded. "Port Stronghold."

"Indeed. That is what happened to my other soul crystal. They are a thing of the Ashlands, but I found two in a shop in Tillgatt. I would like to find more."

"Without going all the way to the Ashlands," Kokko nodded. "I see. Well, Lady, may I tell my men to prepare to depart the day after tomorrow?"

"Yes," Mabinne conceded. "That will do."

The Jutlander general raised one finger to his brow by way of salute, grinned evilly, and left. Clearly the man was anxious to get back into the fray. Mabinne wondered if all his men were so anxious.

Aalis Pummeroy walked around from the back of Mabinne's tent. The girl had shown a knack for leading magic-users in battle and had effectively become Mabinne's second-in-command.

"Lady Mabinne," she said, "I heard General Kokko. What did he want?"

"He and his men, they are anxious to get back in the fray."

"Anxious for loot," Aalis snorted.

Mabinne nodded. "I suppose so. That has always been the primary motivation for armies in war, hasn't it? We can hardly pay them in gold, and not all of our army is driven by revenge. Most of them are not. We have managed to prevent them taking slaves, but yes, they are here for plunder, but we need them, and they know it."

"What will we do when someone else makes them a better offer?"

"They are mostly Jutlanders. Jutland is allied to Beretan."

"They are mercenaries," Aalis argued. "They fight for loot, not for a cause."

Mabinne held up her slender right hand. A gesture, and frost formed on her fingers. "We have over a hundred Beretanian and Mondrian magic-users in camp as well," she pointed out. "I think General Kokko knows better than to try to run afoul of the amount of magic power we have among us."

"Lady," Aalis said, "I hope you are right. If I may ask, what did you tell the General?"

"I told him to wait two days," Mabinne replied. "I think in that time we can stock fresh water and provisions enough. I plan to strike up the Black River to a trading town called Tillgatt. I'm not sure where we will go after that."

"Up a river? How will we do that?"

"Carefully." Mabinne picked up a stick and began sketching in the sand at her feet. "I see it working thusly: The Ikslunder longboats we have will take twenty or twenty-five passengers, and they draw rather less than our Jutlander triremes. We will land near the coast, where we can beach on the banks on both sides. General Kokko can take his troops, evenly divided, up both sides of the river. There is a bridge in Tillgatt; we'll want to make sure that is captured as fast as possible. We will take most of the magic-users up the river in five of the longboats. Our wind-magic users can move us quickly and quietly. With any luck at all, we can fall on Tillgatt before the alarm is raised."

"Are there Ikslunder troops there?"

"Some magistrates and town constabulary, no more than that."

"You sound as though you've seen this place," Aalis observed.

"Yes. When I was the captive of that big Ikslunder Hengist, who you last saw frozen into a block of ice. That was my observation then, and since we have not raided near that area, nor have we gone far up any rivers, I am counting on Tillgatt still being only lightly guarded."

"Why this place in particular? It seems a fair amount of risk to take a trading village."

Once again, Mabinne produced the soul crystal. "You've seen this. It was one of these that enabled me to coat Port Stronghold in ice, but it was destroyed in the process. I have only one remaining."

"You've shown it to me before, of course. What you haven't said is where we can get more."

Mabinne looked up at the younger woman. "In Tillgatt, there in the main market street, there is a magic-user shop run by an Ashlander woman. It was from her that I obtained my soul crystals. If she has more, we will take them; they will be invaluable to us. If she has none, then she will tell me where she got the ones she did have, and we will go there. But one way or another, I will see us with more of these, as they are potent weapons."

"I understand." Aalis smiled. "I'll look forward to trying one."

Two days later, as Mabinne had promised, the raiders boarded their motley collection of Jutlander triremes and captured Ikslunder longboats and set off for the east.

Greenstead, Ikslund

Hengist paused his horse Toothbreaker on the ridge overlooking the port. Behind him, he heard Agneyastra and Kristol Anagsdottir bring their horses to a halt. All three led pack horses bearing clothing and weapons.

How fortunate that I left the horses with my sister, he reminded

himself, and not in the stables in Port Stronghold as I usually do.
If their plow-horse had not died in the spring... A fortunate turn of
events in the end, anyway.

"There it is," Hengist breathed.

"Not much of a town when set against Port Stronghold," Agneyastra observed.

"No," Hengist ground out. "No, it is not."

The twins moved their horses up alongside Hengist's. "Forgive me," Agneyastra said. She bowed her head as Hengist turned to look at her from his one good eye. "I know you were there, at Port Stronghold, when the witch Mabinne destroyed it."

"Don't apologize. What happened to Port Stronghold is what drives me."

"As you say, of course."

"I cannot see the docks very well," Hengist said. "Are there five ships docked?"

"There are two at the docks and three that look to be at anchor in the harbor. There are some smaller boats moving into the harbor that look like fishing boats and the like, but the five ships are sizable. Not the ordinary long boats."

Hengist nodded. "Good. Let's move on. I'd like to find us a place in an inn or something before nightfall. The King said there was some Gustaf Gustafson in charge down there now. I'll find him in the morning."

"It has been a long day," Kristol agreed.

Hengist tapped Toothbreaker with his heels. The big horse, long attuned to his master's prompts, got moving.

The road wound down a long slope to the small town, really only a village, that wrapped around the small natural harbor of Greenstead. There was no chain across the harbor mouth, no ballista covering the opening. Hengist was perturbed to see Greenstead was completely undefended, save for the ships and, presumably, the troops the King had promised; and Hengist intended to move those forces out of Greenstead as soon as possible.

Port Stronghold was supposed to be re-building, but it would be a task of years to restore Ikslund's major port/fortress to its former glory.

Evening saw them safely in the village. There was but one inn, with no kitchen and only four sleeping rooms. Hengist laid down gold for two rooms and use of the small stable. "Where does one find something to eat here?" he asked the innkeeper.

"One street over," the old man said. "There is an eatery. Mostly fish, sometimes they have reindeer, elk, or even mammoth if one is very lucky."

"Living off the country," Hengist mused.

The innkeeper just nodded. "All the soldiers, they are buying up much of whatever produce comes into the town."

"I think those soldiers will be moving on shortly. Can you tell me where they are camped?"

"South of the harbor," the innkeeper replied. "Some in an abandoned warehouse, the rest under canvas. You'll see them if you go to the harbor and take the path to the left."

"You have my thanks." Hengist laid an extra gold coin on the counter. "For your trouble." The old man grinned and made the coin disappear.

Hengist went outside, where the twins were waiting. "We have two rooms," he told them. "We will see to the horses. Then we eat and sleep."

They did so; the only option available at the eatery was a rather tasteless fish stew and a few chunks of coarse bread. "It's not just the soldiers," the woman who ran the eatery told them. "It's Mabinne the Merciless and her forces. They are strangling trade, all up and down the coast."

Hengist nodded and kept his own council.

In the morning, Hengist and the twins saddled horses and

rode out to the encampment south of the harbor. "I am General Hengist Hammer-Fist," he told the sentry that stopped the three of them on the road. He held up the King's commission, rolled and sealed with wax bearing the royal seal. "Kindly direct me to Gustaf Gustafson."

Intimidated by the hulking figure wrapped in bison-skin, one eye covered with a black patch, one hand replaced with an iron hammerhead, the young soldier just nodded. "Go down the lane between the tents," he said, "...and you will see a large tent on the right. You can find General Gustafson there."

Gustaf Gustafson turned out to be a small, spare man, quick-moving and sharp-eyed. He was going over maps of the coast to the south when Hengist entered the tent.

"General Hengist Hammer-Fist," he introduced himself. "Here is my commission to take command of the forces here at Greenstead."

"We had a messenger two days ago; said you'd be coming." Gustafson broke the seal on the scroll, opened it and read the King's commission. "Well. The King has appointed you himself. Much good may it do you; so far Mabinne the Merciless has evaded us at every turn."

"I hope to change that. What do you plan to do now?"

"That, General, is up to you."

"Would you be amenable to staying on as second-in-command?"

Gustafson nodded. "I would. If I might ask—what were you before all this?"

"A summer raider, as most of us were. A farmer. I hunted mammoths in the winter."

"So, your experience is mixed—on water and land, both?"

"It is."

Gustafson regarded his new commander. "I was a sailor," he said. "Served in the King's navy, such as it was. I might suggest, in addition to being your second in all things with this army, that you put me in charge of the ships and their crews? That way you make best use of both of our experience."

"Done!" Hengist extended his damaged right hand. Gustafson took it and proved to have a good, strong handshake; it hurt, but the only expression that reached Hengist's eye was determination.

Gustafson indicated the map table. "Have you a plan?"

"Tell me what you have done to date."

Gustafson traced a finger down the coast, from the ice-locked land to the north to near the border with Beretan. "We have done some patrolling of the coast. Mabinne and her army are clearly using ships to move about and, so far, have only hit coastal communities or towns and villages within a league of the sea. They don't seem to move much overland. But six or seven moons ago, she received reinforcements of several hundred Jutlander mercenaries, and that has greatly enhanced her ability to strike inland."

"Have you been able to engage her directly?"

"Twice. We suffered heavy losses both times, and both times we just barely intercepted her forces as they fled to seaward; they are an army of magic-users, and that makes them very dangerous indeed."

"Have you any magic-users among you?"

"We do not."

Hengist grinned evilly. "I have two. Only the two, but they are powerful." He described the twins.

Gustafson let out a low whistle. "Ice and fire. That could make a difference, if deployed properly."

"I intend to keep their presence a secret until the right moment, lest they be overwhelmed by Mabinne's magic-users."

"Sensible," Gustafson agreed.

"Now. Do you know where they go between raids?"

"We do not. The two times we engaged them they were headed

west, into the unknown expanse of the sea. There must be land somewhere in that direction, but no one seems to know of its location."

"We will have to find it, in time. But first, we must strip away that Jutlander infantry. That will allow us to focus more directly on Mabinne's magic-users."

"We have had no luck pinning them down," Gustafson pointed out.

"None of the King's forces have. But I may have the solution for that."

"You do?"

"Yes," Hengist said. "We make them come to us." He went on for a few moments.

"That could work," Gustafson said with a grin. "That could work very well indeed. General Hammer-Fist, I think you and I are going to work very well together."

Three days later the five ships, loaded with men, weapons and armor, set sail to the south.

The Black River

Mabinne watched from the bow of the longboat as a Jutlander soldier came to the riverbank on the north side of the river. The man waved a red flag, five times, then disappeared. A few moments later another soldier appeared on the south bank and did the same.

Good. They are in position.

Tillgatt was just around a bend, a hundred paces upstream. Mabinne waved at the other long boats following her boat upriver. Wind magic-users on each boat filled the sails and pushed them silently ahead. In the low forest on either bank, Mabinne knew General Kokko's men would be slipping towards the town, weapons at the ready.

The longboat rounded the bend. The trading village lay in view, a cluster of wooden buildings, an arched wooden bridge across the river. Mabinne leaned over the side of the boat, extended her hand to the water, and froze the river.

She heard a shout from the north side of the river: General Kokko, bellowing "Into the village! Put it to the sack!"

The battle lasted only a few moments. Few of the Ikslunders were able to arm themselves before the Jutlander infantry spilled over the bridge and across the river and joined the other cohort charging from downstream. Mabinne's magic-users made their way across the ice and climbed the bank to join them, but the battle was already almost over.

"Follow me," Mabinne ordered Aalis Pummeroy. "The shop I seek is this way." She had described the shop in detail to her forces; all were under strict orders to leave it untouched. With the fire-magic user at her heels, Mabinne walked quickly to the shop and pushed inside.

The Ashlander woman Mabinne remembered stood there, behind her counter, as though expecting customers. "You," she snarled. "I wondered, when I heard about Mabinne the Merciless, I wondered if it was you."

"It was me," Mabinne confirmed.

"You found someone to remove that collar, then."

"My captor. I...convinced him I was harmless."

The Ashlander woman looked down at something under the counter. "Port Stronghold?" she asked.

"Me."

"The soul crystal," the Ashlander said. "They do work, then."

"Yes. And that is why I'm here."

"Too bad for you, then. I have no more. The two I sold you were all I had."

"Where can I get more?"

"Those were the only ones I've ever seen. And if I did know where to get more, I would not be telling you."

"You think so? Aalis, come forward." The Beretanian fire magic-user raised a hand to reveal a blue flame, curling up from her palm. "You think it will take that much to get you to talk?"

"Oh, I'm not worried about that," the Ashlander woman smiled, a nasty smile that bared strong yellow teeth. "I know a trick or two myself." She produced a small bronze globe, about the size of a fist. There was a small wick protruding from the top. The Ashlander had a lit taper in her other hand.

Mabinne watched, not quite sure what was going on.

"Goodbye, witch," the Ashlander woman said. She touched the taper to the wick and dropped the bronze sphere to the floor.

Mabinne stood for a moment, confused. Then, the possibility hit her: "Aalis! *Run!*"

They fled the shop, barely in time, as a thunderous roar blew out the shop's walls and let the roof collapse. Mabinne found herself lying in the street outside. Her ears rang. She heard a voice, but it sounded wrong, as though she was underwater...

"Lady Mabinne! *Lady Mabinne!*" She suddenly realized General Kokko was calling her, shaking her shoulder. "Are you alright?"

"I'm fine. Damn! How is Aalis?"

"She's stunned, Lady. But I see no wounds. She should be well, given some time for her head to stop spinning."

Mabinne sat up. Her ears were still ringing, but she could think clearly. "Tell your men, they have an hour to take personal spoils. No slaves, we can't feed them. Don't kill anyone you don't have to; I want word of this to spread. We will pull back to the coast."

"As you say, Lady." The Jutlander general walked off, shouting at his men.

Aalis lay a few steps away. Mabinne staggered to her feet. Her head was spinning, but she managed to stumble to Aalis' side.

"Aalis? Are you alright?"

The girl's eyes opened. "Gods beneath us, what was that? Some magic we've not seen?"

"I don't think it was. The Ashlander, she touched a lit taper to something. Some thing of the Ashlands, no doubt. Some alchemical potion in that bronze ball? I don't know."

"Whatever it was, I would like to have some."

Mabinne nodded agreement. "Can you get up? We need to move soon. We need to thaw the river."

"I can move." Aalis shook her head and lurched to her feet.

Mabinne looked at the wreckage of the shop. There was no point in trying to look through the ruins, as the roof had fallen flat onto the wreck. It would take hours to clear enough of the roof's debris to be able to look through what was left.

Damn, she thought. *Damn it all. I wanted more of these crystals.*

I wonder what it was that Ashlander bitch set off?

Mabinne was not interested in spoils. Aalis stayed by her side as General Kokko's men—and some of Mabinne's magic-users—put the town to the sack. Several houses and shops were set alight, as was the inn where Mabinne had stayed with Hengist. Outraged feminine shrieks from some of the houses indicated that General Kokko's troops were indulging themselves in other ways, as well. Mabinne frowned at that but let it pass; it was the way of mercenary troops.

An hour later the river ice was melted by Aalis and two other fire-magic users. General Kokko's men had taken spoils but had also gathered food. The longboats were loaded with barrels of salt bison beef and salt pork, earthenware jugs of rendered mammoth fat, bags of yams and onions. With that done, the longboats turned and headed downstream. General Kokko's infantry moved across the country at quickstep.

They were wending their way through the shallow waters

near the mouth of the river when one of the magic-users in the longboat in the lead waved and shouted: "Smoke!"

Mabinne stood up. Several columns of black smoke were rising into the sky, just ahead.

They arrived at the beach to find a disaster. The twenty Jutlander infantry and four fire-magic users Mabinne had left to guard the Jutlander triremes were dead, and the beached triremes were burning, sending into the sky the black smoke they had seen from just upriver.

General Kokko and his remaining infantry arrived an hour later to find Mabinne and her magic-users engaged in burying bodies.

"What happened?"

Mabinne wiped sweat off her brow. "Someone attacked the beached ships and our people we left as guards. There are signs of many attackers; prints in the sand show it was a large force. They must have fallen on our people from the dunes."

"Who were they?" the Jutlander general demanded.

"We don't know. But I would wager on it being Ikslunders. Look around. See if you can work it out."

"Did you know they had magic-users among them?"

"Yes, of course. Can't you see for yourself? The burn marks on the bodies and the scorched sand. And there are remnants of ice on some of the fallen. So, at least two magic-users. I spent a year among the Ikslunders, remember, and as I know -there are few if any magic-users among them. See for yourself, but either way, we must move soon."

"Move? How? We've lost most of our ships!"

"Walk. We'll head south, along the shore, to Beretan. The longboats will carry magic users that can strike at a distance, to protect against attacks from seaward. The rest will march along with your men, down the shore. We must find more ships; we can best do that in Beretan."

"That's a three-day march, just to the frontier!"

Mabinne's temper, already frayed, snapped. "Have you a better idea?"

Kokko stomped off, muttering.

Along the coast, to the south

"It's hard to believe that stroke of luck."

Hengist was in the longboat's bow, leaning on the railing, lost in a brown study. "That may be, General Gustafson. But her infantry is still in the field. Not as mobile, but still in the field. The larger ships, the Jutlanders, were there just off the beach, but from what we've heard they had several longboats. Those could have gone up-river."

"Something else bothers you about this," Gustafson said.

Hengist turned. "It does. Do you know what town lays up that river?"

"No."

"Tillgatt. A trading town. I took Mabinne there, to trade for goods to see us over the winter. Why would she go that far upriver, to strike a trading town? There is nothing else along this river save a few farms."

"I have no idea. A trading town, you say?"

Hengist turned back to his perusal of the gray ocean waters. "There must be some reason. Something lies there that she wanted. My worry, General, is this: Did she find it?"

General Gustafson considered that. "Since we do not know, I can see no reason to change our plans."

Hengist nodded. "You make a fair point. We'll continue south as we planned."

"To Beretan," Gustafson said.

"To Beretan."

Hengist replayed the sudden attack in his mind. When they

had seen the beached ships, his five hundred left his own fleet, crossed a bridge of ice conjured by Kristol and approached from the dunes, but it was the twins that had done much of the heavy lifting; one of Hengist's longboats had approached from seaward, with the twins standing in the bow, holding hands.

The Jutlanders guarding the landing site had launched a volley of arrows, but the twins froze them in place, then incinerated the ships and the frozen men. By the time the Ikslunders crested the dunes and charged, there was little left to kill.

Their power is impressive, Hengist mused. *But I can't ask that of them too often.*

He looked back. The twins were asleep under a bison robe. Using magic at that scale, Hengist knew, was exhausting. But it worked.

They'll want to obtain more ships, he thought. *There's a port a day's sail to the south if the winds hold. That's where they will go. We need to find a spot in between, lay an ambush. Make them come to us. We won't get this lucky again.*

"They know we're after them now," General Gustafson pointed out.

Hengist considered that. "Good." He thought very rapidly for about ten heartbeats. "What do we know of Mabinne's forces? Their numbers?"

"Around five hundred," Gustafson said. "Of course, we confirmed maybe forty dead on that beach, so take that away. From what I've heard of survivors of their raids, Mabinne has a large contingent of Jutlander infantry now—maybe three to four hundred—and perhaps fifty or sixty various magic-users, mostly ice and fire, some wind."

"We outnumber them in conventional forces, then, but they have us badly outmatched in magic. So, we need to minimize their advantage. Magic is best used at some distance, wouldn't you agree?"

"I would."

"A close-in ambush, then. We must negate their magic-users as fast as possible. How many binding collars do we have?"

"Six," Gustafson replied. "The mage who was making them was in Port Stronghold, and now…"

"We won't be able to obtain any more until someone else figures out the making of them. Very well. Most, if not all, of Mabinne's magic-users will just have to be killed, but make it plain to all the men, I want Mabinne alive."

"Set the twins against her?"

"That was my thought." Hengist looked pensive for a moment. "But I would prefer to hold the twins in reserve. If we can take out the magic-users with our infantry, so much the better; the twins can face Mabinne and her fire-user companion, if necessary. To do this, we need to find good ground, lay an ambush. If I remember this stretch of coast, there's a village at a river mouth south of here. Let's try this…" He went on for several minutes.

"Do you think the twins will be ready for a fight again if they are needed? That last action tired them badly, I'm not sure they have recovered yet."

"We are ready."

Both men turned. Agneyastra and Kristol stood there, holding hands. They looked a trifle unsteady in the rocking longboat, but they wore determined expressions. "We are ready," Agneyastra repeated. "If we can do as you say, it may be the last battle."

"We can hope," General Gustafson said.

Hengist nodded. "Very well. Let us proceed."

Two days later

The village proved to be more of a town, with a sturdy dock on the waterfront and houses and shops laid out in a rough oval facing the water. Heavy forest surrounded the town on the side away from the ocean. "Better and better," Hengist mused as the Ikslunders approached.

The town had some magistrates and one elderly woman who wielded wind magic, but they posed little trouble to Hengist's troops. Hengist ordered the longboats run aground, and his troops stormed into the town. The locals who resisted were put to the sword. The rest were herded into a large warehouse near the waterfront and put under guard. "Anyone who makes a sound," Hengist warned them, "will be run through."

The townspeople believed him.

As evening drew on, Hengist agreed to let a delegation from the townspeople gather food and water, which they did under guard. Near the docks and in the trees was a flurry of activity as the Ikslund infantry dug pits, and gathered branches to conceal the earthworks. That work went on through the night, in shifts to allow the men some sleep.

In the morning, when the preparations were complete, Hengist called the captains of the infantry together, along with the magic-user twins. With General Gustafson at his side, he addressed them.

"I want every man to know the plan," he began. "Every swordsman, every archer, every water carrier in the back rank."

The captains nodded.

"You have seen how Mabinne's army operates. In discussion with General Gustafson, we have examined her attack pattern, how she deploys her Jutlander infantry, and how she uses her magic-wielders. You all know she depends on the infantry to act as a screen, behind which her magic-users advance."

"That is what we will take advantage of," Gustafson said.

Hengist went on to explain the plan, walking the captains around the proposed battlefield, pointing out each earthwork, each pit, all the preparations. When this was done, one of them spoke up.

"General," the man said, reluctantly, "...if this works, it will be a great victory. But if Mabinne the Merciless dispositions her forces in any different way, well, we will be at the mercy of her magic-users."

"We have magic-users of our own," Agneyastra snapped.

"Two of you," the captain replied. "Against maybe two-score of Mabinne's."

"That is why the traps we laid are key," Hengist said. "We need you to choose the very best men to carry this out. They will need to move swiftly, quietly, and mercilessly."

"And the lady herself? Mabinne the Merciless?"

"General Gustafson and I will take her ourselves," Hengist replied. "I have faced her in combat before. She is more powerful now, but I also know her better now. I have promised the King I would take her to him in chains, and that is what I intend to do."

"Go and talk to your men," General Gustafson ordered. The captains dispersed, and Gustafson looked keenly at Hengist. "Sure about this, are you? I would never question you in front of the men, but Captain Horst has a point; this plan could go badly wrong in any number of ways."

"I know. But the initiative will be ours. That's half the battle. The best archers will be in place. You and I will be in place. The ships are down the coast, hidden behind that headland to the south. If we can only keep surprise on our side, then this will work. Once it's down to an infantry battle, we have all the advantages."

"Fair enough," Gustafson said.

There was a shout from the top of a tall dune. "Ships in sight— bound our way from the north!"

Hengist turned to a soldier standing nearby. "Pass the word— light the fires."

"At once, General Hammer-fist," the man said, grinning. He ran off to alert several other men who lounged nearby, awaiting this very command.

On a longboat

"Smoke!" A wind-magic user standing in the prow of the lead longboat was pointing to the shore south of their position. Several columns of gray-black smoke were rising there, from where Mabinne knew there was a small Beretanian town.

Again, Mabinne said to herself. *There's someone new in charge of the Ikslunder troops, someone who is taking them on the offensive. Their General, what was his name, Gustafson, he would not be so bold.*

Mabinne shook her head. Whatever was going on, there was a Beretanian town ablaze, and General Kokko's infantry was still straggling down the coast. "Wind users," Mabinne called out, "move us towards the shore. We'll see what's going on."

Aalis Pummeroy stood up, looking at the pillars of smoke. "General Kokko's troops may well be an hour or more's march away. If we land, we won't have his support."

"It may be just bandits," Mabinne suggested.

"But if it's not? What if it's Ikslunder soldiers?"

"We have almost all of our magic-users in the fleet." Mabinne reached into her pouch to make sure the soul crystal was safe inside. "And we can always retreat to the ships if we are outmatched. Our wind-magic users can move us quickly offshore."

Allis nodded. Her face wore a reluctant look, but she held her tongue.

A wind came up, guided by the several wind-magic wielders, and the longboats approached a good landing site to the north of the burning town. As the prows of the boats touched shore, the magic-users jumped off.

"Form a line," Mabinne ordered. "Fire magic, to the left of the line, near the trees. Ice in the center. Wind-magic users on the right."

We should have brought a few of General Kokko's runners with us, Mabinne thought. *If I could get word to him somehow, have him move as quickly as possible to join us…We could wait until he arrives, but there may be people still under attack in the town. No, we'll move in.*

"All right," Mabinne called. "Let's move." The mages sorted themselves out and slowly, cautiously moved down the beach towards the seaside town. Mabinne and Aalis walked a few paces behind the line, watching.

None of them noticed a small movement in the tumbled grass under the nearest trees. There, in a concealed hole covered with woven grass, hid General Gustafson and one of his captains. The younger man was twitching nervously. "There must be forty of them, magic-users all!"

"Let them go past," the General whispered. "Remember the plan."

Hengist had placed a hundred archers in such concealed holes, completely flanking Mabinne's magic users. Every one of the archers had a powerful Ikslunder bow and iron-tipped, barbed arrows. Hengist himself was the only one above ground, watching from a thick patch of brush as Mabinne's line of mages moved slowly ahead. The left flank of the line passed a broken stick stuck into the sand…

Hengist raised a large ivory whistle to his lips and blew a loud blast.

Sixty of General Gustafson's best archers threw back the covers on their holes just inside the tree line. Standing up, they exposed just enough of themselves to draw bows and loose arrows.

Mabinne's force mustered forty magic-users on a long line, facing south along the beach; the Ikslunder archers had them horribly flanked. The first round of sixty arrows lanced into the line, killing or wounding half their number. Before any of the magic-users could react, a second round of arrow stung the line, killing or wounding more.

Mabinne's fire-users, being closest to the tree line, suffered the worst, with not even one of them surviving the two rounds of arrows. The next most powerful group, the ice wielders, fell in large numbers as well, with only three unhurt. The wind-users, while least able to affect the battle, retained half their number.

Hengist blew a second blast on the whistle.

A hundred Ikslunder infantry burst out of the town and charged, shouting like demons.

Two wind-users struck from Mabinne's right flank, conjuring a series of whirlwinds that swept away part of the Ikslunder attackers, sending them screaming off over the ocean to be dumped two hundred paces away from the beach. Mabinne moved forward, Aalis at her side; the two summoned their powers as they ran.

Why aren't the archers targeting us? Mabinne looked to her left. She could see the line of Ikslunder archers, standing in waist-high pits, drawing bows for a third volley. She stopped, grabbed Aalis' arm, pointed. "There," she said, "The archers. Burn them out."

Aalis raised one hand. She took a deep breath. Fire danced over her fingertips.

In the trees, Hengist unleashed the final signal, two short, sharp blasts on the whistle.

Behind Mabinne and Aalis, under the tumbled grass, the sand erupted. Two buried wooden doors, covered with sand and each over a shallow pit in the sand, were suddenly tossed aside. General Gustafson leaped up from one pit and his Captain Munnin from the other. Munnin held a heavy lance. As soon as he was on his feet, he took aim and cast the lance. Gustafson ran forward.

Munnin's lance transfixed Aalis, entering between her shoulder blades and exiting between her breasts. The flame dancing on her fingers went out. She looked down, saw the blood-covered iron point of the lance protruding from her chest. "Oh," she said. She fell to her knees, then to one side.

Mabinne saw Aalis go down. She screamed. *"Aalis!"*

She heard running feet on the sand. Before she could react, before she could even turn, General Gustafson hit her, knocked her to the ground, stunning her.

Mabinne struggled. She raised her hand, frost forming on her fingers, but she felt the cold metal of a binding collar snapping around her neck. Gustafson tapped the contacts, pressed his thumb on the jewel, and Mabinne felt the horribly familiar sensation of her power fading away. She reached into her pouch, grabbing at the one soul crystal she had left, but Gustafson grabbed her wrist. "Oh no," he said, grinning. He took the soul crystal from her pouch. "I don't know what this is, but I think it best I keep it for now."

Gustafson looked up. The Ikslunder infantry was cleaning up the magic-users. All was going according to plan. He turned towards the tree line, placing one boot on Mabinne's waist. "General!" he roared. "We have her!"

"Good," came a voice from a shadowy figure under the trees. The voice was gravely, damaged somehow, yet strangely familiar...

Mabinne gasped as Hengist stumped out onto the beach. "You! How..."

Hengist limped to where General Gustafson held Mabinne the Merciless to the sand. He looked around; her magic-users were either dead or collared. There was still the matter of her infantry, presumably closing in, but Hengist had a moment to gloat. "Yes, my sweet, it's me. Surprised to see me alive, are you? Well, I am. You hurt me, Mabinne, you hurt me badly, but I'm alive."

He reached down, grabbed the collar, hauled Mabinne to her feet.

"Now," he said in a conversational tone, "Tell me, Mabinne, where you and your army have been hiding in between raids?"

Mabinne suggested Hengist perform an act that was both unhygienic and anatomically impossible.

"Now now," Hengist chided her. "That's not very polite."

Meanwhile, General Gustafson was shouting orders. "All of you," he roared at the infantry, who were just finishing the clean-up of Mabinne's magic-users. "Form a line on the beach facing north."

"I'm moving Mabinne the Merciless off the beach," Hengist called to his second-in-command. "We'll take one of their longboats. Call off a crew for me. We'll wait a hundred paces offshore."

"Very well." Gustafson pointed at ten men. "You lot. Go with the General."

"And us?" Hengist turned to see the twins, who had been left out of the battle.

"Come with me."

One of Gustafson's soldiers came forward with a length of hemp line. He bound Mabinne's hands, tightly, uncomfortably, behind her. "Come on," Hengist ordered Mabinne, shoving her towards one of the longboats; the ten-man skeleton crew was already swarming over the captured boat. "Get in. Agneyastra and Kristol, come along."

A scout ran down the beach. "Infantry coming," he shouted. "Three to four hundred. Maybe a half-hour away."

General Gustafson started shouting his men into line.

Behind him, Aalis stirred. She took a bubbling, agonizing breath, extended a hand. General Gustafson was enveloped in flame, transforming him in an instant to a screaming torch. Aalis waved her hand; the bulk of Gustafson's soldiers burst into flame.

From the longboat, Kristol gestured and encased Aalis in a block of ice, but the damage was done.

"Shit," Hengist breathed. He shouted at the remaining infantry; no more than forty had survived the fire-users' final, overwhelming blast of power. "Seize the longboats! We move away from the coast!"

How suddenly things can change in war. Hengist turned back to Mabinne. "Tell us where you have been hiding," he ordered. "Tell me now, or I'll pitch you over the side."

Mabinne thought very rapidly for a few seconds. She hadn't left the island untended…

"South by southwest," she said at last. "Sail south by southwest. There is a chain of islands. The largest is on the north of the chain. That's where we have been resting."

Two days later - at sea

"How fast the hunter becomes the hunted," Hengist mused. He stood at the back of the captured longboat, watching four ships full of Mabinne's soldiers a league or so away, in pursuit. The early-morning sun was casting long shadows from the ships onto the sea, making them easier to locate. A few paces across the water was the second captured longboat, bearing thirty-six soldiers.

We'll have to find this island, Hengist reminded himself. *Find someplace to set up a defense. Some spot where the twins can use their powers to their best advantage. They have that crystal they took from Mabinne. They claim it enhances magic-users' power. Will that be enough to tip the scale?*

Hengist shrugged. All would depend on how far ahead of Mabinne's troops they could make landfall, and so far there was no land in sight. He walked forward and seated himself across from Mabinne.

Her hands were now free, necessarily as she had to eat, drink, and perform necessary tasks. She sat now, leaning against the side of the boat. She gave Hengist a speculative look.

"Was I really so bad to you," Hengist said, a slight smile on his face, "that I drove you to this?" He held up his hammer-fist, and then used it to tap his wooden leg.

Mabinne frowned. "You killed my husband. You *took* me, and then took me as your slave."

Hengist leaned forward. "And then I made you my wife. I bequeathed my lands and property to you. I *loved* you."

"I know." Mabinne looked down. "I know that, yes. But I ask you, were our positions reversed, would you have ever stopped seeking revenge?"

"I suppose not. But you had your revenge against me, and then went on to seek it against my people."

"As did you, raiding into Beretan?"

"A fair point." Hengist looked up at the blue sky. "I suppose we are both to blame."

"But you…" Mabinne stopped suddenly. She remembered Hengist's narrative of the war in his father's time:

> *"Sweet," Hengist said gently, "the town we are heading for was occupied by Beretanian troops for three years. Beretan invaded the south side of this peninsula, along with Mondria, while the Jutlanders came at us from the west. Port Stronghold held out, but the invaders swept over most of the countryside. Towns, villages, farms were burned, whole families taken into slavery. This academy you speak of, it's on the south end of Beretan near the coast, yes?"*
>
> *"On a cliff overlooking the ocean, yes."*
>
> *"And many of the workers, the cooks, stable-men, drovers and so on are Ikslunders, yes?"*
>
> *"Why, yes," Mabinne replied in some confusion; she had noted that as a girl in the academy, but had never given it any thought; the tall, fair Ikslunders were just servants and workers, surely?*
>
> *"Slaves," Hengist said.*

"Gods beneath us," Mabinne breathed. "Where does it stop?"

"I fear it does not," Hengist said.

"We're all quite mad," Mabinne whispered.

They sat in silence for some time, with only the wind in the sails for company. Then:

A shout came from the front of the longboat: "Land!"

Mabinne and Hengist stood. Mabinne squinted, looking at the faint green strip of land visible to the west. "That should be it," she said. "That should be our island."

Hengist nodded. "Oarsmen! To the oars! Move us to that land, as fast as possible!"

They landed in the early afternoon. Hengist's boat touched the beach first, with the second longboat arriving minutes later. The four ships of Mabinne's fleet had closed the gap, and with them only a few hundred paces from the beach, Hengist's forces only had moments to spare.

There was a row of tents just off the sand, under some odd-looking trees. The sun shone down brightly from a clear sky. "No cover," Hengist mused, "save one big rock. Wonderful."

Agneyastra and Kristol came to stand by his side. "Where do you want us?"

"I'm not sure yet. Let's get off the boat. Mabinne, you're coming with me. No, don't look at me like that; I'll carry you if I must, but I'd rather not."

They clambered over the sides of the ship, dropping into the shallow water and wading up to the beach. Hengist watched Mabinne; she was looking at the row of tents, a little too intently to suit him.

What was left of the Ikslunder infantry leaped off their longboat and scurried towards the trees.

Hengist stopped. He held Mabinne by one arm, but she was ignoring him, watching the tents.

Why is Mabinne watching those tents? She's powerless...

...unless she left someone behind who is not...

Hengist pulled on Mabinne's arm. The big rock outcrop he

had noticed was a few paces away; it was the only natural cover in sight. "Come on," he urged her. He looked over his shoulder at the twins. "Follow me. Stay alert."

There were only two guards on the camp, but both were accomplished magic-users. They waited until the line of Hengist's remaining infantry was almost to the tree line before they struck. They stepped a pace away from the row of tents, two young women, both Beretanian from their looks and dress. They raised their hands. A skirl of wind picked up sand and blasted it at the infantry, blinding them. A blast of fire followed, incinerating half the line.

Kristol reached towards the Beretanians and gestured. Spears of ice shot from her fingers, skewering the Beretanians. Agneyastra followed with a blast of flame that reduced Mabinne's magic-users to screaming, bubbling torches.

Behind them, Mabinne's soldiers were landing. General Kokko was in the forefront. He looked up the beach, saw a big, obviously crippled Ikslunder dragging away his army's leader. "Lady Mabinne!" he shouted.

Agneyastra gestured; Mabinne's general went up in flames.

"Form up!" Hengist roared at what was left of his troops. There were, maybe, twenty, to withstand what appeared to be a hundred or more Jutlander infantry.

The soldiers looked around them. Half of their comrades lay in the sand, burning into char. The trees were nearby, offering cover and perhaps escape, but they were Ikslunders, warriors born, and so they formed a line and drew swords.

Mabinne's men did likewise.

Hengist dragged Mabinne behind the one big rock outcrop. He could barely see over the monolith.

The Ikslunders, screaming like furies, charged down the beach. The Jutlanders, the last few of them still jumping down from the beached ships, hurried to form up to meet them. Both sides came together with a great clashing of steel.

In front of the rocks, Agneyastra and Kristol looked at each other.

"As good a place as any," Kristol smiled at her sister.

"As good a place as any," Agneyastra agreed.

Agneyastra took the soul crystal from a pouch on her belt. She held her right hand out to her sister, the soul crystal in her palm.

Kristol took her sister's hand in her left hand. They walked forward, slowly. Halfway to the water, they shared one last look. Then they clasped their hands, tighter, until the soul crystal crushed.

The twins threw their heads back, screaming, as the power raced through them, overwhelming their control. Flames and ice burst from them.

Hengist grabbed Mabinne. He threw her to the sand behind the great rock and threw himself on top of her. "Keep your head down," he ground out. "Close your eyes. This will be bad."

The twins exploded, the mass of their bodies lost in a maelstrom of fire, ice and steam that wiped the opposing forces away. Flames rushed and crackled, down the beach, over the ships. Ice spicules rose from the sand, skewering infantrymen before flashing away into steam. The water of the sea itself boiled, froze, and boiled again. The Jutlander ships and Ikslunder longboats alike shuddered, burned, cracked apart from frost, then burned again. The very ground shook.

Finally, a blast of steam rolled away from the beach. Hengist and Mabinne were caught up in the fringes, rolled a few paces away from the rock, lifted in the air and slammed down again. The last thing Hengist saw was an Ikslunder longboat, blown a hundred paces out to sea, burning furiously, while a Jutlander ship lay across the beach, broken open by a dozen spikes of ice.

On the beach

Hengist woke to bright sun in his eyes, and sand in his mouth. He sat up, spat, and spat, then looked around.

He was still on the island, lying in the sand behind the great rock outcrop that had saved his life. A few bodies floated in the surf. The fires were all out, only a few thin banners of smoke rose from what was left of the tents. The ships, both his and Mabinne's, were destroyed; only wreckage lay washed up on the shore or bobbing gently in the surf. He saw no living person, save one, who sat in the sand a few feet away, watching the surf roll in.

Mabinne.

It took a few moments before he could work up enough spit to speak. "Well, sweet," he said at last. "Er, I mean, Mabinne. Mabinne the Merciless, I should say. I suppose you'll still want to kill me."

Mabinne turned. She smiled. "It matters very little now." she said. She tapped her neck. "I cannot freeze you. The binding collar your general put on me is still in place. And since he is dead, I am powerless, for the rest of my life."

Hengist looked around. "It would seem General Gustafson has a lot of company in death."

Mabinne nodded. She returned to her study of the waves.

"Of course, you could try to kill me with a knife, or a sword. There would seem to be plenty lying about."

"Have you not seen enough killing?"

"Have you not yet claimed your revenge?"

Mabinne shook her head. "I've walked that path. You can see," she waved a hand at the floating bodies, "where it has taken me."

Hengist struggled to his wooden feet. He walked slowly to Mabinne's side, lowered himself to the sand to sit next to her. "I must say, you walked that path very effectively. Even to here."

Mabinne shrugged. Then, she laughed. "As one warrior to another, you say?"

"Even so. I underestimated you once. I learned a hard lesson from that."

"Then we have both learned some hard lessons."

They sat in silence for some time. Then:

"I confess, I'm amazed you survived at Port Stronghold."

Hengist held up his left arm. The iron hammer head that took the place of his hand was still in place. "I am rather amazed myself. You certainly did some damage. You are strong, Mabinne, but you should have known my own strength, which is great."

"I could hardly doubt that now." She looked over her shoulder at the trees nearest the shore, waving slowly in the wind. "I don't suppose you can build us a ship to return to the mainland?"

"Sweet," Hengist lapsed back into addressing her in the old way, "Building a ship that will survive a sea voyage is the work of a craftsman, and an able-bodied and properly equipped one at that. I am, candidly, a cripple. With half an arm, half a hand, half a leg, a missing foot. We have no tools. We can make no canvas for sails. We have no crew to sail a ship. We are, I am afraid, marooned, on an island that only we two know exists."

"I see. So, then. What happens now?"

Hengist shrugged. "As I see it, we have two choices. We can go on as we just were and try to kill each other."

"And the other?"

"We live. We two, here, on this island. There is food here. We have fire. Building shelters is within my ability, I think. We can live here for some time. Even the rest of our lives, should it come to that."

"Should it come to that," Mabinne repeated.

"We lived together before, after all. We can surely do so again, even if not so...intimately."

"Given that the alternative is to fight to the death, I suppose it's the better choice."

Hengist looked at her for a moment; there was a twinkle in his eye. "You know, I promised to drag you in chains before the King. It looks as though that will not happen now."

Mabinne laughed. "No," she said. "No, I suppose it won't."

"Well. To the task at hand, I suppose." Hengist pushed himself again to his wooden feet. "I should look to building some simple shelters. Nightfall can't be that far off."

"I'll help."

"Search among the wrecks, if you would." Hengist asked. "See what you can find by way of cordage, any unbroken planks, cooking pots, anything useful."

"Very well."

An hour later, they sat in front of a fire in the shade of the trees. Two simple lean-tos stood back in the woods a few paces away, and over the fire, a small bronze pot simmered with a stew of some dried bison meat and Beretanian yams. They ate in silence, side by side, facing the sea, as the sun sank slowly behind them.

"Well," Hengist said at last. He spooned out the last of his stew and swallowed it, then tossed the bowl in the sand. "Here we are. Sailing in a ship of our own building, with our destination unknown to all but the gods."

"You may be right."

Hengist looked out over the waves, still gently rolling in on the beach. Behind them, the sun was setting, and the reddish-gold light played on the sea. "You know," he said, "I really did love you."

"I know."

Mabinne looked down at Hengist's mangled hand, in the sand next to her. She hesitated. Then she laid her own hand on his. "Everything we have done has brought us here. And left us here."

Hengist looked down at Mabinne's hand on his. He frowned. Then he smiled, but it was a humorless, bitter smile. "Together," he said. "The gods' own joke."

"The gods' own joke," Mabinne agreed.

Behind them, the sun slowly sank into the trees.

Twenty years later

Floki Haraldson, second son of old King Harald Iron-Jaw, knew and would freely tell anyone that listened that he was the greatest navigator in the history of Ikslund. He had compiled extensive maps of the coasts of Ikslund and Beretan, as well as star charts that encompassed the entire year. That, along with a device of his own creation that used a sliver of lodestone to indicate true direction, emboldened him to drive his longboat to places hitherto unknown.

This summer, eighteen years after the final peace between Ikslund and their Ashlander allies and the Beretanians, Jutlanders and Mondrians, he drove to the west, across unknown seas. And now his search was rewarded: New land, unknown to all who had gone before.

Or so Floki thought.

"We'll land," he directed his crew. The sun was high in the sky, near midday. "It will be good to stretch our legs. When we land, Gunther and Bjorn, see if you can find us some fresh meat. Jorn and Vigdar, start fires, see about some shelters."

They landed the ship on a broad, gentle stretch of sandy beach and climbed out. Past the beach was forest, oddly straight trees with a spray of broad leaves at the top. Underneath one of the trees, amazingly, stood a girl.

She was tall, fair, with not quite the look of an Ikslunder despite her blonde hair and blue eyes, dressed in a ragged, knee-length tunic that looked as though it had been made from woven packing bags.

She walked forward, slowly, cautiously, with an old, stained bow in her hand, an arrow nocked. "Who are you?" she asked in an oddly accented Ikslunder.

"Floki Haraldson," Floki replied. "Son of the late King Harald Iron-Jaw, brother to the present King Knut Haraldson. We came out of Port Stronghold. We mean you no harm. Who are you? How did you come to be here?"

The girl lowered the bow. "Me? Mabinne Hengistdottir. How did I come to be here? I've always been here."

"Where is your family, child?" Floki asked. "Where are your people? Are there others?"

"No. No longer, at any rate. My parents were marooned here. My mother died of a fever when I was two summers of age. My father died last year. They are buried back there, in the trees. I am alone."

"Well, no longer," Floki said. "We will be returning to Port Stronghold with news of this new land. You are welcome to come with us."

Mabinne thought about that. She remembered her father telling her of his farm in Ikslund, and how he had appeared before the King, and all his other stories...

Imagine the daughter of Hengist Iron-Fist and Mabinne the Merciless, returned to Ikslund. By the brother of the king, no less.

"Yes," she said. "Yes, I think I'd like that."

Shadow
Inspired by Bob Dylan's "Trust Yourself."

A warm place, a human place

Looking out through the invisible wall had gotten boring. It was wet on the other side; she could not smell that through the barrier, but she could see it easily enough. She could hear it, too, the drops of water falling from the sky, splatting on the stones, pattering on the dead leaves. She was much more comfortable on this side, and yet the other side beckoned to her somehow.

Instead, she went to the large pillow her pets kept for her, drawn cozily up to the fire. The Man usually kept the fire going. She didn't like the Man very much. While it kept the space warm by managing the tame fire, its voice was jarring, deep and rumbling, and it did not pay her proper courtesy. The Woman was kinder, petted her, and most of all, fed her. It was enough that she was able to overlook the annoying barking sounds the Woman made, and the deeper droning sounds the Man made to it in reply.

Both of them had sounds they used to address her. The Woman made the sounds gently, at least as gently as it could, and when the noises were soft and gentle, if it pleased her, she would respond to the Woman, to come and be petted and have her ears scratched. When the Man made the sounds, it was generally upset, usually at some small matter such as where she chose to sharpen her claws. It was an ignorant beast and did not understand the necessity of keeping her catching claws sharp in case some prey presented itself.

In her own head, she had not a sound, but a thought, that she used when thinking of herself. It was an image, a concept, that took in her dark, dark fur, her noiseless walk, her bright eyes, and how she could drift silently through the darkness unseen, unheard, alone.

If there was a human word that could begin to capture that concept, it would be Shadow.

There was another animal in the place. Shadow definitely did not like the other animal. Like her, unlike the humans, it walked on all four legs. Like the humans, unlike her, it was noisy and rude. And most unlike her, it was dirty. It went outside through a swinging piece of the wall, and when it came in it frequently had been rolling in the dirt. Even when reasonably clean, such as just after the Man would take it into a small room near where Shadow ate and pour water and some white foam on it, it still had a sharp, rank odor. What's more, it looked at her sometimes as though *she* were the prey animal.

Shadow did not trust Dog, and never would. But then, she didn't trust the Man, either, and trusted the Woman only slightly, only to supply her with food and petting.

Shadow only really trusted herself.

This was not without reason. The Man, the Woman, and Dog were clearly her inferiors. They were not beautiful, like Shadow. They had not her glossy black fur, her shining golden eyes, or her silent, padded feet. They were noisy, where she had the sense to be quiet. They were awkward, where she was graceful. Shadow walked quietly and could vanish at will into any slightly darkened corner.

Clearly, she was the superior being.

She laid down on the pillow. The fire was warm. Dog came and laid in front of the fire as well. Shadow wrinkled her nose at the bad smell, but for the moment Dog was content to leave her alone, so she concentrated on her grooming. When she had cleaned herself and groomed her fur into glossy loveliness, she gave Dog a fearsome glare—the beast was oblivious—and went to sleep.

Some time later, the Woman came into the room. It had some kind of container with a drink of some sort in it, as it often did, and the drink smelled sharply sweet, like some kind of fruit left too long on the vine. The Man came in a few moments later. It also had some sort of drink. The Man's drink smelled sharper, with a bitter smell. It was nasty.

The Man and the Woman sat on the big, long pillow that faced the fireplace. Their pillow was high off the floor, with an upright portion at the back to support their long, awkward upright bodies. They made noises at each other for a while. Shadow ignored their noisy rudeness and tried to go back to sleep.

In time, as they always did, the Man and the Woman went off into the other room where they slept. Dog, as it always did, went with them, to sleep at the foot of the huge, raised pillow where the Man and Woman slept. Soon after, Shadow heard their breathing slow and deepen as they slept. The Man made loud snarling noises in his sleep, which Shadow always found annoying.

Shadow lifted her head. Her golden eyes opened wide. It was her time.

Most times, when night fell and they went off to sleep, the Man would draw some kind of stick across the swinging piece of wall Dog used to go outside. When it did this, the piece of wall was blocked shut. But some nights it forgot, as it had done tonight.

Shadow left her pillow. She jumped back up to look again out of the invisible wall. The rain had stopped. It still looked damp outside. Shadow lifted her front paws, reflexively, and shook them, even though the sill she sat on was dry.

I will put up with the wet, she mused, as long as water is not falling from the sky. Others will be outside.

Shadow hopped down to the floor and went to the place where the wall opened. It was heavy. The Dog pushed it open easily. For Shadow it was an effort, but then, she did not need to push it open very far. She pushed, felt it give way, and slipped outside.

The ground was damp, but not unbearably so. Shadow perked up her ears. She could hear the big beasts that ran on the stone path nearby, but at night there weren't as many of them. But that wasn't what she was listening for.

There, she realized. She jumped up on the wooden divider behind the human place, then dropped down into the grass on the other side. Another of her kind, one she knew well.

There you are.

And there you are, the other one replied. It was another female like herself, about her size, with fur of dark yellow, orange, and white. Shadow thought of her in terms of her color, and if there was a human word that could begin to capture that concept, it would be Ginger.

Wet, Ginger indicated with her paws and a flick of one ear. *Under the trees is better. Others will be there.*

We should go there, then, Shadow agreed.

Shadow did not trust Ginger. Ginger had the same preference for being out of the wet that Shadow did, and the same desire for the occasional company of her own kind. But Shadow did not really trust her.

Shadow only really trusted herself.

The two moved together, silently, staying in the shadows. Not far away was a woodlot, where the great trees grew together to block out the sky. They went there, into the woods, to a small area where the grass was short. Others were there. One was a small, slim female, tan with black face, paws, and tail. Shadow always thought of her in terms of her eyes, which were like no other's eyes Shadow had ever seen, and if there was a human word that could begin to capture that concept, it would be Blue.

Two others were there—males. Shadow thought of them as she thought of all males, and if there was a human word that could begin to capture that concept, it would be simply Tom. Shadow was not in season at the moment, nor were Ginger or Blue, so the Toms were relaxed and peaceful.

Shadow did not trust Blue, nor did she trust the Toms. Shadow only really trusted herself.

Shadow sat at the edge of the open space. Above, the great pale light in the sky came out from behind the clouds. Shadow looked up at it, Ginger came and sat beside her.

Blue approached. *Can you see how beautiful my points of seal are tonight? I had just finished my grooming before I came here.*

You are beautiful, Ginger indicated, *but not so beautiful as my stripes of white and my bands of orange.*

You are both beautiful, Shadow agreed. *But I am black like the night, and therefore the most beautiful of all.*

Before things could turn unpleasant, one of the Toms jumped up on the stump of a tree. *I have things to say*, he indicated with the wave of a paw and inclining his head just so. *Things that will affect all, the community of Cat.*

There is no community of Cat, Shadow replied by waving her tail and cocking one ear. *There are only us each alone. As has been with Cat forever, we walk by ourselves. As has been with Cat forever, all places are alike to us.*

I will say my things I came to say, the Tom nodded. *Things of truth, and of beauty. Then you will see. Then you will know.*

Shadow did not like the Tom presuming what she might think. She did not care for such a plain beast with dull gray fur telling her anything of beauty, when she was clearly the most beautiful of all. Shadow did not really trust the Tom to say any of these things.

Shadow really only trusted herself.

But to be polite, in the manner of Cat, she perked up her ears, and composed herself to listen.

The Clearing

It is of the path forward for Cat that I will speak, the Tom began.

Which Cat? Blue asked, inclining her triangular head just so.

Cat, the Tom replied. *All of us. The community of Cat.*

There is no community of Cat, Shadow repeated. *There is only each of us, alone. Go on, anyway. We will listen.*

Tom nodded. *We are of one kind,* he went on. *All of us live nearby to humans. It is of this that we Toms are concerned. It is of the humans I will speak, in truth and beauty, so you will understand.*

Ginger's tail puffed up, just slightly. *So you've been saying,* she indicated. *We're still waiting.*

You all live among humans, Tom said, indicating Blue, Ginger and Shadow. *You live in their homes. They feed you what and when suits them. They take your kittens away, before they are grown and ready to hunt on their own. Why do you do this?*

It is what we have done always, Blue said. *My ancestors lived in palaces. Now I live in a small place with two elderly humans. But it is the way of Cat to live among them. They serve us. They are our beloved pets. We have kept humans for pets since the beginning of Cat.*

That is what we would change, Tom said. The second Tom, this one with black stripes among his gray fur, hopped up on the stump beside the first. *We should live in the wild, as once was,* the second Tom said. *Hunt for our own food. You could raise your kittens as a free cat should. The humans have enslaved you long enough.*

Enslaved? Shadow asked. *We keep them as pets by choice. Our choice, not yours. When winter comes, we are warm. When our kits are born, they are safe, away from predators. The humans feed us and shelter us in return for keeping their homes free of vermin. This is a trade, not an enslavement.*

You would be better off living as we do, the Tom insisted.

Fine, then, Shadow replied. *You have the night before us. Show us how you live, in this free way in the wild.*

Shadow did not trust the Tom. She really only trusted herself. But she was willing, for one night, to follow, to see this 'truth' for herself.

Come, then. Both Toms jumped down from the stump and led the way out of the woods, back into where the humans had their homes.

This is the wild? Shadow asked. *Are these not the human dwellings*?

They are, the gray and black Tom said. *You will see.*

The Tom led them between the human buildings. There was a narrow passage, and in it were several tall containers emitting a strong odor—bad meat, some remnants of fish, and other foul odors. Shadow's nose wrinkled in disgust.

This isn't good, Ginger indicated.

Blue stopped in her tracks. *Oh, no*, she shook her head. *I'm going home. I've seen enough.* The slim brown and white female turned and left.

Shadow and Ginger followed on. Shadow was curious, as cats are, and knew Ginger would be curious as well. But they two followed the Toms at a distance. Neither of them really trusted the Toms. Ginger, like Shadow, really only trusted herself.

The Toms went down the narrow alleyway. They stopped at a reeking canister, from the smell obviously full of waste. One of the Toms jumped up on the bin, braced, and pushed against the wall, knocking the container over, spilling the reeking contents on the ground.

See? The Toms jumped into the refuse. *Food for the taking.*

Shadow and Ginger kept their distance and looked on in disgust. The Toms picked through the refuse until a light came on in an opening in the wall above, and a human voice shouted something. An object—one of the odd coverings humans wore on their big, ungainly flat feet—sailed out of the window and landed on the ground near the pile of refuse.

Now we go, said the grey Tom. *Find another place.*

It was a disaster. The Toms were used to feeding out of human refuse bins and making a great amount of noise while doing so and added the risk of being struck by something flung from the human dwellings into the bargain. *This is not freedom*, Shadow indicated to Ginger. *They depend on the leavings of humans. They scrounge among waste for their food. Where humans serve us, these Toms depend on humans.*

Yes, Ginger agreed. *They may as well be dogs.*

You go, Shadow said to the Toms. *We have seen enough.*

We're leaving, Ginger said snootily.

The two cats turned and walked away, tails upright, lashing the air in indignation. They walked back through the clearing in the woods, back to the place where they had first met. There they nodded to each other, touched noses delicately, in the manner of Cat, before each turned towards their own homes.

Shadow pushed though the piece of wall that opened into the human dwelling where her pets were. Dog was sitting just inside, clearly having sensed Shadow's approach. The beast could not really communicate, certainly not with the beautiful grace and nuance of Cat, but it could manage to make basic concepts known.

You, it indicated, *were out.*

Yes, Shadow agreed. She sat, looked down her nose haughtily at the stupid beast. *I was out.*

What doing?

My own affair, Shadow replied.

Dog just sat there, tongue lolling out, his breath reeking. *Humans not sleeping*, it said.

So?

Listen.

Shadow flowed quietly, gracefully through the darkened dwelling to the closed panel behind which the Man and the Woman slept. Dog followed, his claws clicking loudly on the floor, his panting loud enough to be heard on the other side of the dwelling.

Shadow paused; Dog was correct, from behind the panel came the odd straining, struggling sounds that the humans sometimes made in the night.

This does not affect me, Shadow thought. Dog sat down, evidently willing to wait slavishly until the Man and the Woman emerged in the morning. Shadow went off to sleep in front of the fireplace, on her own comfortable pillow.

Over the next few days Shadow forgot about the Toms and their abject dependency on human garbage, the life they considered "free." They believed they were free, but they were just scavengers.

What could be better than to have her human pets serving her, in this warm dwelling, with good food? Oh, Dog could be annoying, but all in all she was content with her two pets and her soft pillow by the warm fire. Surely nothing could disrupt this comfortable, peaceful existence.

Then, one morning, Shadow was sitting comfortably in a ray of sunshine in the big room the humans used for preparing food. The Woman came through, got some sort of drink for itself out of the big white box they kept food in.

It called to Shadow as it left the room. Shadow recognized the crude barking; it was the sound that the humans used when addressing their mistress. Shadow considered things for a moment and decided that some petting and ear-scratching from her pet may be worth leaving her sunbeam, so she followed the Woman into the room with the fire.

The Woman sat down. Shadow jumped up on to the big

pillow next to her, then paused. The Woman, somehow, smelled different.

Shadow sniffed, then sniffed again. There could be no doubt about it.

The Woman was going to have a kitten, or whatever the human equivalent was.

One year later

The human kitten was wailing again.

Shadow was annoyed. Not only was it the middle of the day, her preferred napping time, but the kitten once again had distracted the Woman, who up until a moment ago had been gently petting Shadow as she lay next to it on the big human pillow.

The Woman got up and left. Shadow jumped down off the big pillow and went over to her smaller one, which was colder now as the Man had apparently lost interest in keeping the fire going. The pudgy, noisy, helpless human kitten took up too much of their attention. They were clearly only thinking of themselves—selfish creatures!

Shadow was disappointed in her pets, but not terribly surprised. She had never really trusted them in any case.

Shadow only really trusted herself.

One night, the Man forgot again to place the stick across the section of wall that opened to the outside. As this happened after a long day during which Shadow's pets mostly ignored her, she made to go outside after the Man and the Woman had taken their kitten and gone into their sleeping room.

Where go? Dog met her at the panel, looking stupidly inquisitive.

Out, Shadow told the beast. Dog made no move to stop her, so she pushed open the panel and left.

Outside it was a pleasant night, at least. The sky was clear, the great nighttime light shone brightly, and there was no wind. Shadow did not sense Ginger or any other of Cat around, so she walked away from the human dwelling towards the woods, her tail waving pleasantly in the air. It was chilly, but Shadow had her thick pelt of glossy black fur to keep her warm.

She did not stop in the clearing where the braggart Toms had sung their deceitful song of freedom. She went on up, away from the place where the humans had their homes, into the wooded hills above.

This is good, she said, as she walked through the forest. She could hear rustlings all around. There were small animals in the leaves on the forest floor. Shadow had caught mice in the humans' house; the humans did not like mice and capturing and eating them was a boon she deigned to extend to her pets.

But now she realized that the Woman would not be feeding her in return, as long as she stayed here in the hills. So, she stalked, and after several unsuccessful attempts she managed to catch a mouse. It was not like the mice from the human dwelling, being brown and white instead of gray, and it even smelled cleaner. She ate the mouse and found she enjoyed it.

Shadow found a thick patch of brush, crawled in, and spent the balance of the night there, sleeping peacefully, with no squalling human kitten to interrupt her slumber. *This*, she told herself, *this is good. I will stay here, in this forest. I am Cat, after all. All places are alike to me.*

The next night she found a hollow log that was the perfect size to shelter her when she slept. She explored the area thoroughly each night as she hunted. There were mice and low-nesting birds to eat. A clear stream sparkled over round rocks nearby, so she had clean water. Here and there she smelled the acrid scent-marking of a Tom, but otherwise saw no others of Cat in the forest.

It was a good place. Shadow was pleased, even after the loss of her pets, as she had chosen this place for herself. She relied on no other creature now, which was good, as in the nature of Cat, she did not trust any other creature.

Shadow only really trusted herself. Now, in the forest, she found that trust rewarded.

Came the time of year when the leaves dried and fell from the trees, and then the white flakes fell from the sky and left the cold white blanket covering the earth, but Shadow's fur grew thick and luxuriant, and she slept snug in the hollow log. There were always mice and other small creatures, and tracking them through the white blanket was easy. Shadow fed well. Outside it was cold, but Shadow slept warm in the small space afforded by her hollow log.

One morning a strange creature appeared at the opening of the hollow log. Shadow was awake but still curled up, enjoying the warmth her body generated in the small space, when the creature poked its head in. It was an odd-looking beast, black with white stripes leading from its head down its back to its tail, which was a brush of white and black. A foul odor preceded it.

Shadow bared her teeth and hissed. *Stay away*, the hiss conveyed. *You smell bad. See how sharp my teeth are?* She extended a front paw, claws flexed. *These can scratch out your eyes. Go away!*

The creature left. Shadow did not see it again, although she smelled it for several days.

In due course the weather warmed as spring came, then early summer. Shadow took to sunning herself on top of her hollow log in the afternoons, and as happened that time of year, her season came. The big Tom she had sensed showed up in response to her calls. Shadow normally had no time for Toms, but as she was in her season and receptive, she found this one handsome. His head was large and rounded, his brown and tan striped fur well groomed. They mated, and sometime after he left, as summer was in full bloom, Shadow delivered four kittens, in the comfort of her hollow log.

The kittens were growing rapidly. Their eyes were open, and they were starting to explore the confines of the hollow log when disaster struck.

Early morning, and Shadow had just returned from a nighttime hunt. She had brought a mouse for the kittens; they were still dependent on Shadow's milk but were old enough to start getting the feel of prey.

Shadow's ears perked up. Something big was out there, outside the hollow log, and it was moving closer. She smelled the air. Whatever it was, it had something of the sour smell of Dog, but somehow thicker, stronger.

The hollow log suddenly rolled. Huge claws were tearing it open. Shadow glimpsed the creature in the first pale light of morning. It looked something like Dog but larger, heavier, and vastly stronger. It was black, with a tan face, and impossibly huge.

It exposed the hollow log, opening the nest of soft grasses and her own fur that Shadow had made for the kittens. The kittens looked up at the monster, curious.

The beast bared teeth: Huge, yellow, carnivorous.

Shadow knew she could not fend off this predator. Ignoring Shadow's hisses, the beast grabbed a kitten, crunched it, and swallowed.

There, close by, was the largest of the kittens. It was a female, healthy, strong, with a coat of mixed black, white, and orange. Shadow had a concept for this kitten in her head; if there was a human word that could begin to capture that concept, it would be Calico.

She grabbed Calico by the scruff of the neck and fled. Behind her, she could hear the monster tearing apart the nest and devouring the rest of her young.

Shadow ran through the woods. When she came to a tiny

brook, she stopped for a moment, so she and Calico could drink. Then she picked up Calico again and ran on. When night came, they hid in an abandoned burrow under a rotten stump; it smelled faintly of the black-and-white beast she had seen before but the smell was old and barely tolerable.

The next day, they came across a human dwelling, a small one, deep in the forest. There was a Woman working outside, doing something with plants growing in rows in the black dirt. A Man walked around the side of the dwelling, said something to the Woman, then went into a smaller construct to one side. *Enough,* Shadow decided. *If I can make these humans my new pets, we will be better off.*

She watched the humans for a few moments. Both had white hair. Their scent revealed that they were elderly, but healthy and strong. Their voices were not like the pets Shadow had abandoned; theirs were softer, quieter, gentler.

Shadow finally picked Calico up, went to where the Woman kneeled on the dirt, set the kitten down and called softly.

The Woman looked up. Its eyes opened wide. It called out something, and the Man came. Both made soft, sympathetic noises. The Woman gently picked Calico up and started towards the dwelling. The Man walked beside it. It looked at Shadow, said something in his quiet voice, and, surprisingly, made a motion with its big, awkward paws that she understood: *Come with me.*

Inside the dwelling, there was a faint smell of Cat, but old. The Woman held Calico while the Man looked in some enclosure on one wall and brought out a pillow. Shadow could smell Cat on the pillow, faintly. It placed the pillow on the floor near a big black device that radiated warmth. Again, it motioned: *Lay down.*

Shadow laid on the pillow. The Woman placed Calico beside her. The Man opened a container that gave off a delicious smell, placed food on a plate, put it next to Shadow's pillow.

Thus, Shadow and Calico found a new home and new pets.

While Shadow knew that she was Cat and that all places were alike to her, she found she preferred this place to most others. But sometimes, in the night, Shadow slipped out into the dark woods and hunted, teaching Calico the things she needed to know, how to be Cat.

It was a good home, for the time being, and a good end to her journey.

But Shadow didn't really trust her new pets. Shadow only really trusted herself.

Changing Times
Inspired by Bob Dylan's
"The Times, They Are 'A Changin'."

Sector Five, Level Eight, Thunberg-121

Denver G-126 (he/him) was excited as he left his Minimal Personal berth. Helena R-223 (she/her) was meeting him for a quiet dinner, and Denver had reserved a personal booth in the Sector Five Refectory. The dinner would be largely soy patties and 3-D printed proteins, with nothing but recycled water to drink, but Denver was excited all the same.

As he walked through the crowded corridors of the self-contained Modern City of Thunberg-121, he mentally reviewed everything he had gone through to arrange the date:

> Before speaking to Helena, Denver had checked with the Cultural/Racial Rectification Authority and confirmed that Helena R-223 (she/her) was certified compatible with Denver in racial and cultural privilege level, gender identification, and amativeness.

> Denver had properly filled out the Social Interaction Permissions form, Helena had countersigned without any alterations to the agreed interaction guidelines (personal contact by handshake, hugs allowed on spoken assent of both parties) and had submitted the completed form to the Social and Sexual Interaction

> Regulation Authority. After the date, both Denver
> and Helena would have twenty-four hours to confirm
> that those guidelines had not been exceeded, on pain
> of fine and/or confinement.

> Denver's Weekly Ration Allowance contained enough
> credits to cover his planned protein draw to go along
> with the soy ration.

This was dating in the 22nd century in one of the Modern Cities of the North American People's State.

Denver looked up at the great dome covering the city. As usual, the sky was a dark red; gusts of wind blew black dust over the dome. The environmental calamity brought about by the selfishness of the capitalist governments of the early 21st century was still, as always, right there outside the safe, protected, self-contained city dome.

Denver harbored some doubts about that. The winds never seemed to change direction, and one gust of black dust seemed much like all the others. *Wouldn't the weather change from day to day?* He was careful to keep those thoughts to himself; voicing doubts about the history inculcated in them in the People's Academies would lead to demerits in his Social Credit Score, and a concomitant denial of services.

Indeed, just his insistence on traditional pronouns had already prompted some interviews with officials of the Cultural/Racial Rectification Authority, concerned about Denver's "adherence to patriarchal norms associated with the racist and sexist standards of the past."

His Social Credit Score had taken a five-demerit hit after the latest of those interviews, but Denver felt some pride in standing firm. He was a Kinsey 1.2, confirmed in the mandatory Sexual Preference testing he had taken at ages six, ten, sixteen and twenty, and felt the traditional pronouns best suited him.

Overhead, the display of environmental ruin gave way to the

afternoon newscast. The face that took up the display was (for most people) comfortably androgynous and neutral in skin tone.

The newscast began:

"This is Fionellia B-344, 'they/them.' Communications with neighboring Modern Cities are still disrupted by the ongoing environmental conditions outside the dome. A carefully chosen team of experts, selected by the People's Bureau of Equity in Repair and Maintenance Functions, have now been approved as having an acceptably diverse mix of gender identities, cultural and racial backgrounds, and sexual preferences. Work on restoring communications is expected to begin in the next Designated Work Week."

"The People's Equity Court today sentenced captured thought-criminal Gerard T-226 to six months in penal retention and one year in accelerated re-education and re-orientation, after xe was found guilty of expressing incorrect thoughts about the gender identity of another xerson using the Sector Six Refectory. The People's Equity Court released a statement condemning the presumption of gender expressed by Gerard T-226, and all nine members of that Court will be retiring for extensive therapy for Post-Traumatic Stress Disorder brought on by their reading of the transcripts of the thought-criminal's statements."

"In other news, the People's Council for Spreading Truth and Preventing Disinformation has made a statement..."

Denver tuned out the rest of the newscast. He was so sick of the approved news. *Every day*, he thought, *it seems to get more bland, more approving of anything the People's Councils do, more ignoring of all of us down here in the corridors. Sooner or later, everyone will be sick of it. I wonder what will happen then?*

He knew he was supposed to stop and pay attention to the approved news, but he had other things on his mind, and was willing to risk another demerit on this Social Credit Score if anyone noticed his disregard of the approved news. He could see

Helena R-223 ahead, near the entry to the Sector Five Refectory, waving to him.

Helena was, to Denver's improper thinking, attractive. She was a little shorter than Denver, who would have been considered very small by 21st century standards; generations of restricted, environmentally conscious diets had seen to that. Both young people were thin and pale despite their enforced "diverse" ethnic backgrounds, with wavy black hair. Helena was a tad lighter-skinned than Denver, and he was afraid that her lighter skin tone may have cost her points on her Social Credit Score, but he had never asked her about it.

Denver had heard rumors that in olden times, men were noticeably taller and stronger than women, but he wasn't sure whether to believe it. He smiled tightly to himself as he hurried towards Helena. Despite exercise plans being proscribed as "ableist," he had spent the last few months doing surreptitious push-ups and sit-ups in his Minimal Personal's tiny bathroom, the only place in his quarters not "observed" by government-run cameras. The government repeatedly denied that these cameras existed, but everyone knew they did. He knew Helena had been secretly exercising as well.

Denver and Helena were planning something.

"I greet you, Denver G-126," Helena said as Denver walked up.

"I greet you, Helena R-223. How was xir day?"

"Fine. Shall we go in?" Helena winked at Denver.

They presented their approved Social Interaction Permissions form to the attendant and were shown to the small booth, surrounded by "privacy screens" that both knew did little to ensure privacy. So, to evade curious eyes and ears, they spoke in an informal code while eating their soy patties and protein blocks.

"Are you ready for the next Designated Work Week?" Helena asked, meaning: *Have you thought about the plans we discussed*?

"Of course," Denver replied. "I'm always ready to do my part for society." *I'm ready to do it. I've saved enough protein and soy to last three days, like we talked about.*

"Everyone I know feels that way," Helena agreed. *Our co-conspirators are ready, too.*

"Do you know where you're working yet?" *Do we know how to get outside the city dome?*

"Soy harvest, like usual." *Brietta U-626 has plans for the lower maintenance levels, including the access ports and egress hatches.*

"Do you have your work uniform ready?" *Have we got the respirators and protective gear for the environment on the Outside?*

"Oh, yeah. I'm ready."

They made small talk over the balance of the meal, and when the standard meal timer chime rang, they vacated the booth so the next shift of diners could move in.

"Shall I set another time for us to eat together?" Denver asked as they went back out into the teeming corridor. *When are we going to make the attempt?*

"Sure, I'd like that. A week from tonight? That gives us time for meal arrangements and the social permissions." *One week from tonight, we'll do it.*

The two young people smiled and went their separate ways, without so much as a handshake to draw the attention of the Social Interactions Assessment cameras.

We've waited long enough, Denver thought as he walked away from the Refectory. *Long enough. It's time something changed. It's time people learned that things* can *change.*

0200, the Maintenance levels, Thunberg-121

Brietta U-626 (she/her) proved to be cautious enough; she had copied the plans for the city's maintenance levels onto a large piece of paper, which she now took from her coverall pocket, unfolded, and examined. She didn't explain where she had actually found the paper, and her compatriots didn't ask. Denver had asked where she found the plans for the Maintenance spaces. "We four," Brietta had replied, "...aren't the only ones unhappy with the way things are in the Modern Cities."

Now, she studied the plans. "This way," she said after a few moments.

The maintenance shaft—it was too narrow to call it a corridor—was dark, hot, and uncomfortable, especially to four young people dragging bags loaded with food, water, and protective equipment.

Denver G-126 and Helena R-223 walked behind Brietta U-626 and Romano H-988 (he/him). The co-conspirators were making their way through the maintenance spaces underneath the lower level of the Modern City of Thunberg-121, where all four of them had been born and where they had lived all their lives. Now, they were risking everything to get out of that city.

Romano H-988 was still scowling. He had been furious when they had met near an access hatch on Level 2. An hour earlier, he had burst out with the news to the others the moment after they had disabled all their personal electronics: "I got two demerits on my Social Credit Score!"

"How?"

Romano looked at Denver. "How? I'll tell you. I was in an Approved Vendor buying some snacks." He had been augmenting their rations for the undertaking, but he left that part out. "I gave my name and pronouns so the vendor could debit my Social Standing Credits, and three non-binaries and an otherkin started yelling at me, claiming my pronouns were artifacts of the heteropatriarchal past, and that I was ignoring the pain and suffering they suffered from hearing those hateful pronouns used. I told them to leave me alone, I had the right to name my own pronouns, but a Monitor overheard the whole thing. I got two demerits for inadequate remorse for my representation of the racist, sexist, heteropatriarchal past."

"That's not right," Brietta said. "I mean, we've all taken heat for our traditional orientations and pronouns, but I never heard of anyone getting demerits for it."

"Yeah," Denver agreed. "They're getting worse."

"Oh, yeah," Helena said. "Didn't you hear? The term 'traditional' is now problematic, as it normalizes past injustices. We're supposed to use 'archaic' now."

"Oh, great," Romano snapped. "Just great."

"Come on," Denver urged. "Let's get going."

Brietta had somehow obtained the code for the access hatch. After one last look to make sure no one was watching and that no Eyes were operating nearby, the four young people crawled into the hatch and pulled it closed behind them.

"We've got maybe twelve hours before someone notices our quarters have been empty and we haven't popped up on any facial recognition cams."

"Hold up," Brietta whispered. There was a flickering light ahead.

"What is it?"

"Don't know. There shouldn't be anyone working down here now. It's not a Designated Work Week, and it's the middle of the night."

"Let's look. Stay quiet."

They crept ahead, slowly. A few paces ahead, the maintenance shaft intersected a long room, over twenty meters tall, with a row of odd-looking devices in each one. A blinking indicator on a control panel near the maintenance shaft was the source of the light.

"What are those things?" Romano asked.

"I think they're transformers," Brietta said. "They step down electricity from the big transmission lines to a level where we can use it for our electronics, heating, that kind of thing."

"Why are they all the way down here? Our electricity comes from the solar panels and windmills on the top of the dome. That's what we were all taught, right?"

"I don't know. None of this is on the plans I got from Maintenance. Oh, hey—look back here." Brietta pointed. "Look at those big transmission lines. They aren't coming from above. They're coming from the same direction we're going. Why?"

"We're already going that way—maybe we'll find out." Denver took one last look around the big, puzzling space. "Let's keep moving. Keep a look out. If this stuff is down here, there may be other things we aren't expecting."

"Straight ahead," Brietta directed. "We should come to a four-way junction. When we do, go straight ahead. About three hundred meters and we'll hit a T junction; take a right, and it's about another hundred to the egress hatch."

"Good," Romano said. "Let's get out of this place. We're never gonna get another chance."

Ten minutes later they were at the egress hatch. "OK, it's time," Denver told the others. "Let's get our protective gear on. It's going to be nasty out there."

"We *think* it's going to be nasty out there," Helena corrected him. "One of the reasons we want out is to find out how much of what the City government tells us is true."

"Better safe," Brietta said, "than sorry. Let's get the gear on."

The four struggled in the right confines of the maintenance space to put on their protective gear: Heavy, coated coveralls, respirator masks, rubberized gloves and boots.

Finally, it was done. "OK," Brietta said, her voice muffled by the mask. "This is it." The egress hatch was not locked; it was presumed no unauthorized people would be down in these levels.

Only a simple steel wheel hatch closed the port. Brietta spun the wheel and swung the hatch outwards.

"Shit! Close your eyes!" A bright, white light was streaming in through the port, blocked partly by Brietta as she looked outside.

Denver spoke up. "Is it bad?"

Brietta squinted, stuck her head outside, looked around. Then she looked back over her shoulder. "No. It's beautiful."

One by one, they climbed out.

The vista that greeted them was unbelievable. A gentle breeze waved knee-high grasses, which stretched away from the city down a gentle slope to where a line of trees grew along a small stream. In the distance lay gentle, rolling hills, covered in green. The sun shone brightly in the eastern sky.

"Should the sun be up?" Romano looked at his timepiece. "It's only 0256."

"They've been lying to us," Denver said. "They lied about the conditions outside. Why not lie about the time? Do you think there is anything they *weren't* lying about?"

Slowly, he unfastened this mask and removed it. He took a deep breath.

"The air," he marveled. "It smells so good."

"Look," Helena pointed. "Over there. Electrical lines." A line of metal pylons supported several heavy cables, running off into the hills. "They aren't coming from any solar panels, or windmills, either."

Denver thought about that. "More lies," he said. "Forget that for now. We need to get moving. They may be looking for us."

"At least we can get rid of this gear," Romano said. He started removing his heavy coverall.

"Wait." Denver looked back into the hatch, then closed it. There was no way to seal it from outside; to anyone that looked, it would be obvious that someone had left. "We can take it off, but we should take it a ways from here before we dump it. Otherwise, they'll know for sure we came this way."

The other three nodded. "Makes sense," Romano agreed.

They removed their protective gear, stuck it back in their carrying bags. Then they struck off into the grass.

Helena walked beside Denver. As they walked away, through the tall grass, through the brilliant sunshine, she reached out and took Denver's hand.

Denver smiled at Helena. "Hey," he said. "We haven't filled out a Social Interactions Permission form."

"To hell with Social Interactions Permission forms. We're free now. Free to do as we please—not as the City government approves."

Denver smiled and squeezed her hand. *We have to let people in the City know about this*, he thought. *We must tell them the truth. We must bring this system down. It has to change—all of it.*

Ten days later—the forest

Learning to get along in the Outside had occupied much of the escapees' time. But the gentle country proved friendly. There were fish in a stream near the big rock overhang where they had made their camp, and after several false starts, they learned to catch fish, and found some edible herbs, nuts, and berries. And somehow, by some unspoken consensus, Denver ended up being their informal leader.

After the first night in the overhang, the four constructed a woven screen out of brush to separate the area into two sleeping areas—one for Denver and Helena, the other for Romero and Brietta. To commemorate the occasion, they took new names, announcing them one evening after they had eaten:

"Denver and Helena Paine."

"Brietta and Romero Franklin."

The days were spent foraging and improving their camp under the overhang. The nights were spent exploring other new aspects of their newly free lives—and not a single Social Interactions Permission form was filed.

On the tenth day they walked to where they could see the big electrical transmission towers, and followed them over several steep ridges until they found the source.

"What is that?" Denver asked. They were at the edge of a wooded area on a hill overlooking a large, open valley.

Brietta chuckled. "Don't you remember? The classes we had on pre-Green energy production. Remember all the ways they said people were destroying the planet?"

"Sort of."

Brietta pointed. "That is a nuclear power plant. That's where the city is getting its electricity. And look, there's another row of towers heading off the other way. Bet you there's another City out there that's getting their power from this nuclear plant."

"So, who's keeping the plant running?" Denver wanted to know.

"Look. To the right. There's a bunch of buildings. Bet you anything it's a town for the workers in the plant."

Helena spoke up. "What's that on the other hill? Over there, to the left?"

"Another building?" Denver examined the larger structure. "No. Not just a building. You reminded me of our classes; do you remember what they showed us, about how the mega-rich lived back in the 'dark days of capitalism?' That's a mansion. And not a relic, either; it's well-kept. Look, you can see gardens, and the grass around it is cut short. Someone lives there."

"Someone who is making sure that power plant keeps working," Denver said.

"Look—there's another one. You can see the roofline just over the top of that hill." Brietta looked at her 'phone. "No signal. I've got this in isolation mode anyway. Nobody should be able to track it. Should I take pictures?"

"Yeah," Denver agreed. "Take pictures. Of everything. Need to get a little closer?"

"I don't think that's a good idea. I'll get what I can from here."

Brietta moved up and down the tree line, taking pictures from several angles. When she was done, they pulled back into the forest.

"Let's head back to camp," Denver suggested. "We need to talk about this."

It was growing dark by the time they returned to the rock overhang. Brietta started a fire, and the others brought in two large fish. After they ate, the four young fugitives sat around their fire and looked at each other for a while.

As he usually did, Denver voiced the thoughts that had occupied all of them throughout the afternoon. "Lies," he began. "All of it. Everything they told us. All lies. The old world, what they did—all lies. The Modern Cities, how they were built for inclusiveness and equity, all lies. You all saw that for yourselves; the elite still have their mansions. The environment, how the old society destroyed it, how the Outside was unlivable because of their selfishness—all lies. The new green energy plans, the wind and solar power—all lies."

"We've seen it all," Helena agreed. The others nodded.

"Why?" Romero asked. "That's what I want to know. Why?"

"Why do you think? Control. Oh, the one thing they didn't lie about was the elites. You saw for yourselves, they still have their mansions in the nice, clean countryside, while we have Minimal Personal cubicles in the Modern City, and have to fill out a bunch of forms before we can hug someone."

"They did all this, just to keep the regular people under control?"

"Why else?"

"So, what are we going to do about it?" Brietta held up her 'phone, showing a picture of the mansion. "I presume you think we ought to do something about it?"

"We have to let everyone in the City know about this. Things will change quickly if we can spread the word."

"You think?" Romero laughed. "How many people are going to want to leave their nice, warm, comfortable cubicles to come out here? We did, sure, but I bet we're in the minority. Also, now that we're on the topic, remember that they used to have something Outside called 'winter?' What are we going to do when cold weather comes?"

"What are you saying, Romero? Do you want to go *back*?"

"No, Brietta, I don't want to go back. Why would I want to go back?"

"To tell the truth," Denver repeated. "Let's see if people still trust their government when all this comes out. I mean, we 'vote' for the same people, over and over again, they keep promising changes—and what ever changes? It's time for a *real* change."

"Fine, then. How do we go about it?" Romero demanded.

"Well," Brietta said, "I might know a way. But we'd have to get back into the City."

"Think that hatch will still be open?" Denver asked.

"Only one way to find out. We haven't had a Designated Work Week since we left, so maybe nobody's been down there."

"Good, then," Denver said. "We'll leave tomorrow morning."

He grinned. "Let's go rattle some cages."

Outside the dome

Denver tried the edge of the hatch experimentally. It moved. "Well, the hatch is still open."

"Told you."

"They'll be looking for us by now," Romano pointed out.

"Let them." Brietta laid a hand on Romano's arm. "I know where we can hide—at least for a while. And I can contact my friend who works in Maintenance. He may be able to get us into the computer net."

"So just how do you know this guy, anyway?"

"Relax, Romero. His sibling was a classmate of mine in school." The four had already slipped effortlessly into the use of 'archaic' pronouns. "She told me when he was selected for Engineering and Maintenance training. Then, when he had been working there for a year, he was released and assigned to work in waste disposal, because there weren't enough 'traditionally disadvantaged' ethnic, cultural, and sexual preference members in that department. So, he's not very happy with the system."

"Why didn't he leave with us, then?"

Brietta blushed. "I think he was…interested in me. But I made it clear I wasn't into it, so…"

Romero grinned. "I see."

"Let's go on in," Denver said. "Brietta, show us to this hiding place you mentioned. Then you can see if you can reach your friend."

Interestingly, the hiding place proved to be a heavy-equipment storage compartment on the main level. The equipment stored was mostly earth-moving and farming equipment, which had set idle since the Modern Cities had forsworn the use of fossil fuels. Most of the machines ran on something called 'Diesel fuel.'

Brietta's contact, Julian D-455, met them in the big compartment, showed them around, pointed out bathroom and shower facilities, and a compartment he called a "break room" where they could store and prepare food. He had even managed to secure some protein blocks and soy paste for them. "Nobody comes here," he assured them. "Most of this equipment hasn't been touched for a couple of generations." The thick dust that lay everywhere spoke eloquently to that.

Denver noted one other thing on the other side of the big compartment. "What are these? Doors? They're huge."

"Doors," Julian D-455 agreed. "So they can roll the equipment out when they need to."

"Out?"

"Outside. Out of the City."

"Well, that might be convenient."

"They're sealed," Julian pointed out. "Have been for decades."

"Seals," Denver said, "can be broken."

"Where can I charge my 'phone?" Brietta asked. "I need to get our photos and videos sorted out."

Julian looked at her for a moment. He looked at Romero, then back at Brietta. He shrugged, then smiled. "I'll show you."

Over the next day Brietta, with Denver and Helena helping, carefully edited all of the photos and video they had taken before their 'phones had gone dead. Romero, while they were doing that, examined the equipment. "I think I may have an idea how they work," he told Denver. "At least, most of them. But it's like Julian said—no fuel."

On the second day, Julian D-455 returned to the compartment with a tall, imposing figure he introduced as Marielle K-120 (she/her.) "Marielle," he said, "works in the computer network, in Disinformation Control."

"Is that good?"

"I know how to bypass all the filters and blocks," Marielle said. "And I brought this." She handed Denver a small object. "That's a storage chip. Use this cable, attach that to the chip and the charging port on your 'phone, and you'll see how to copy your information onto the chip."

"Can you show me how?" Brietta asked.

"Yes."

That evening, the four of them sat alone in the 'break room' and talked as they munched on protein blocks.

"You know," Denver pointed out, "If this works, we're going to bring everyone that listens to the message right here. If it works, we'll bring the City Security and Disinformation Control people here as well."

"We'll just have to hope there are more of the people than there are Security troops," Romero said.

"Soon enough, we'll find out. Marielle will be here in the morning for the chip. She promised to put it in the system at noon tomorrow, when most of the people will be surfing while they're having lunch."

"At least we picked a good name to give everyone," Helena said. "The Freedom Caucus. It has a great ring to it."

They slept. Then, they waited.

Shortly before noon, Julian and Marielle showed up. "Whatever happens," Julian said, "we'll face it with you."

At noon, Helena held up her 'phone. They gathered around to watch. A prompt popped up; Helena tapped it, and the video began to play.

"People of Thunberg-121," Brietta's distorted voice began. The screen showed scenes of tall grass waving in a gentle wind, of tall trees under a blue sky, of gentle evening rains. "The images you are viewing are not from the distant past. These images were taken within the last few days, outside the City. The environment outside the City is not ruined. The City's power does not come from the 'green' installations of solar panels and windmills atop the dome, but from the nuclear power plant you see here. You have been lied to…"

The video went on for ten minutes. It began to repeat—then was suddenly cut off. The seal of the Disinformation Control Bureau replaced it.

"Well," Romero said, "it's done."

They waited.

A short while later, someone entered the compartment. A small person, pale, tentative; he approached the six rebels timidly.

"I'm Gregor B-344," he said. "Uh, he/him. Is it true?"

"It is," Helena said.

More people came. It began as a trickle, but it quickly became a flood. The compartment filled with people, all with the same question: "Is it true?"

Denver climbed up on one of the big machines. "Everyone, listen to me. Everything you saw, everything you heard, it is all true."

An electronically amplified voice suddenly rang out. "Everyone here! Listen carefully."

The crowd turned. Two people in the black uniforms of Security stood, flanking another in the white uniform of the Disinformation Control Bureau. The one in white held a megaphone.

"What you have heard is disinformation! Do not believe these people, these terrorists..."

A roar from the crowd cut him off. "We saw the images! We saw the video! We *heard* birds singing!"

"And it's all there," Denver shouted. He pointed at the big doors. "Just outside those doors! You can see for yourselves!"

The crowd surged forward. They pressed against the doors, which bulged, and finally gave way.

To a person, the crowd stopped. Amazement was on every face.

Outside. A gentle wind was stirring the grass. The sun shone, low in the sky. Evening was coming, but somewhere, a bird sang.

"It's all there," Denver shouted. "It's all there. Don't believe their lies any longer! Come with us! Come and see!"

The crowd surged outside.

Thunberg-121 - Outside

Almost as one, the crowd turned on the two Security troops and the Disinformation Control bureaucrat, who had followed them outside.

Denver found a handy rock sticking a meter or two out of the ground, climbed up on it. "Well?" he shouted. "We were all told that the environment outside was destroyed. We were all told that previous generations burning fossil fuels made the Earth unlivable. We were all told that the population crashed, and the only survivors were in the Modern Cities. Does this," he waved a hand at the peaceful evening meadows outside the walls, "does this look unlivable to you?"

"It may not be safe," the Disinformation Control bureaucrat began, but he was rapidly shouted down:

"There isn't anything wrong with the environment out here!"

"You lied! You all lied!"

"You kept us all sealed in that dome for generations, and you all lied!"

One of the Security troops put a hand on the Disinformation Control bureaucrat's shoulder and spoke quietly for several seconds. Then: "We'll be closing the doors," the Security man called out. "If you remain out here, you won't be allowed back in."

"Oh, no," Denver called back. "You're leaving the doors open. No more lies. No more keeping people locked up in here. If any more people want to come out, they can come out." The crowd, by now a couple hundred strong, roared. "You'd better get back in there. I can't guarantee your safety if you stay."

The City officials looked around, and then pulled a fast fade back inside.

"All right," Denver called out once the crowd's attention turned back to him. "I'm proposing we all move away from here. The four of us in the Freedom Caucus have been living in the woods, but we'll need to find a better place for all of us. And we'll need some supplies. Does anyone here know where the refectory's food is stored?"

Several shouted in the affirmative.

"How about clothing? Shoes?"

More raised hands.

"OK. Here's what we're going to do. Anyone who knows where to get food, water, medicines, clothing, tools, raise your hands. We'll go back in groups of at least ten. Arm yourselves with whatever you can find in the warehouse there—wood, metal, whatever. We will meet back out here in one hour. They we'll move off to the south."

"Why the south?" someone called.

"We know there is a nuclear power plant and some houses to the west. To the north, it may be colder. I don't really know, but I've always heard that it's colder when you go north. To go east we'd have to go all the way around the City, and I'm not sure what they may try. So, we go south as soon as we have supplies. Ready?"

A roar of approval.

"Let's go!"

One year later

Two hundred and twenty-one people had left Thunberg-121.

Two days walk to the south, they had been fortunate enough to come across an abandoned town from the old times, which gave them tools, shelter, some medicines, and even some viable seeds for crops. The Freedom Caucus disbanded, as Denver told the group, "you don't need to be led by the noses. Everyone here can see what we need to do. It won't be easy. We have a lot of work to do. The one promise we'll make you all is this: The fruits of your labor, everything you make, will belong to you. No more 'collective' crap. We'll produce our own goods, and we'll trade freely with one another."

The year that followed was lean and spare, but now the colony was beginning to prosper. Team Deere had formed first and was specializing in developing and growing grain and truck crops. Team Wayne found wild cattle roaming the hills and captured some for breeding, so the colony would soon have meat.

Team Watts formed with three members who had worked on maintaining wiring in the City, and they were exploring ways to restore electrical power; a river nearby was a promising candidate for a small-scale hydroelectric setup. Best of all, Helena's Team Guttenberg had found the abandoned library and had scoured the town for any books that might prove useful, so the colony's knowledge base was growing.

They named their community Freehold.

Best of all, Brietta Franklin had recently delivered the colony's first new citizen. "His name," a grinning Roberto Franklin had announced, "is Benjamin. Don't ask his pronouns. He is our son, and we will raise him to be a man."

The pale, poorly nourished group that had left Thunberg-121 had transformed into lean, strong, capable adults.

There was just one disappointment, as Denver voiced to Helena one evening as they sat on the small concrete patio at the rear of the house they were restoring for themselves. "I'm surprised we didn't have more people come with us. There were probably a quarter of a million people in Thunberg-121. And most of them seemed content to just stay there."

"That's the thing about cages," Helena offered. She laid a hand on her stomach. Her own baby was due soon. The five members of Team Hippocrates were about to get their second chance to oversee a birth. "They're safe. Lots of people don't like to leave their comfort zones."

"They're slaves," Denver objected.

"No. They chose to stay. We can't feel bad for them. They had a choice between a difficult freedom and a comfortable captivity. They chose captivity."

"It's sad. It's disappointing."

Helena leaned over and kissed Denver. "We're here. Our child will grow up here. Let them choose captivity. We chose freedom."

The next day at midday, Freehold was handed a surprise, when forty people showed up at the outskirts and asked to talk to whoever was in charge. "Nobody is really in charge," they were told, but for lack of a better idea, they were taken to see Denver. "After all," they were told, "this was all his idea."

"Wow," Denver said when he walked to the edge of town to meet the group. "Hi, everyone. I'm Denver Paine. Where are you all from?"

A small, thin woman stepped forward. "I'm Georgetta G-333. We're from Thunberg-108. We broke out two weeks ago, and four days ago we came across a nomad who said there was a town here. Is what he said true? You're all free people? You all work only for yourselves?"

"It's true. It's all true."

"Can we stay here too?"

"That," Denver smiled, "is up to you. You're free now."

The Painter

Inspired by Bob Dylan's "When I Paint My Masterpiece."

Beelitz, Germany - 1919

It was less than a year since the Great War ended. It would have been so easy for the young man to have slipped away to anger, to dissolution, to join the unrest that swept Germany. In the horror of the trenches, he had almost forgotten his pre-war fascination with painting, but his patron had not; while the young man was serving in a Bavarian regiment, while he was being awarded the Iron Cross First Class, while he was being wounded, being gassed, someone had been patiently tracking down and purchasing all the paintings the young man had produced before the war. He had heard of the collector third hand, from his sister, from his mother, and from his few remaining acquaintances in Austria.

Then, once the Armistice was in place, while the young man was still recovering from the gas attack, the buyer of the paintings had tracked him down in the hospital in Beelitz. The young man had been lying in his bed, soaking in anger and self-pity, when the gray-haired, portly man in what looked to be an expensive suit walked in and took a chair next to the young man's bed.

"My name," the older man had told him, "Is Avram Goldberg."

The younger man gave his name. He regarded the older man suspiciously. "Why are you here?"

Goldberg produced a large brown envelope and handed it to the recovering soldier. "Look at these."

'These' turned out to be a series of photographs. The young soldier, squinting through the remaining visual haze remaining from his gas exposure, nevertheless identified the subject of the photographs. "These are my paintings," he said in some amazement. "You are the one who has been buying them."

"I am. You have a rare gift, young man," Goldberg said. "Since 1915, I have purchased every one of your paintings that I was able to locate."

"Why?"

"Because I am a German," Goldberg pointed out. "Because *Mein Herr*, you show the beautiful side of Germany and Austria so well. During the recent...unpleasantness, the world came only to see Germany as a military power, and the Kaiser as a warmonger. You show the other side of Germany—the culture, the architecture, the daily life in the towns and cities. I want to promote that. The war is lost. Germany must move forward now. To do that, I am willing to underwrite you as an artist. You will need not worry about expenses, about food or shelter, or supplies. I will provide that. I will promote your career. I have contacts all over Europe. I can easily do all of that."

The young soldier leaned back against his pillow. "You want me to present Germany's best face to the world?"

"Yes," Goldberg said.

"I must think on this," the soldier demurred.

"I will return tomorrow."

Munich, six months later:

The *Pinakothek* was Munich's premiere museum of art. The young man who was hurrying through the crowded morning streets of Munich towards that museum, the young man whose patron had set up this exhibit of his work, still couldn't quite believe how quickly his fortunes had reversed.

The *Pinakothek* was still closed when he arrived. A knock on the door brought a sleepy-looking clerk, who peeked out at the young man.

"Who are you?" the clerk demanded. "What do you want?"

"*Herr* Goldberg has organized an exhibit of my paintings here today."

The clerk pulled out a scrap of paper and consulted it. "Your name?"

"Adolf Hitler."

"*Ach*. Yes. Here you are. The painter." The clerk held the door open. "Come in. *Herr* Goldberg is waiting for you."

The venue was impressive. The results of the exhibition were rather more so, and Adolf came away from the day with several commissions, including one from the Lord Mayor of Munich, Eduard Schmid. "It's hard to believe," Adolf told his patron at the end of the day.

"Indeed," Goldberg replied. "You have done very well. It does not hurt that you have a certain…charisma, when speaking to groups of your attendees. You have a knack for gaining and holding their attention."

Adolf considered that for a moment.

"Now," Goldberg went on, "Let us discuss moving you onto a larger stage."

Adolf looked at the older man. He blinked; his head was still spinning with the figures, the amount of money involved in the commissions he had just agreed to. "What larger stage?"

"Europe. To start with. Here," Goldberg handed Adolf another brown envelope.

Adolf opened the envelope. Inside were train tickets to…

"Rome?"

"Indeed. It is one of Europe's major cultural centers. We will have at least two exhibitions in Rome. I have already found and leased a studio there for you. I can meet these expenses for a year, perhaps eighteen months. Judging from today's performance, I am confident you will be quite well-off on your own effort by then."

Adolf nodded, his expression serious and determined. "I will."

"May I give you one piece of advice?"

"Of course."

"Do something about the mustache. Either grow it out properly or shave it off. You look as though you were growing a toothbrush on your lip."

"I will consider it."

Two weeks later found him in Rome—and clean-shaven. Previously, Adolf had only experienced German food, culture, and history. Staying in Rome was a new experience. History surrounded him, and he had taken up an informal study of the Roman Empire, inspired by visits to local sites and fueled by reading what books he could find on the Roman Emperors.

Evening, and Adolf was hurrying to an appointment. A local businessman, one who claimed descent from a famous Italian artist, had retained Adolf to paint a portrait of his twin nieces. Adolf had not previously done a personal portrait, but the businessman had readily agreed to the figure Adolf had named. He had, in effect, made Adolf an offer that was too good to refuse.

The nieces had a room somewhere near the historic Spanish Steps. Adolf was running late for his appointment to start sketching the twins, so now he was hurrying through a damp, chilly evening.

Since that first exhibition in Munich, Adolf felt as though he had hurried everywhere. *I have no time to do my own work*, he reminded himself. *To paint what I want to paint. To show what I want to show. Goldberg said he wanted me to show the better side of Germany. How am I doing that by painting a rich Italian's nieces?*

Soon, he thought. *Soon. I'm making money with these tasks. My name is becoming known across Europe. One day I will be known as the one who showed the world the pride and the beauty of Germany and the German people.* He smiled, slightly, as he hurried through the drizzling rain. *Maybe these Italian twins will even realize the glory of Germany.*

Rome - 1926

"And this," Adolf pointed out to the exhibition guest, "is the Reichstag building in Berlin. I did the sketching when I was there last year, and finished it here in Rome."

"Excellently done, *signore* Hitler," Italy's new dictator complimented the artist. "You do the German people credit." The bombastic Italian moved on to another painting, standing before it with his hands behind his back, rocking back and forth on his heels. "And this?"

"Schloss Charlottenburg, *Duce*," Adolf replied. "A seventeenth century palace in Berlin."

"Beautiful." Benito Mussolini leaned in, examined the painting closely. "You have an eye for detail."

"Have you been through the section on Rome, *Herr* Mussolini?"

"I have. You are gifted, *signore*."

"Rome gives one much to work with." That much was true; Adolf was increasingly a German partisan, but the architecture and history of Rome was inescapable. *If only Germany could attain the greatness of the Roman Empire*, Adolf thought. *Then the other nations of the world would see something.* So far, his work had not been terribly successful—oh, Adolf had achieved no small commercial success, especially as his work improved through practice. But the Europe-wide recognition of his vision of Germany had not yet come to pass.

There was another matter. Adolf had, in 1923 and 1925, given exhibits in New York and Boston, and in between had traveled through that country; he saw for himself the steel industry in Pennsylvania, the manufacturing might of Detroit, and the impossibly vast sweeps of rich farmland in the upper Midwest. He had seen the booming growth of the USA as an industrial and economic powerhouse. The United States' growing might was—or at least, should be—a matter of the greatest concern to any European power, including the hamstrung Weimar Republic. America had the potential to become the next great lion of the world economy, and having seen that country for himself, Adolf could scarcely overlook that possibility.

The Americans were fractious, undisciplined, incorrigible— but somehow it worked for them. Adolf found it difficult to resolve that seeming contradiction.

"How long have you been painting, *signore* Hitler?" Mussolini asked.

Adolf snapped out of his reverie. "Since I was a boy," he replied. "Beginning with street scenes in Austria, where I grew up. As you did, *Duce*, I served in the Great War, which delayed my work. But after the war, thanks to the patronage of *Herr* Goldberg—he sadly passed away last year—I resumed my career as an artist."

"*Signore* Goldberg would be proud to see all you have achieved," Mussolini agreed.

"I hope so," Adolf replied.

Mussolini wandered away, his small retinue following. Adolf spent the balance of the evening talking to other viewers of his work, finally leaving the exhibit at about ten o'clock and walking alone through the darkening streets of Rome.

His studio was dark and deserted. Adolf walked around aimlessly. The faint noises of the street outside intruded only slightly. He was lost in thought.

Nearby stood his largest easel. On it was a canvas, covered with a piece of cloth. The canvas, Adolf knew, was blank. For all his efforts, for all his work, for all the success he had achieved, the one great masterpiece he longed for still eluded him.

He sat on a hard wooden chair for an hour, regarding the blank canvas. Finally, he gave up. *Sleep*, he told himself. *Sleep, and tomorrow will bring fresh perspective.*

The next day brought no new perspective; there was too much to do. The next few days were instead occupied with taking down the exhibition, removing the paintings back to the studio, and arranging shipping of those that had been sold. Adolf was pleased and bemused to find that Benito Mussolini had purchased one of his paintings, a large study of the Roman Coliseum.

With that finally done, Adolf sat down for his typically Spartan supper—a bowl of vegetable soup and a boiled egg. He ate at a small table, from which he could still see the blank canvas.

Mussolini, he mused, *he would have the Roman Empire restored, with himself as Caesar, no doubt. Why should Italy be so glorified, when the German people still suffer under the rule of Weimar? Why, when Germany still suffers under the treaty at Versailles?*

Paul von Hindenburg, the pompous, obese old Field Marshal, was now President; as far as Adolf could see, the old man had done little to retrieve Germany's status in the world of nations.

He finished eating, washed up in the studio's tiny sink, brooded over the empty canvas for a while, and then went to bed.

Adolf awoke early the next morning. He washed and ate, then sat down to work on a painting of a street scene he had sketched in Munich the year before and was mildly annoyed when there was a knock on the studio door. Dropping his brush, he stumped to the door and opened it, a testy look on his face. "*Jah*? What is it?"

"You are *Herr* Adolf Hitler?" The caller was a portly man with dark hair, thick glasses, and a distinctly Bavarian accent.

"I am," Adolf replied.

The man stuck out his hand. "I am Anton Drexler," he introduced himself. "Chairman of the German Worker's Party."

"I've heard of you," Adolf admitted. "Your group attempted to seize control of Bavaria, is that not true?"

"We did. We paid the price for that attempt. May I come in?"

Adolf stepped back and held the door open. "Very well." He led Drexler into the studio and indicated a chair. "I have no coffee," he apologized. "There is tea, if you like."

"Not necessary." Drexler dropped his battered hat on the narrow table Adolf used for eating and sat down. He pulled out a pack of cigarettes and raised a questioning eyebrow.

"I have no ashtrays," Adolf said testily.

"As you wish." Drexler put the cigarette pack away. "I have come from Munich to talk to you about your work on behalf of Germany."

The man has a bit of Mussolini's bombast, Adolf thought. "*Ach. So?*"

"So, we would like you to put your talent to greater use."

"To promote another putsch?" Adolf's face clearly displayed his distaste.

"No." Drexler shook his head. "We learned many hard lessons from that attempt. No, *Herr* Hitler, now we will seek the resurrection of Germany through political means."

"I am an artist," Adolf pointed out, "not a politician."

"And a good portion of your art portrays your Fatherland," Drexler pointed out. "You do want to present Germany not as it is, but as you hope for it to be, is it not so?"

"I wish to," Adolf admitted. "I strive to. It is my struggle, that much is true."

Drexler leaned forward. "Tell me, *Herr* Hitler, how may we help you in this?"

Brussels - 1932

The Fokker tri-motor aeroplane touched down at the Brussels aerodrome, gently, as though it was a great bird settling slowly to Earth. Adolf looked curiously out the window. For all his travels, he had never been to Brussels before. He knew, of course, of the great port at Antwerp, and the huge arms manufactories at Liege. He had received, as a gift from the Lord Mayor of Munich, a beautiful autoloading fowling piece made in Liege but apparently designed by some American named Browning.

Today he was here for a small showing of some of his works resulting from a tour of northern France and southern Belgium. The timing worked out well, as he had finally tired of Rome. Just a week earlier, Adolf had signed a lease on a large studio in Berlin. His art supplies, works in progress and his modest inventory of personal effects were even now in a boxcar, making its way across Europe's rail system from Rome to Berlin.

Adolf waited for the other passengers to clear off the aeroplane before standing up. He picked up the one painting he had carried by hand, a depiction of an oak grove that supposedly had been sacred to one of the old pagan tribes of northern France. He marched off the aeroplane, down the steps to the tarmac. Jozef-Ernest van Roey, the Archbishop of Mechelen, was there to meet Adolf, clad in his flowing robes. Behind him was the normal crowd of admirers, including the inevitable crowd of young women calling for Adolf's signature in their personal diaries.

Adolf walked over to greet the Archbishop. "Your Eminence," Adolf smiled, shaking the older man's hand. "A pleasure to finally meet you in person." The year before, the Archbishop had commissioned Adolf for three studies of Belgian landscapes.

"Indeed," the Archbishop greeted Adolf gravely. "Ah—you have the painting of the grove at Gournay-sur-Aronde that we commissioned." Adolf nodded, handing the clergyman the painting. "It was an interesting commission; I spent several days in the grove, finding the correct perspective."

"It is beautiful," the Archbishop beamed. He turned to Adolf. "Quite excellent. *Herr* Hitler, I wonder if you would consider taking supper with me tonight?"

"Of course," Adolf replied. He had been raised Catholic, although his faith had suffered badly from his experiences in the Great War; that part of his personality had been replaced by his immersion in art. But the Archbishop wielded much influence.

The Archbishop walked away, trailed by two parish priests, still beaming at the painting. Adolf made his way down the row of admirers, signing diaries, shaking hands. He was now, after all, one of Europe's greatest figures in the world of art, and he knew it; greeting the public was one of the requirements that went with that status. Finally, he was able to make his way through the throng to find two large *gendarmes* holding away a number of scruffy-looking young men wielding notebooks and cameras: The press.

"*Herr* Hitler," one of them called. "Is your work portraying the industrial sector of the Ruhr meant to glorify Germany's exit from the Treaty of Versailles?"

Adolf normally ignored reporters, but that statement demanded an answer. "I have no influence in Berlin, nor does Berlin have any influence on me, I assure you." That last was a thumping lie; his depictions of the new factories in the Ruhr were done at Drexler's request. "But I will say this: Germany has the right," he called to the reporters, "to rebuild her industrial capacity. The Great War ended fourteen years ago."

"What about Germany's imperial ambitions?"

"Please. I am only an artist. I depict what happens; I have no say in policy. I will say this, *Herr* Drexler and *Herr* Göring have only peaceful intent. The annexation of the Sudetenland and the land corridor to East Prussia were done peacefully."

"Isn't it true that you are just a propagandist for the German Worker's Party?" another reporter called out.

The *gendarmes* moved in. "All right," one of them called. "That's enough. Move along, *meine Herren*, or you will be moved along."

Adolf looked ahead. As usual, a car was waiting to whisk him away to his Brussels exhibition. Following that, he reminded himself, he would return to Germany, this time for good. Much work already awaited him there.

Berlin - 1945

Adolf would have been more impressed at meeting the *Reichskanzler* had he not already met Hermann Göring on any number of occasions; as Germany's foremost artist, he had attended any number of events hosted by or in honor of the Greater German Reich's leader. The former fighter pilot had ascended to lead the German Worker's Party after Anton Drexler's death in 1943, and now, following the passage of the Enabling Act, stood alone as the leader of the Greater German Reich.

"*Herr* Hitler," the pompous, overstuffed Great War hero greeted the artist.

"*Mein Fuhrer*," Hitler replied. They shook hands.

"I must thank you again for your work showing the Wehrmacht's peaceful occupation of Austria," Germany's leader said. "The displays of your work helped swing public opinion in your favor both in Germany and Austria, and indeed, even in France and Britain. There has been no backlash from any of the old Allies."

"It was my honor and my duty to the Fatherland, *mein Fuhrer*," Adolf said modestly.

Göring placed a hand on Adolf's shoulder. "Thanks to you, and of course thanks to the Wehrmacht and the Luftwaffe, the reunification of Germany is complete. We have back the Ruhr, thanks in part to your efforts in portraying that region. We have back the Rhineland, we have our corridor to East Prussia, the Sudetenland and now Austria. All without another war."

"It has been well done," Adolf agreed. He was thinking of twenty years earlier, when he had seen for himself the New World's growing might. "Are you thinking, *mein Fuhrer*, of any further expansion? I ask only so I can begin to plan my next work, of course."

"For now, I am content," Göring replied. "We have ample breathing space for the German people. Any further expansion would mean war with Britain and France, and possibly the United States. You read the papers, *Herr* Hitler. You have seen how badly the Americans have trounced the Japanese in the Pacific. They have built so many ships that one could almost walk from Pearl Harbor to Tokyo without getting one's feet wet. No, we will focus instead on making Germany the world's foremost industrial power. For now." He smiled, enigmatically; he was thinking privately of a physicist named Heisenberg, and some very interesting work he was engaged in...

Adolf nodded. He had seen the Americans' potential for industrial might years ago.

"So," Göring said. He snagged a champagne flute from a passing waiter, handed it to Adolf, and seized one for himself. He held up the drink. "To peace!"

"*Jawohl, mein Fuhrer*," Adolf Hitler saluted Germany's leader with his champagne flute. "To peace."

Adolf excused himself and blended into the room. He was thinking of something the Fuhrer had said. *Breathing space*, he thought. *Now that is an interesting turn of phrase.*

That night, Adolf awoke suddenly. He looked at the cheap wind-up clock at his bedside; it was not quite four o'clock in the morning. He sat up, blinking away the remnants of a dream: The wide-open steppes of Ukraine and Russia, the golden fields, now overrun with the latest German panzers, with the newest jet-powered fighter-bombers passing overhead…

Breathing space, he remembered. *The Fuhrer is not interested in expansion. That is regrettable. But while only he can make policy, I have shown that I can influence matters, as well…*

He got out of bed and dragged on an old evening robe. He walked over to his work area. His largest easel stood to one side, still holding the big, blank canvas that had made the move from Rome years earlier and was still empty.

Adolf was holding an image in his head. Uncovering the blank canvas, he gathered his materials and began to work.

Ten Minutes

Norman Taggert was my best friend.

That's why I'm leaving this record. After witnessing the events of the last hour, someone has to leave some kind of written record behind...well, just in case.

Norman fancies—fancied—himself an inventor. In all honesty, he had some successes in inventing various gadgets. You've probably heard of the Taggert Multipurpose Water Dehydrolizer, and who hasn't used a Dendritic Atmospheric Distortion Analyzer to predict that perfect golf swing? Even the common Ultrasonic Cockroach Disintegration Hotel—that was Norman's baby, too.

You may have even seen Norman's picture in Popular Gadgetry when they ran that feature on him—you'll remember him as that funny-looking guy with the trademark round glasses, gap-toothed grin, obnoxious checked jacket and bow tie. Norman was proud of being an inventor, and wanted to look the part.

Scarcely a week went by without Norman cooking up some new gizmo or another; a few of them even worked. He had a modest string of patents hung on his workshop wall. His few "real" inventions returned enough in license fees to enable Norman to tinker full-time.

Until today, anyway.

I'm writing this on a Friday afternoon. Tomorrow is Saturday, but after the last hour, I'm not sure what kind of Saturday to expect.

Most guys look forward to Fridays. For me, it's just a day that brings the prospect of spending two more days at home with my wife instead of at the hardware store where I've worked for nineteen years. To put this bluntly, I'd rather be at the store. A man learns to face the inevitable, though, and so I left work today as always and drove home, hoping to slip away by myself for a few hours of peace and quiet at some point during the weekend. See, all I had in mind an hour ago was fishing. Now I'm not even certain I'll be here an hour from now. I'm afraid anything could happen.

Let me tell you why.

I was in my basement workshop when Norman showed up at my house. He was in an obvious and, for Norman, perfectly characteristic state of excitement.

Norman was always excited about something, usually whatever gizmo he had more recently "invented," so I wasn't too surprised when my wife Belinda ushered an eager Norman downstairs to my shop, where I was winding new line onto a fishing reel.

"George!" Norman leaped into the little cement-floored workshop.

Behind him, Belinda glowered at us both. I looked at her with a weak grin.

It was an intimidating sight. Twelve years ago, when we married, Belinda was tall, thin, a trifle horse-faced, and a trifle hard. Now, she's still tall, even thinner, even more horse-faced, and much more forbidding. She glared at me from behind her stainless-steel rimmed glasses and tapped one foot in its solid brown leather shoe.

"No smoking down here," she snapped, "or there's gonna be trouble."

"I know, dear," I answered her. I long ago stopped trying to argue with Belinda; there's no way to win. "We won't smoke." Belinda glared at me for a moment, then turned away and clomped up the stairs, her heavy shoes thumping each riser like a hammer.

I walked over to the little refrigerator I keep in the shop—a necessity since I also sleep there quite regularly—and pulled out two cold beers. I handed Norman one. "What is it, Norman?" I asked him. "What have you cooked up now?"

Norman looked back to the door at the top of the stairs. Belinda shot him a glare. She didn't like Norman, or anybody else much for that matter—and slammed the door shut.

Norman grinned and pulled a small black box out of his pocket, handed it to me. "I just finished this," he said. "I rushed right over to show it to you. Almost had an accident on the way over, too—guy blew through a stop sign, he almost hit me!"

"Traffic is getting bad around here," I agreed.

"Crazy," Norman said. "This guy, he drove like he was blind drunk. Anyway. Have a look at that. What do you think?"

I looked over Norman's new gizmo. It was just a small black plastic box, about six inches by three by maybe an inch deep, with a small dial on the top, a toggle switch, and a red button. Norman had scribed some markings around the dial—from zero to ten minutes, marked off in ten-second increments. The toggle switch was marked "ahead" and "back." On the top of the box a tiny blue light glowed softly.

The red button was just a red button.

"All right," I said. "I'll bite. What is it?"

Norman popped open his beer and took a long pull. "Thirsty," he said, "I've been working on that all day."

"So what is it?"

"Isn't it obvious? Look at the markings."

"You've got it marked in minutes and seconds…Don't tell me you've…Norman, that's not possible."

"That's what everybody thinks, but everybody was wrong," Norman grinned. "It is what it looks like. It's a time machine."

I handed him the box back. "Very funny. What is it really?"

"I'm completely serious. It's a time machine. There's a problem, though—it will send you forward or backward in time, but only a maximum of ten minutes. Well, actually ten minutes and sixteen point three-five seconds; that's the way the programming and power constraints worked out. You can't manipulate the space-time continuum all that much with four double-A batteries, you know, even with a raritanium-based agrodomatic rectifier."

"Even so, ten minutes? It will send you forward or backward in time ten minutes?" I looked at the dial markings again. "That's how you've got it marked—what good is that?"

"Haven't you ever wanted to take back a comment? Make a last-minute bet on a football game? How about playing poker? Think of the possibilities!"

I thought about the last twelve years with Belinda, of all the comments I wished I hadn't made—and of all the shouting matches that resulted from my not saying anything at all. "Better if I could go back twelve years. Anyway, I suppose it could be handy. Have you tried it yet?"

"No," Norman said. "I need a witness. That's why I came to you, buddy—I wanted you to be the first to see it."

"All right," I conceded, "let's say that it works. What do you intend to do with it?"

"The possibilities are endless," Norman said, "but I did have one thing in mind. Don't you have some vacation time coming to you?"

"Sure," I said. "About three weeks." Not much point in taking time off work when I'd spend it at Belinda's beck and call.

"I've got a lot of work that I've been putting off for lack of funding," Norman said. "Three of my patents expire this year. So, when I made this little gizmo, I got to thinking." He grinned.

"How's about you and me taking a little trip to Las Vegas in a couple weeks, make a few hundred thousand at the crap tables?"

"I don't like the idea. Could get rough if they get any idea we're cheating."

"Not if we're careful—take a few hundred here, a few hundred there, spread it out over different tables and casinos. Anyway, think about it. This little gadget," he held up the black box and shook it, "could change our lives. Hell—it could change everything."

An image of Belinda's horse face swam in front of me for a moment. I shook off the thought before it could form. "How does it work?"

Norman grinned. "I stumbled on the principle while I was trying to recalibrate the Ipswich field strength on my multi-phase kababulator—you remember that, I invented it to produce wave-phase variations in alpha-theta band neutrino emissions from my Jones-Utz particle stability desensitizer?"

"Uh, if you say so."

"Anyway, I noticed that my particle tibufibulatrices monitor was picking up chronographic irregularities from the desensitizer—so I removed the Kohoy-Bopp circuits from my desensitizer, rewired it to be a destabilizer instead of a desensitizer—merely a matter of reversing the phase polarity of the krepulator guide—and cobbled up a field projector that should move the mass of a medium-sized human body. It's set for my body specifications, to be specific, although anyone of about my mass could probably use it safely."

I sat down at the workbench and opened my beer. I reached for the pack of cigarettes that lay on the bench, remembered Belinda's scowling face, and thought better of it. "All right," I said. "Let's see if it works. How do you plan to test it?"

"I'm going to set it to send me forward in time, one minute. All you have to do is to sit here for a minute and wait for me to show up."

"Don't you think you should try it on something inanimate first? A hammer or something?"

"Might not work," Norman said. "I've calibrated it for someone or something of about my mass. The field follows discrete surfaces using a topopgraphic apoplexomatic area-mapping yetzolagrophic dodulizer, so it will send whoever's holding it and nothing else around them. If you tried it on a smaller mass, the field strength won't be right—on something the mass of a hammer, it might either send it back to the late Jurassic or completely destroy everything within about ten light-years. Better to stay with the designed mass. So, I have to touch it to push the button; the only way to use it is to use it on myself. Don't worry, though—I'm confident that my calculations are right. It'll work."

I took a long drink of beer. "All right. Go ahead."

Norman flipped the toggle to "Ahead," turned the dial to one minute, and handed me the machine to check the settings. "One minute ahead," I confirmed. Norman took the device back and, grinning like a big ape, poised his finger over the red button. "See you in one minute," he said, and pressed down.

The machine fizzled and buzzed for a moment, then stopped. Nothing else happened.

"Well," I said.

Norman looked disappointed. "I don't get it," he said. "I was sure it would work."

"Maybe your batteries are dead."

"They're brand new."

He walked over to the workbench and scrutinized the machine in the light form the window. He pushed the red button again. Nothing.

"Dammit," Norman muttered. He tugged his tie loose. "I'll have to take the thing apart—must be a bad connection. The jodhpur-gigaferkastatic circuit may have gone out; it was pretty much jerry-rigged. I kind of cobbled it together with solder and electrician's tape."

"Have another beer," I offered.

"In a minute. Have to go to the john." Still looking disappointed, he walked out of the workshop and disappeared into the little half-bath he and I had built in my basement the year before. I went back to winding line on my fishing reel.

A few seconds later, I was startled by a voice behind me. Norman's voice. "See?" he said, real joy in his voice. "It works!"

I turned to see Norman standing there, holding his time machine. "What do you mean? You just said it…"

I stopped dead. I'd seen Norman loosen his tie—now it was tightly knotted. I looked past him—the time machine was still lying on the workbench where Norman had left it.

Then there was a faint shimmer in the air by the window, and another Norman appeared out of thin air, holding another time machine. "See," he said, "I knew it would work!"

"What the hell!?" the first Norman burst out. The second Norman turned to see the first; his jaw dropped.

Then the original Norman, tie loose in his collar, walked out of the bathroom. The other Normans turned to face him. The original Norman—my friend, the inventor Norman—took one look at them and fainted.

It took a while to get Norman to come around.

Once the three of us—the other two Normans and I—managed to get the original Norman sitting upright and sipping feebly at his beer, I went to my workbench and found a big black permanent marker. "OK," I told the Normans, "First things first." I pointed at the original Norman. "You're Norman-Prime. You," I indicated the first of the duplicate Normans, "are Norman-One." I marked a large '1' on his forehead with the marker. "You're Norman-Two," I said to the second, and marked him with a '2.'

"So, Normans," I asked them, "What happened, and what do we do now?"

All three Normans started talking at once.

"I built the machine to send a body physically through time."

"But it seems to only send an image of the body…"

"…probably due to a flux in the floccanihistation index…"

"…this could have been caused by the reversal of the sustephapolitrix vertices…"

"…causing an irretrievable contrafibularity of quantum data transfer…"

"…in the Gompers-Keldfield continuum…"

"…causing a duplication of quantum states…"

"…sending an image of the body…"

"…through time, and reconstituting a duplicate at the destination…"

"…not the original. So you end up with a…

"…non-paradoxial…"

"…duplication of identities."

"That shouldn't be possible."

"Well, it's obviously possible," I belabored the obvious, "but none of you have answered my question. What do we do now?"

"How long has it been since I first pushed the button?" Norman-Prime asked.

"About three minutes," I said.

Norman-Prime stood up. "Well, then," he grinned weakly, "All I have to do is go five minutes into the past and stop myself pushing the button. That should put it all right."

"What will happen to us?" Norman-One asked.

"You're me," Norman-Prime said, "nothing can happen to you."

"I don't like it," Norman-Two answered.

"We're messing with the primary time streams," Norman-One

observed. "There are, theoretically, millions—billions of alternate possibilities, and..."

"...we don't really understand what..."

"...happened in the prime chronal stream..."

"...that is, our time stream..."

"...to cause the duplications."

"Maybe you should think this over some," I cautioned Norman-Prime, but caution has never been Norman's strong point.

"It can't miss," he said. Before I could move to stop him, Norman-Prime turned the machine's dial, flipped the toggle to "Back," and pressed the button.

And nothing happened.

Norman-Prime stood there as before, a befuddled look on his face; his eyes were focused on something behind me.

"Damn it."

I closed my eyes, gritted my teeth, and turned. Another Norman stood behind me. He was holding another time machine.

"Hold still," I told him, and marked a '3' on his forehead. "All right," I said, "what's your story?"

"I've never seen anything like it, George. It was like watching the whole thing on television – I saw myself come in, saw myself push the button, but I couldn't do anything about it. I even saw the other two pop in, but I couldn't move, couldn't talk, couldn't do anything until I—well, Prime—pushed the button that last time."

"So we've learned one thing," I said, "namely that, bad science-fiction notwithstanding, you can't change anything that's happened in the past."

"Agreed," all four Normans chimed in. "Unless..."

"...the chronal vertices are somehow..."

"...realigned during the Phanse pulse insertion..."

"...of the physical representation of..."

"...quantum states at the level of..."

"...the zenojargonastic wavelength of..."

"...osawaddoteppic material transfer."

"So," I went to the fridge and pulled out another beer—I didn't even remember finishing the first one— "what do we do now?"

All four Normans started talking at once. "Stop!" I shouted.

I pointed at Norman-Prime. "You. Talk. Everyone else, shut up."

"Well," Norman-Prime began, "You know, I haven't moved at all since I pushed the button to go backwards. Now, remember, when I pushed the button the first time, I was standing there;" he pointed at the spot where Norman-One had appeared, "And then I pushed it the second time, I was standing at the window there." He pointed at Norman-Two, where he stood by the window. "And Norman-One and –Two appeared right where I'd been where I pushed the button. Makes sense, right?"

The other Normans and I agreed.

"So, when I pushed the button to go back – why did Norman-Three appear over there, instead of where I'm standing?"

"Well," a Norman began,

"...it's not possible under classical physics for two..."

"...masses to occupy the same..."

"...portion of space-time without..."

"...causing a major quantum flux event that would annihilate..."

"...all of the normal matter in both masses..."

"...and destroy pretty much everything else..."

"...for a pretty wide radius, and so..."

"...it's likely that the mass conflict started..."

"...a rearrangement of the space-time matrices around..."

"...the previously existing masses in the..."

"...time frame of the moment where the..."

"...duplicate reappeared, so that he..."

"...materialized in an area where there wasn't any conflict..."

"...and that's interesting, because it indicates..."

"...that there is some adjustment of the time stream in..."

"...each instance where we've used..."

"...the device, proving an unknown..."

"...effect on causality that we can't..."

"...understand or predict..."

"...without a lot more experimentation..."

"STOP!" I shouted.

I heard the door at the top of the basement stairs open, and my wife's voice barked down the stairs. "What's going on down there?"

"Nothing, dear," I called. "Just looking at Norman's new invention."

I heard Belinda's hard, sensible shoes thumping down the wooden stairs; in a cold panic, I managed to shove Normans One through Three into the little storage closet at the end of the workshop before my wife stalked into the room, scowling (as usual.)

"What are you doing?" Behind her, Norman-Prime smiled feebly.

"Nothing, dear."

She sniffed at the air and frowned at the beer I still held in my hand. "You better not be smoking down here."

"We're not."

Belinda walked over to the workbench. "What a mess," she snarled. "What is this thing you're fooling around with now, anyway?"

"It's a..." Norman began.

I grabbed his arm. "It's just a way to improve TV reception, dear. No big deal. I'm helping Norman with the electronics, that's all."

"So you're working on something useful for a change? That's a new one for you, Norman," Belinda said. Norman blinked but said nothing. He knew better.

"All right, then. Don't make a mess. Not any more mess than you've already made, anyway." With a final glare, Belinda turned and stalked out of the workshop. As soon as I heard the door at the top of the stairs close, I let the three duplicate Normans out.

"All right," I said, "we have to figure a way out of this mess, and fast. And whatever else happens, none of you push any buttons."

"Well," a Norman began,

"We have three devices now instead..."

"...of one, so that means we can parallel the hooplaster derivators, and..."

"...daisy-chain the tiplimiter diodes into the..."

"...chronfrannistatic gillister pads..."

"...with the vodulatic voltimeters in reverse..."

"...and the cases grounded to the parallel ports..."

"...of the power supplies, and then..."

"...reverse the inductor polarity..."

"...that, and the removing the chronological verifier circuit..."

"...and tripling the power input..."

"...while boosting the resolution of the wave-form regulator..."

"...of all three devices hooked up in parallel..."

"...might undo everything we've done..."

"...if we can program it right."

"George, can we borrow some tools and your laptop?"

I got them a screwdriver, a soldering iron, and my old laptop computer. Then I sat, sipped beer, resisted the urge for a smoke, and watched. The four Normans took the time machines apart, extracted the circuit boards and wired, soldered, programmed, and just generally fiddled with it all for a good half-hour.

"All right," Norman-Prime said at last. "I think we're ready."

"Yes," the other three Normans chimed in.

"What did you do?" I asked.

"Well, it's kind of hard to explain. We reprogrammed the left-hand cycling on the setacetical chronoprogession and reversed the frannistatic wave-phase inhibitor gronification pathways. That should retrace the ophetic chronal alternative pathways and shut off the dimensional shunts that are allowing more than one of me—of us—to be in one β-axis time stream at one moment."

"No," I said, "I didn't get any of that."

"We fixed it up to undo everything we've done," Norman-Two said.

"OK. That I understood."

"All of you—me—gather around, the field won't go far." The four Normans crowded around, Norman-Prime in the middle surrounded by doppelgangers.

"See you in a minute, buddy!" Norman-Prime assured me again and hit the red button. The four Normans shimmered briefly and vanished in a flash of light.

A fraction of a second later, there was a second flash of bright white light. It blinded me for a moment; I rubbed my eyes, squinted, fidgeted and in a moment was finally able to see clearly again.

Eight Normans stood there, blinking at me. I felt my jaw drop. Two Norman-Primes, with no mark on the forehead. Two Norman-Ones. Two Norman-Twos. Two Norman-Threes. Two combined, cobbled together time machines.

"It repeated the whole process," one of the Norman-Primes said.

"But it should..."

"...have unraveled the dimensional..."

"...time stream disruptions..."

"...caused by the repeated influx..."

"...of chrononavigational particles..."

"...unless we forgot to reverse the leptotransmogrifier pathways..."

"...and timed the Moss-Steinfeld pulses to negative wave-form..."

"...which would have initiated a quantum wave pulse..."

"...that could conceivably have completely..."

"...disrupted the fabric of space time and..."

"...eliminated all baryonic matter within a ten or twelve light-year radius..."

"...or just as likely, generated a killer strangelet..."

"...particle that would suck the entire solar system..."

"...down into a miniature black hole..."

"...which would be a bad thing,"

"Very bad," I interrupted. "Listen, Norm—Norms—this is rapidly going from bad to worse, and it's getting crowded in here. Can you figure out what's wrong and fix it without destroying the Earth, or do I have to explain your mysterious identical octuplets to Belinda?"

"We can figure it out," one of the Norman-Primes assured me. "We've got twice as many minds working on it now."

"One mind," I corrected him, "duplicated eight times."

"Only technically," a Norman-Two answered. "Since we were inserted into the time stream some moments ago, we've been having somewhat differing experiential streams..."

"...which leads to the establishment..."

"...of differing quantum states in each..."

"...of our material forms, which now that I think of it..."

"...may require another adjustment of..."

"...the Tergaster field-strength level and..."

"...the polonium plasma particle rectifiers..."

"...polarity, which may serve to..."

"...rewind the chain of alterations to the main time frame."

One Norman-Three looked at me, his face reposed in supreme confidence. " We just need to do some reprogramming."

"That's right," three or for more Normans agreed, while the others stood there nodding.

"Well, get to it. I don't have enough beer for all of you."

They got to it. With a lot of gesturing, muffled arguments, and tapping on the laptop computer, which was wired up to the time machine through a USB port, they got to it.

I went out to the back yard for a smoke to calm my nerves. Visions of the Earth, the Moon, the Sun, all the planets swirling down into the vortex of a black hole like cigarette butts being flushed down a toilet bowl assailed me, along with the idea of a titanic explosion obliterating all matter from Earth to half-way to Alpha Centauri. The cigarette didn't do much to calm my nerves; both scenarios were only marginally more palatable than explaining eight Normans to an outraged Belinda.

When I went back inside about ten minutes later, the Normans all looked up at me with a series of identical triumphant grins.

"I think we have it now," one of the Normans said—I'd long since given up trying to keep track of who was who. Why would I? They were all Norman.

"Will it work?"

"It should…"

"…as long as our presumptions are correct…"

"…of course it's possible…"

"…that the multiple manifestations of one identity…"

"…having their own experiential realities in the time stream…"

"…since the initial incident…"

"…and the various incidents since…"

"…might have irreconcilable…"

"…conflicts of causality…"

"…as the event matrix rewinds…"

"…and recalibrates…"

"…to reality, whatever that is."

"All right," I said. "But will it work?"

All eight Normans shrugged. "Only one way to find out," one of them said.

One of the Norman-Primes picked up the consolidated device and fiddled with the dial.

Another Norman Prime pointed over his shoulder, said something in a low voice.

The first Norman-Prime nodded, flipped a switch, looked up at me and grinned. "This will do it. Everything's going to be all right now." He pushed the red button.

There was a gathering whine. A swirling, polychromic whorl of colors began, slowly, to surround the Normans, moving slowly from the floor upwards to surround them. A sparkling, opalescent field of energy formed over them, following their body surfaces, tracing over shoes, trousers, jackets, faces, until the Normans were encased in the gleaming mother-of-pearl film. The whirling colors vortex slowly contracted, closed in, and tightened, the opalescent field shimmered brighter and brighter.

Then, there was a sudden flash of light, and the dull pop of air imploding into the space where, moments before, eight Normans had stood. The workshop was empty. No Normans stood in front of me. No consolidated time travel device lay on the workbench, or anywhere else. And worst of all…

"Dammit," I muttered. "Wherever they've gone, they took my laptop with them."

Well, I figured Norman—hopefully only one Norman—would turn up in a few moments, so I took the last cold beer from the fridge, flipped on my radio and sat down to finish winding line on my fishing reel.

After a few minutes, I was surprised to hear Norman's name mentioned on the top of the hour news:

The lone fatality in a hit-and-run accident at Highway 4 and Oakton Avenue earlier today has been identified as Norman

Taggert, 48, of Springfield. Taggert was driving east on Oakton Avenue when...

I didn't hear anything more after that.

Somehow, Norman—the Normans—had done the impossible. They had reprogrammed their little black box—black boxes—to violate causality. In trying to undo a chain of increasingly unlikely events, they had somehow set an entirely new timeline into motion, an entirely different chain of events.

In this new chain, Norman was killed in an accident on his way to my house. The near-miss he described to me on his arrival actually happened. Somehow, the device changed the outcome, slowing Norman's reflexes, speeding up the oncoming car, changing the timing just a little—it didn't matter how. That was how whatever impossible software in the guts of that damned little black box had undone the chain of endlessly repeating Normans.

Norman was a bit of a crackpot, but he was a brilliant man—and my best friend. Now he was gone, killed by his own genius.

I laid my head on my workbench, and just stayed there for a while.

Eventually I decided to go upstairs. There would be a funeral; I owed his daughter and son a call, I had to be ready to do my part in the memorial service—all those thoughts were going through my head as I slowly, so slowly, dragged up the stairway out of the basement and into the kitchen.

In the kitchen, I heard something I hadn't heard in years— Belinda's braying laughter. Before I could give that a moment's thought, something on the kitchen counter caught my eye. A hammer lay on the counter, and next to it...

No, I thought, it couldn't be... It's not possible.

But it was.

Scraps of black plastic and pieces of shattered circuit boards lay scattered on the granite countertop. As I sorted through the wreckage with horror, I found the remnants of two red buttons.

In the back of my mind I heard a Norman's voice, "We have three devices now instead…"

That was Norman-Three, I thought, fighting down a growing panic. There were four Normans then—Prime, One, Two and Three—they should have had *four* devices…

Belinda's laughter floated in again, from the living room. I could hear voices over the television.

Voices? Belinda hated company. She has never liked anyone—except herself. She thought she was the cat's own pajamas, even if nobody else did. So who would be visiting her? What were they laughing about? I looked back at the shattered remains of two of Norman's time machines. Could she have? Would she have?

A feeling of horror gripped me like a fist of dry ice. I wanted to turn and run from the house. Instead, I walked into the living room.

Three Belindas looked up at me from the couch. Three Belindas looked at each other and laughed. Three Belindas stood up, walked towards me, and barked in unison, "George! You haven't been smoking, have you?"

"No," I stammered.

"Good. You know I hate you smoking…"

"…it stinks up the house, and my carpet is in…"

"…bad enough shape as it is, and…"

"…you know I've been after you for weeks to get them cleaned anyway, and…"

"…you've spent most of today messing around with that no-good Norman…"

"…when you promised me that you would get the garage cleaned…"

"…and fix the kitchen drain…"

"…and replace the garbage disposal. Why can't your worthless…"

"…friend invent something practical, like a TV set that won't…"

"...cut out every time the neighbor starts up his lawnmower? Speaking of which..."

"...you need to cut the lawn, too."

"What are you standing there staring at us for? Get busy!"

I looked at the three of them, nodded, and fled back into the kitchen.

They're in there now, watching television and laughing, as I write this down. I've got the wreckage of Norman's time machine—machines—down on my workbench, but I already know it's hopeless. All the King's horses and all the King's men couldn't put that thing—those things—back together again. I'd need Norman to do that. Instead, I've got three Belindas and no Normans.

God only knows what might happen next.

Three Days of Snow

Nick Eldridge lives alone in a tiny house on the bank of a trout stream in western Colorado. While he enjoys material success as a nature writer, his memories are drawn back to his senior year of high school, to the girl Ceilidh O'Connor.

It's been almost 30 years since Nick has last seen or heard from Ceilidh, but not a day's gone by without her entering his mind.

One day a blizzard strikes, screaming down from Canada. A car has gone in the ditch on the highway a mile from Nick's house, and out of the howling wind, a distant figure from the past comes to Nick's door.

Friday October 9

The weather forecast had called for snow, and sure enough, it started on Friday afternoon, big fat flakes drifting down out of a gray sky. By nightfall, the wind had picked up, and the snow turned hard and gritty, blasting sideways against my cabin windows. No matter—I had a big stack of firewood, a full LP gas tank, and plenty of food. My cabin isn't big, just a front room, a tiny kitchen, a tinier bathroom, and a bedroom—but there's always been just me, so it's always been big enough. "Bring it on, Mother Nature," I called into the wind when I went out for an armload of wood.

That's when I saw the headlights coming down the highway.

Not too many people drive down my stretch of state highway at the best of times, and certainly not during a blizzard. The road always turns icy in these kinds of storms, and sure enough, the headlights wavered as the car skidded—right into the ditch about a quarter mile down the road.

The mountains have a code, just like the sea, so I went inside, got my parka and my big searchlight, and went out to help. My old green Bronco started right up, but I had a heck of a time getting the front hubs locked—they were half-frozen. By the time I got them hammered loose, I looked up to see a parka-clad figure walking up my drive, face turned away from the wind, a small overnight bag clutched in one hand.

I couldn't see anything other than a parka, a pair of blue jeans, boots, and an expanse of darkness in the hood's opening. "Come on in—it's warm inside," I shouted over the wind. "I was just coming down to see if you were all right. Is there anyone else down there?" The figure's head shook.

We went inside. I took a moment, stomping snow off my boots, and turned around to greet my unexpected guest. She had her back turned, and was just taking off her parka, letting a cascade of deep brown hair fall out of the hood. She turned and smiled at me, her eyes shining brilliant green in the light.

"Thank you so much," she said. "I was afraid I'd freeze! I never guessed there was a house out here."

"I, uh, guess you'd like to use the phone," I stammered. It couldn't be—could it?

"Yes, please," she beamed. I showed her to the phone on my little desk in the front room. She picked up the handset, listened, turned the phone off and on again, and then frowned. "No dial tone."

"Phone's kind of iffy way out here," I told her. "Storm may have taken the lines down. Do you have a cell phone?"

"I tried it when I went in the ditch. No signal."

"My name's Nick."

She didn't answer. Her back was turned to me, and she was

standing very still. When she moved at last, she turned around, holding a framed portrait of a young, green-eyed girl in her hand.

"Nick Eldridge," she said at last.

"How've you been, Ceilidh?"

There were a few streaks of gray in her hair, but the lopsided smile was still the same. "Nick, Nick Eldridge, who'd have ever thought it, after all these years?" She laid the picture down and came over to hug me.

"How long has it been?" she asked. I thought a moment. "Twenty-eight years, four months, and eighteen days," I answered, and we both laughed.

"You've got my senior class picture on your desk? Nick, it's been almost thirty years!"

"For old time's sake, I guess. Who wouldn't keep a picture of their best friend from high school? Please, sit down!" I scrambled to move a stack of magazines off my battered old couch. "Sorry about the mess—I don't get many visitors out here." We sat down facing each other.

"So, what do you do out here?" Ceilidh asked, breaking a moment of uncomfortable silence.

"Ever heard of Owen Bradley?"

"The writer? I've heard of him, nature and outdoor guides, right?"

"Yes." I picked up a copy of my latest, *Colorado's Secret Wilds*, and tossed it to her. "That's me. It's a pen name."

"Nick, that's wonderful! You're famous!"

"Well, not really. Owen Bradley is famous. Good old Nick Eldridge is known around here as some odd old hermit that lives in a cabin on the Uncompaghre. I've come a long way from Prairie Ridge, Minnesota."

"I'm really very happy for you, Nick. Do you ever get back home?"

"Not since Mom passed away. And you? What have you been up to the last twenty-some years?"

"Oh, nothing that exciting. First medical school, then a horrible internship, a worse residency, and now I've got a practice in St. Paul."

"Sounds exciting enough to me. So, it's Doctor O'Connor now, then?" I knew better, but I had to ask. I could swear Ceilidh blushed before she answered, even though I'd spotted the ring when she took her coat off.

"Well, actually, it's Doctor Ross," she said, looking down for a moment.

Why are you looking away from me now, Ceilidh? I thought to myself—at one time I'd known her better than I knew myself. How much could change in almost thirty years?

A lot, I had to admit. Still…

"Anyone I know?"

"Ryan Ross," she smiled now, looking at me with a faintly defiant air.

"Well, that's good news!" *No, it isn't.* "How is Ryan? Last I knew he was all hot and heavy with, oh, who was it? Beth English, wasn't it?"

"Back at Prairie Ridge he was, yes. But Beth stayed in PR, and Ryan went off to Iowa, like me, and since we knew each other already, we just took to hanging around together—we were driving home on weekends together, and so on."

"And the rest is history?" I teased her, but gently.

"Yes," she answered, "the rest is history. We had our twentieth anniversary last year."

"Kids?" *Please say no.* I'm not sure why that thought popped into my head.

"Tom's seventeen, Ann's fifteen."

"And you said your life wasn't exciting!" I laughed. "Sounds pretty exciting to me! Two teenagers, an M.D., your own practice!

So, what brings you out here to the middle of the Uncompaghre anyway?"

"Well, that's a long story. I was in Durango for a conference—the Third Annual Mountain Medical Conference—and I decided to get away to spend a little time by myself when the whole thing wrapped up. I was actually heading for Vail when this hit."

"You were taking the scenic route, coming up here through Montrose, weren't you?"

"Well, sure! I've only been to Colorado one other time. It seemed like a good idea until this snowstorm hit. I guess I should have listened to the weather report."

"First rule of the mountains," I chided her. "Always know what the weather is supposed to do, especially in the winter. It gets pretty wild out here." I realized I'd left her an opening.

"So, what are you doing out here, all on your own? Don't you have a family, Nick?"

"Me?"

"Yes, you!" She reached out to poke me in the chest.

"No, Kaye," I answered, retreating to an old nickname I'd used for her, way back in high school. "No family. No wife, no kids, no girlfriend. Mom passed away the year I left for college."

"I remember."

"Well, that's it. If you recall, Dad disappeared when I was fifteen. Mom was the only family I had."

We sat in silence for a few moments, both of us a bit uncomfortable. So many years, so much water under the bridge. Ceilidh had gone so far, and I had gone, well, into myself. I'd retreated into a tiny cabin in the Rockies, making my living writing about rocks, trees, and birds under an assumed name. I was just an anonymous hermit alone on the Uncompaghre.

We talked about Colorado, about the mountains, about Ceilidh's practice, about my books, until it was quite late. The fire burned down to coals as we sat there, talking oh-so-seriously about things neither of us really wanted to discuss, avoiding the questions we both really wanted to ask.

After some debate, I managed to persuade Ceilidh to sleep in my tiny bedroom, while I made myself comfortable on the couch. "I sleep here lots of nights anyway," I lied, "It's closer to my desk, anyway, in case an idea hits me in the night." The bedroom is only a few feet away from the living room, of course, but Ceilidh was polite enough to leave that unsaid. Without further ado, we said our goodnights, and I lay down to stare at the cabin ceiling until well into the small hours.

My first love, the only girl I'd ever really loved, had just walked back into my life after almost thirty years, thanks to an early Colorado blizzard. But way back then, I'd never been able to tell her how I felt.

What was I going to do now?

It was past three before I finally fell asleep.

Saturday, October 10th

I awoke the next morning to the sound and smell of bacon and eggs cooking in my tiny kitchen, just around the corner. I followed the smell around to the kitchen/dining room—such as it is, in my tiny place—to find Ceilidh, long hair tied back, wearing my ancient bathrobe, padding back and forth from the stove to the little table with bacon, scrambled eggs and toast.

"Well, good morning!" she chirped at me, smiling warmly. I tingled right down to my toes. Almost thirty years and more than a few gray hairs later, her smile still made me feel weak in the knees. "Have you looked outside yet?"

I stole a glance at the window and saw a solid sheet of white. The wind rattled the glass, and when I stopped to listen, I could hear the tin chimney from my little gas furnace rattling in the gale.

"I bet it's ten below out," I said.

"Almost twenty below," Ceilidh confirmed, "according to your little indoor-outdoor thermometer in the bathroom."

"I'll have to go out and get some wood. The living room gets cold fast if you let the fire go out."

"Well, you can eat first. Although, Mister Eldridge, as a doctor I should take you to task for your diet. I didn't see any dry cereals, no bran, just eggs and about four pounds of bacon in the fridge. Do you eat this way every day?"

"Well, a lot of days," I demurred, "but I work it off. You don't think I just sit here and write all day, do you? I've got almost three hundred acres of land to take care of."

"Well, all right. I guess you do look pretty fit."

We ate in silence, accompanied by the howling wind outside. I don't own a television, but I did dig out my weather radio and we listened for a while:

> A Canadian cold front has stalled over the central mountains and the Western Slope. Much of the area is experiencing winds of up to 60 mph, and whiteout conditions. Today's highs will range from an expected sixteen above in Grand Junction to twenty below in Aspen, Leadville, and Eagle.
>
> Vail reports twenty-two inches of snow in the last twenty-four hours, Eagle twenty-five, Glenwood Springs twenty-four, Leadville twenty-five and Grand Junction nineteen.
>
> Travel advisories remain in effect for most of western Colorado and Wyoming. The storm system is expected to remain stalled for another twenty-four to forty-eight hours, bringing as much as an additional thirty-six inches of precipitation to the area.
>
> Mountain residents are advised to remain at home.

Most state and county roads are impassible. I-70
remains closed over Vail Pass until tomorrow.

"Well, I guess I won't be back on the road today, will I?"
Ceilidh looked down at her plate.

"Are you complaining about the company?" I teased.

"No, not the company," she laughed. "I just wish we could
have run into each other under better circumstances. I mean, here
I am, sitting here in *your* bathrobe, with my car buried in six feet
of snow down the road and no way to even let anyone know I'm
alive!"

"Speaking of your car, is there anything in there you need?"
I asked. "I've got to go out to get some firewood, so while I'm
dressed up, I could just as easily walk down to your car."

She shot me a wry look. "Well, I've got most of what I need in
my overnight bag, right here. I may have to borrow a clean shirt if
we're snowed in another day, but other than that..."

"Ceilidh, I live up here, remember? It might be three or four
days before the highway gets cleared."

Thirty minutes later I was dressed to go out in my felt-lined
pacs, my old Swedish Army parka, an ancient pair of insulated ski
pants I'd picked up someplace, and my heavy mittens. "I'll pile
some firewood up right outside the door first," I told Ceilidh, "And
then I'll take a hike down the road to your car. I've got a good pair
of snowshoes right outside."

"Be careful, Nick."

"Hey," I told her, "It's me!"

That bit of bravado was a little over the top, as became
apparent the moment I stepped outside. The wind was screaming
in from the open ground across the highway.

The first real gust hit me right as I walked around the corner
of the cabin towards the woodpile, snapping me sideways and
tearing away my breath with a sharp *pah*. I gasped a couple times,
and forged on for the woodpile, which I could just make out as a

lump of white surrounded by white, glimpsed through the howling white of driven snow.

I made at least a dozen trips, slogging back and forth with armloads of wood dug from under the drifting snow. Each trip, my footprints had almost disappeared by the time I beat my path back to the house with another load.

I stacked a pile six feet wide at the base by about four feet tall before I decided that it was enough. At least the overhanging roof of my porch would keep the wood reasonably free of snow. My snowshoes were stashed in the rafters of that overhang, so I retrieved them and lashed the old willow and rawhide frames to my boots.

Ceilidh's car was three or four hundred yards down the highway. I figured I could trace the driveway the hundred yards to the highway, and then follow the highway south to the car. It worked, after a fashion—I strayed into the ditch twice from my own driveway. The highway was a little better, kept blown clear by the wind for a stretch in front of my property. I floundered through two big drifts, though, the snow so powdery that even my snowshoes didn't help all that much. It seemed like a year before I found Ceilidh's car, a brand-new blue Lexus, nose-down in the steep ditch near where a tiny creek passed under the road.

Her big suitcase was in the trunk, right where she said it was. I got the trunk open without too much trouble and manhandled the big case out. Another ordeal—I had to get back up to the highway. I only fell twice and managed to fill my ski pants halfway up with snow, but at least carrying the big suitcase back up the highway and driveway to my house sufficed to work up a sweat.

Ceilidh was waiting in the house when I fell through the door. She looked anxious. I imagine I looked exhausted—I was. And I hike 'fourteeners' all summer long, just for fun. I'm in great shape for a man of forty-six.

"It's worse than I thought," I told her. "The highway is sure in bad shape." I shucked off my boots, parka, and ski pants. My jeans were covered with melting snow that dripped on the rug.

"Are you all right?" she demanded. "Here, I've got some hot tea waiting for you—you don't have any coffee."

"No coffee, I never touch the stuff," I gasped. A long gulp of the hot lapsang souchong lit a fire inside me. "You know what? I'm going to take a hot shower. Do you mind?"

"Not at all," she answered, laying a hand on my arm. "You shouldn't have gone out there, but thank you for bringing my case in." She dimpled. "Now I won't have to drag around in one of your shirts, anyway."

"Or my bathrobe," I added, and headed off for the bathroom.

A long, hot shower restored me. At least the gas was still on! I hopped into the bedroom, put on an old pair of sweatpants, a heavy sweatshirt with a bull elk on the front, and a thick pair of fleece boot socks. A thought hit me, and I grabbed a second pair of the heavy socks and headed for the living room.

Ceilidh had changed as well. She was standing in front of my tiny stereo stand, glancing over my music collection, dressed again in jeans and a black t-shirt.

"You've got quite a collection."

"I don't have a TV, but I do like to have music, especially when I'm snowed in." I picked up a CD. "Remember this one?"

She laughed. "I remember you playing it in that horrible old Chevy of yours!"

I handed her the socks, noticing her bare feet. "Here. My floor gets pretty cold. There's just concrete under the carpet pad."

She put the socks on hopping on one foot at a time, giggling a bit as she almost lost her balance. I caught her arm to steady her, and I could have sworn she blushed a little. She picked up another CD from the rack.

"Oh, Bob Dylan!"

"Yeah, I got into his music in college. Boulder's kind of an odd place," I explained. "I guess you'd say it's kind of eclectic."

I put an album on to play, and we sat on the couch again.

"So how did you end up writing your Owen Bradley books, Nick? I remembered you were going off to learn to be a newspaper journalist—it's all you talked about."

"It's a long story."

"We would seem to have plenty of time, Nick," Ceilidh answered, gesturing towards the window. A particularly nasty gust of wind rattled the pane.

"Good point," I had to admit.

"So, give," she said. "Tell me your long story."

I told her. While Stevie Nicks sang "Gypsy" in the background, I told her about my five years at Boulder. I told her about running out of money and joining the National Guard to pay for school. I told her about my six months in the Persian Gulf, and how I wandered from place to place for five years or so after my return. I told her about the job as a reporter with the Baltimore Sun that only lasted three months before I was laid off. I told her about driving through Prairie Ridge once—only the one time, to visit my mother's grave in the little cemetery north of town. I told her about my year in Denver, living in a crummy apartment on Capitol Hill, tending bar in a lower downtown watering hole while I tried to find a job with one of the city newspapers.

About three albums and a big plate of sandwiches later I got to the point where I took up backpacking one summer, hoping to get some fresh air and exercise.

"I had pretty much given up on finding the reporting job by then," I told her. "My heart wasn't in it anymore. The city was too much of everything—too much crowding, too much noise, too much pollution." She nodded, eyes closed, as though she knew just what I meant. "But when I got out into the mountains, it's like everything came together for me, like I finally knew where I ought to be. So, since I was spending more and more time up here, I moved. I got an apartment in Eagle first of all and made a living tending bar there—a bartender can always find work—while I wrote my first book, *Summer on Hardscrabble Mountain*. I was still in Eagle when I wrote *Autumn in the Holy Cross*, and when that book started selling, I had enough money to come out here. This piece of land was for sale, so I picked it up and lived in a camper trailer one summer while I got the cabin built. I've been here for eight years now. I wrote *Walking Winter Wildernesses* and *Spring in the Maroon Bells* right there at that desk."

I got up and went to my bookshelves, retrieving copies of all four books. I dropped them on the couch next to Ceilidh. "Here," I smiled at her, "signed originals. Those will tell my story better than I could tell you here."

"Aren't you lonely out here, Nick?"

"Me?" I tried to look astounded. "Lonely? No, not me."

"Come on, Nick," Ceilidh admonished me. "I know you, we were best friends once, remember?" She picked up one of the books and waggled it at me. "You're pouring everything of yourself into these books, and you aren't even putting your own name on them." She stood up, leaning over me. "You've built yourself into this little cabin, and nobody around here even knows what you do. Everything about you is turned inwards!"

"It's easier that way, Kaye."

"Why? Why is it easier to tell the whole world who you are anonymously, than to tell who you are with one person for real? The Nick Eldridge I remember never had that problem!"

"I don't know, Kaye!" I was a little flustered by her response. "Maybe it's because the one person I was ever able to open up to walked out of my life thirty years ago, and never came back. Maybe the Nick Eldridge you remember just never had that problem because that Nick Eldridge had a best friend he could always turn to."

Ceilidh had walked over to stare into the fireplace, and now she turned to look at me. Her eyes were red and brimming with tears.

"I'm sorry," I said. "That wasn't fair."

"It's OK," she answered. "I'm just a little concerned about you, Nick. You're out here all alone. I had thought…Well, I had thought you'd have found someone."

I did, thirty years ago.

"Maybe we should change the subject," I offered.

"Is that really how it's been for you, Nick?"

"It's not like that, Ceilidh. I've got a great life up here. I'm not tied to a job or an office. I hike and backpack all summer, I live out here away from the city, and I make my living writing about things I love. What more could I want?"

I could see that she wasn't about to answer that one, so I dodged. *I'm such a coward,* I thought to myself bitterly.

"Listen," I said, "I've got a deck of cards around here someplace. You still play peanuts?"

"Yes," she smiled, wiping her eyes. "Oh, it's been years, but I think I still remember how to play peanuts."

I rifled my desk looking for a deck of cards, all too aware that Ceilidh was looking over my shoulder at her senior picture framed next to my computer monitor.

"Here we are," I said, producing a deck of cards. "Would you believe I got these in Las Vegas? I spent a week there while I was writing an article about the Desert Wildlife Range north of town." Giant hotel-casinos aren't really my cup of tea. That week had been a real eye-opener.

"I've never been there," she answered.

"Vegas, or the Desert Wildlife Range?"

"Either one. You know, I've only left Minnesota twice since I finished medical school? I've taken one skiing trip to Vail, and one trip to St. Louis for a conference. This trip was the first one I've ever taken alone."

"Yeah, well, I've been around rather more than would suit me. Iraq isn't anything to write home about."

"I don't expect I'll ever find out!"

We sat at my tiny kitchen table and played cards while the wind howled outside, and the snow drifted up. I had to duck out twice for firewood, and the drifts were piling up across my drive. "Good thing I went out to your car this morning," I reported as I tossed some wood on the fire. "Drive's drifting shut now."

"How do you get it cleared after a snow like this?"

"I've got a little old tractor with a loader blade on the front in that shed back of the house. I can get out to the highway easy enough, but it doesn't do any good to get out there until the road crews get the highway plowed."

We kept on with the card game while the windows slowly grew dark, and the storm raged on. Ceilidh took her turn to bring me up to date on what medical school was like, how her practice ran in an upscale area of St. Paul, a city I'd never visited, and how her two teenagers were a constant source of frustration.

"And what's Ryan up to these days?" I finally asked. She hadn't mentioned him twice since she walked through my front door the day before.

"Lost in his career," she told me. "He's a sales rep for a big pharmaceutical wholesaler in Minneapolis, he travels a lot. Some weeks the only time I see him is when he drops off samples at *my* office." She smiled. "This week he got stuck at home with the kids, though."

"I remember how he was in school," I reflected. "Hell of a guy—always driving, always focused. A real type A personality, wasn't he?"

"Oh, he still is. *Peanuts!*" she shouted the last word, slamming a card down.

"You always were better at this than I was," I grumped. "Tell you what, why don't you have a look through the books I gave you, and I'll get us some supper? It's, what, six o'clock already."

"That's a change, having someone cook for me!" Ceilidh laughed. "Sure, I'd love that. The summer book is the first one, right?" I nodded and headed for the freezer.

Fortunately, I'm a quick rough cook. Years of living alone have seen to that. Forty-five minutes later I had a pair of elk tenderloin steaks broiled, a salad mixed, and some hot garlic bread and steamed vegetables ready. Ceilidh poked her head around the corner from the living room as I was setting plates on the little table.

"Smells wonderful."

"I've had lots of practice," I explained.

We ate in silence for the most part, except for an account of the source of my elk steak—a big cow elk I'd brought out of the Flat Tops Wilderness the previous month, during the archery elk season. "I'm a pretty fair hand with a bow. I use a hand-made English longbow, there's a guy I know in Michigan that makes them. Keeps it interesting."

Ceilidh insisted on cleaning up— "You cooked, it's only fair." I brought in some more wood, stoked the fire up, and tuned in the weather radio again.

> A Canadian storm front remains stalled over the
> central Rockies. Severe winter weather has resulted
> in a Traveler's Advisory being put in place until
> Sunday evening. Vail, Rabbit Ears, and Loveland
> Passes remain closed.

> The weather front is expected to move to the east
> beginning Sunday afternoon. The winter storm will
> be followed by a high-pressure system that should

bring some sunshine and rising temperatures to the Western Slope by Monday morning.

"Looks like this will last most of tomorrow," I called to her.

She walked into the living room, drying her hands on a towel. "Then it lasts until tomorrow," she said. "And no, I'm not complaining about the company."

There was a lot we needed to talk about that evening, and nothing else to do but talk. We sat on the couch and talked about the old days, about Prairie Ridge. All the funny memories, all the sad memories, everything we'd both half-forgotten. It took a while for Ceilidh to get to the question I'd been expecting.

"So how come you never asked me out, Nick?"

"What do you mean?" I dodged. "We went out lots of times. Sheesh, Kaye, we were together all the time."

"You know what I mean," she replied, very serious now.

"Would you have said yes?"

"Yes." She nodded. "I would have. That's what I wanted all along."

I didn't need to know that now, Kaye, after all this time. I felt the weight of my life's biggest missed chance slamming down on me now, and I guess it showed. Ceilidh leaned over and hugged me hard.

"I'm sorry, Nick, I shouldn't have dredged that up. I've just always wondered…"

"It's hard to explain, Kaye. How do you tell your best friend something like that?"

"Like what?"

"I guess I was afraid of losing what we had, the friendship. I didn't want to take a chance on losing my best friend in a messy break-up. Do you know how often high school relationships crack up in a big mess? I couldn't take that chance."

"You didn't answer the question, Nick. What couldn't you tell me?"

"How crazy I was about you. How I went weak in the knees every time you smiled at me." *Or how I still do!* "How my heart raced when I walked in the school every day, knowing you'd be in the building waiting for me?" *Or how much I loved you*?

She was holding both my hands now.

"That's what I was afraid to tell you, Kaye."

"I wish you had, Nick."

"Would it have made a difference, Kaye? We both had our own directions to go in life. We were just kids. We didn't know any better." *And we do now*?

"We already had our lives planned out. You were going off to Iowa to pre-med, and I was going to Colorado. That's what we were going to do, and that's what we did. Nothing was going to change the plans we made."

Reluctantly, it seemed, she let go of my hands. My fingers tingled.

"You're right, I shouldn't have brought it up. I guess I just needed some closure on that…I've always wondered."

"It's best this way, Kaye," I told her. "We were best friends. We still are friends now."

"And, my old friend, I have to admit, I'm exhausted," Ceilidh stretched her arms, yawning. "Would you believe it's ten-thirty? Where has this day gone?"

"It's been a day well spent," I had to admit. "What could be better than catching up with your best friend?"

I had to insist on Ceilidh taking my bed again, and once again I stretched myself out on the couch and lay down to stare at the ceiling again.

Unbidden, my mind wandered back to the young, dark-haired, green-eyed girl that had haunted my thoughts for the last twenty-eight years. On some level I realized I was being handed a second chance of sorts.

But a second chance to do what?

Sunday, October 11th

I woke up to the sound of the wind blowing as it had the previous thirty-six hours, but the light from the windows seemed a little brighter. I got up and peeked out the front door. The wind was dying down however slowly, and the sky was brightening up. I could see across the highway now, and when I leaned out to look around to the south, I could even make out the back of Ceilidh's car sticking up out of the ditch. I brought in some more wood, hopping from one foot to the other on the cold boards of the porch, got the fire roaring up again, and then I went looking for Ceilidh. She was still asleep.

I stood in the bedroom doorway for a moment, riveted to the spot.

Ceilidh was laying on her back on the old double bed I'd picked up a few years before at a garage sale in Grand Junction. Her dark hair played out across the pillows, like a spill of some dark honey. Her chest rose and fell, softly, as she breathed. She was wearing some kind of black silk nightgown, and the effect was shattering.

As I watched, enthralled, she roused slightly, rolled to one side, and pulled the covers up. I shook myself, and turned away, closing the door softly. I felt all the old feelings; my heart pounded like a jackhammer in my chest.

"Oh, crap."

I caught a quick shower and put on some water for tea. By the time the kettle started to whistle, I heard noises from the bedroom. A moment later, just as I was pouring hot water into the pot, Ceilidh came into the kitchen, wrapped up once more in my old robe.

"Good morning," she said, brushing my cheek with her lips.

"Sleep well?" I asked.

"Pretty good. The wind's dying down, don't you think?"

"Yes, I had a look outdoors. I can see all the way down to the creek now. In fact, I can see your car. If things brighten up, I'll get the tractor out and see if we can't get it out of the ditch this afternoon." *And then you'll drive away out of my life again.*

"Are the phones working yet?"

"No," I answered. I hadn't tried the phone, but I had looked at the computer. The Internet connection was down, and I still use a phone line for that connection.

"That's OK," she said, sitting down across the table from me. "I'm not in that big a hurry. Won't it take another day or so for them to get the roads cleared?"

"The radio says the road crews will be out late this afternoon," I said. "That is, if the storm moves off to the east the way it's supposed to. It will be morning before the passes are open again, though."

"And it's a four-hour drive from here to Vail, right?"

"In good weather, yes," I answered. "Right now, better figure on six."

"So, it looks like you're stuck with me at least another day, Nick." She smiled at me, making me feel all weak and watery.

"I guess so."

"Good," she said, sipping her tea. "That will give us a chance to talk some more."

We didn't talk much more for a while. We had some toast, and Ceilidh went off to take a shower, emerging in jeans and a white sweater. She sat on the couch with my *Summer on Hardscrabble Mountain*, paging slowly through the book as I spent a little time at my desk catching up on some correspondence.

It was strange how comfortable the silence was, as the morning passed with only the sound of my computer keyboard tapping and Ceilidh turning pages. It was as though, in silence, we regained a measure of the intimacy that we'd left in that small town in Minnesota all those years ago. I felt like I had my best friend back again.

But for how long? The question nagged at me.

I was finishing up answering letters and thinking about lunch when Ceilidh finally spoke up.

"I think I understand you a little better now, Nick Eldridge."

"You always did, Kaye."

"No, I don't mean the high school Nick Eldridge." She held up *Summer on Hardscrabble Mountain.* "I mean the guy who writes as Owen Bradley. Today's Nick Eldridge."

"Is that right?" I had to smile.

"Yes, that's right." She stood up, walking to the window.

"And what have you figured out about the new, improved Nick?"

She stood, looking out the back window of the cabin to the dim form of the mountain, just now beginning to be visible through the snow.

"You haven't changed as much as you think you have, Nick. You're still that shy kid in lots of ways."

More than you know, I thought, but kept it to myself.

She turned away from the window to smile at me again.

"You put everything of yourself into your writing. You always were a generous soul, Nick. There wasn't anything you wouldn't do for a friend."

"And?"

"And you're still doing it. Your writing works because you're writing about something you love, and you're writing as though you were telling it to your best friend. Your heart just flows out onto these pages, do you know that?"

"That's pretty much it," I answered.

"And yet, it's a one-way street for you, Nick. You pour all this love you have out into the pages, but nobody's returning the favor."

"That's not quite true," I told her. "The mountains are always there for me. The meadows, the aspens, the dark timber, it's always there when I need it to be."

"And you've never felt the need for a person in your life? Someone special to share all this love with?"

"Not for a long time now, Kaye." *Not for twenty-eight years.*

"I'm glad we ran into each other again, Nick."

We stood for a moment, looking into each other's eyes. The sparkling in her green eyes was familiar enough. I'd seen it often enough, way back then. I didn't know what it meant then. I was afraid I did, now.

"You know, I think we might be able to get your car out now." I was beginning to sweat. Ceilidh looked out the window again, at the slowly clearing sky.

"OK, let's give it a try."

We bundled up—it was still around zero outside—and I got the old tractor out. Ceilidh sat perched on the fender as we chugged down the driveway, using the snowplow blade to clear the snowdrifts.

The Lexus was buried worse than I'd thought. We shoveled snow for at least two hours, trying to clear the wheels. Finally, I got a log chain fastened to the car's rear axle, covering myself in snow in the process. I hooked the other end to the drawbar on the rear of the old Ford tractor, and we were finally ready.

"OK, start the engine and watch the chain. When you see me take up the slack, put it in reverse and give her just a little gas, just enough to keep the wheels turning. Keep the front wheels straight, and I'll try to pull you right out onto the highway the way you went in. As soon as you're all the way up on the highway, we'll stop so I can unhook you."

Amazingly, it worked. I stuck the tractor in low gear and pulled gently, and in a few moments the Lexus slowly began to move, wheels slipping and spinning, easing slowly out of the ditch, backing finally on up to the highway. I put the tractor in neutral and dropped the blade on the pavement.

"OK, back up a few feet," I called. Ceilidh's mitten-clad hand waved out the window, and the Lexus eased back a little. I climbed under and unhooked the chain. I bundled the heavy chain back into the toolbox behind the tractor's seat and walked up to the car.

"Drive right on up to the house," I told Ceilidh, "Park right in front. I'll follow you up the drive and put the tractor back in the shed."

She was waiting for me when I came around the corner from the shed. A snowball hit me right in the chest, followed by Ceilidh's triumphant shout.

"Oh, it's like that, is it?" I grabbed a handful of snow, flinging it after her retreating, laughing form. I let out an old Prairie Ridge High battle cry, "*Boo-yah!*" and raced after her.

We ran back and forth for the rest of the afternoon, throwing snowballs and laughing. At least growing up in Minnesota gets you used to snow and cold at an early age, and a good thing, too, because we were both covered with snow by the time the sky began to grow dark. I finally caught her as she ran into a drift at the edge of the aspen grove behind the house, and we both ended up falling into the snow, rolling over a few times, laughing.

She lay in the snow, her green eyes glowing. "OK, Nick," she mock-scolded me. "Now my jacket's full of snow, and I'm freezing, and it's getting dark. You're going to have to build that fire up." She blushed suddenly, perhaps realizing her unintentional double meaning.

"Beats shopping in Vail, doesn't it?" I asked, helping her to her feet.

We went inside, bearing armloads of firewood, the last of the pile I'd stacked up on Saturday morning. After we both changed into dry clothes, I built the fire up to a roaring blaze that radiated heat into the tiny living room while Ceilidh bustled about in the kitchen, heating up some canned soup for our supper. We drank our chicken soup from mugs as we sat on the floor in front of the fireplace. A faint steam rose from Ceilidh's snow-dampened hair.

"I suppose you'll be able to be on your way again in the morning," I finally said. "The road crews will be out all night now that it's clearing up. They'll have the passes open by morning."

"Yeah—so much for my little vacation at Vail," Ceilidh laughed. "That's OK—I wouldn't have missed this reunion for anything."

"Me either."

She leaned against me, her hair warm and fragrant against my shoulder.

"I wish we were still seventeen," she sighed.

"Why? A chance to do some things differently?"

"Yes, Nick. At the least, I'd like a chance to do one thing differently. At least a chance to tell someone how I felt about him, way back then."

"I know what you mean."

"I thought you would."

"Oh, hell, Ceilidh," I confessed. "There hasn't been a day gone by that I haven't thought about you. You wanted to know why I'm up here all by myself? Hell, I've had relationships. I lived with a girl for a year in Boulder, even. But it just never worked."

She took my hand. "Why not?"

"Because I never met anyone who I felt about the way I felt about you, Kaye. The way I guess I still do."

"The picture on your desk," she said.

"Yes, the picture on my desk. There's more than just the love I put in my books, Kaye, more than the love I have for the mountains. I could tell people about that. I never had anyone I could talk about my best friend; about how much I loved her."

"You just did, Nick."

"Yes, I just did. But that's all there is ever going to be to it. Kaye, you're going to leave in the morning," I husked. "There's a place in here," I tapped my chest, "that will always be yours, Kaye. But tomorrow morning, you're going to get in your new Lexus, and go back to St. Paul, to Ryan, to your kids, and your practice. And I'll stay here, in my mountain cabin, writing my books."

"But not until morning." She stood up, pulling me to my feet. "Nick, I think we've waited long enough, don't you?"

"Long enough?" It took me a moment to understand.

"Long enough," she repeated, and led me to the bedroom.

Monday, October 12th

I woke up that next morning to find her gone, only the faint scent of her on the sheets. My framed print of her high school senior picture lay on the pillow she'd used, with a note on the letterhead of Ceilidh Ross, MD of St. Paul. Her neat, flowing handwriting had changed hardly at all since high school. My vision misted as I read her message.

> Nick,
>
> I've always loved you. I always will. Someday, please let someone write something for you.
> Goodbye – love always,
>   Ceilidh.

I went to the door and looked out to see the tire tracks in the snow where the Lexus had gone down my drive and turned north onto the highway, towards I-70 and Vail. *Someone has written something for me, Ceilidh. My best friend finally wrote me something that took her twenty-eight years, but it was worth the wait.*

I folded up the note, tucked it under her photo in the frame, and placed her portrait back on my desk. I realized, suddenly, that for the first time since I'd moved in, the little cabin seemed empty. For the first time in my adult life that I'd spent mostly alone, I was lonely.

After the snow

In the months that followed, I thought of many things, entertained many notions. I thought of getting in my old green Bronco and heading for St. Paul. I thought of calling her, at her home, at her office, just to hear her voice. But I didn't do any of those things. I just buried myself in my work, getting through the rest of the fall and winter as I usually did. Working, a bit of snowshoeing on nice days, a trip to town once a month for canned goods.

Spring came, as it always did, and summer, and in July I decided to pack my gear and head up into the Holy Cross Wilderness. I drove out to a trailhead up the road from Edwards, and spent a day hiking into Rainbow Lake, where I'd camped many times before. One sunny day found me perched on a ridgeline, sitting on a granite outcrop eating a strip of elk jerky, watching chipmunks play and thinking, as I often did, of Ceilidh.

The afternoon slipped past as I sat on the ridge, and the sun dropped behind me, shadows marching up the face of the mountain across from me as the light faded. I sat there until dark, thinking, watching the endless cycle of light turning to shadow, thinking how the light would come back in the morning, striking down into the valley below me through the firs on the mountain to the east. I thought about how fall would bring the snows again, how Rainbow Lake would freeze over, and how this valley would lie frozen until the sun came back in the spring.

Everything has a cycle, a season, I thought to myself. *Everything has its time. Ceilidh and I had our time, all those years ago. We left some things unsaid, and it's good that we got to say them, at last.*

But that snow has melted. It's time my own spring finally came.

A boy never really forgets that first love. I'll never forget Ceilidh – not my best friend from school, not the three days in the storm. But now I realized what happened that last night, the acknowledgment that what we had between us wasn't of the future, or even the present, but of the past. We were tying the last loop in a knot we'd begun thirty years before—and now that loop was closed.

Now I realized that after almost thirty years, it was finally time to move forward. For the first time since that October night, I smiled, as a million stars began to wink on overhead. I laughed once, feeling suddenly free, and got up to pick my way down the ridge to my camp.

When I got back home four days later, I took Ceilidh's portrait, wrapped it carefully in tissue, and packed it away.

The End (for now)

About the Author

Ward Clark grew up in the hills and trout streams of northeast Iowa's wooded uplands, gaining a keen interest in wildlife, camping, hunting, fishing, and the outdoors.

Clark served in the U.S. Army in the last years of the Cold War, including service in the Persian Gulf War. Captain Clark concluded his military career by serving on the staff of the Command Surgeon, U.S. Army, Europe. Along the way, he obtained a bachelor's degree in biology.

Writing as Anderson Gentry, Ward Clark's first major novel, *The Crider Chronicles* received a 2005 Preditors & Editors Reader's Choice Award for Top Ten Science Fiction Novel. The Galactic Confederacy series has continued with the 2008 release of *Sky of Diamonds*. A spin off work, *Barrett's Privateers* was released in 2008. Ward Clark's vision of the future combines a high-tech, planet-hopping world presented in a gritty, real style that has led some to call him the "Tom Clancy of Sci-Fi."

Also under the pseudonym Anderson Gentry, Clark released the first of the Nova Roma alternative history series, *Nova Roma 1: De Itinere in Occasum* in 2021, followed in 2023 with *Nova Roma 2: Quaestu pro Nova Terra.*

His fast-paced, hard-hitting style combines a unique blend of outdoor savvy, real-world military experience, and realistic character development.

Learn more at https://andersongentry.com

Other Books by Ward Clark
(writing as Anderson Gentry)

Barretts Privateers
Times Almost Forgotten: The Nick Eldridge Stories

<u>The Galactic Confederation Series</u>
The Crider Chronicals
Sky of Diamonds

In the depths of space, a new era of exploration and colonization has begun. With the invention of the Gellar Star Drive in 2130, mankind opened the door to new worlds and civilizations. While settlers struggle to survive on strange planets, the new worlds face new variations on old problems that arise with the advent of interplanetary commerce. Mankind must find a new way to govern themselves.

The Grugell, with an aggressively warlike culture, have also been spreading their reach and are determined to become the rulers of the galaxy.

Then, events bring to light an ancient guiding influence that affects both races.

The Galactic Confederacy series is a thrilling journey through the vastness of space. Don't miss out on this action-packed tale of survival, politics, and the struggle for power.

<u>Nova Roma Series</u>
Nova Roma 1: De Itinere in Occasum
Nova Roma 2: Quaestu pro Nova Terra

49 B.C.

Julius Caesar has crossed the Rubicon with his army. In Rome, the Optimate Senators, representing the cream of the Roman nobility, decide to flee before Caesar's forces. At the last moment, their leader, General Gnaeus Pompey Magnus, decides to go to Spain, where Pompey has gold, property, and men. But a freak storm interrupts their trip and takes them across the vast ocean to a new land.

Since they have no alternative, they begin building a new roman society. Little do they know how difficult that might be.

**Find more about
Crimson Dragon Publishing's Books,
sign up for news, sneak peeks,
giveaways, and more!**

https://crimsondragonpublishing.com

www.ingramcontent.com/pod-product-compliance
Lightning Source LLC
Chambersburg PA
CBHW061654190726
48289CB00006B/1876